T0283232

Praise for *Isaac's Song*

"*Isaac's Song* is an absolutely beautiful book. It's a beautiful song of generational pain and love, a novel that is thrumming with truth and life."

—Nana Kwame Adjei-Brenyah, *New York Times* bestselling author of *Chain Gang All Stars*

"*Isaac's Song* continues the tradition of Daniel Black making absolute beauty out of the so-called unspeakable. Here, though, the execution and soulful interventions create the most superb writing we've read in a long, long time. Daniel Black is a magician."

—Kiese Laymon, bestselling author of *Heavy: A Memoir*

"*Isaac's Song* is a beautiful, all-consuming novel about the complex relationships between fathers and queer sons, loss, grief, identity, friendship and love. I will read anything Black writes."

—De'Shawn Winslow, award-winning author of *In West Mills* and *Decent People*

"A heartbreaking journey that grips and holds you to the bitter end like a weighted blanket, reminding me of the lyrics from a gospel song, 'We Fall Down but We Get Up,' and try again."

—Sanderia Faye, author of *Mourner's Bench*

"As Isaac's story unfolds, his song moves from its roots in pain, fury, and yearning and leads him toward knowledge, forgiveness, and a love of self that liberates as it lifts. This book is balm and tonic, impetus and light."

—Jabari Asim, *New York Times* Notable author of *Yonder*

"*Isaac's Song* is not just a novel; it is an intimately personal story buried inside a multi-generational saga. It is a detailed account of a journey of self-discovery and a collective oral history. Dr. Daniel Black beautifully chronicles one man's heroic quest to find the source of his generational trauma, a cure for his pain, and ultimately, himself."

—Michael Harriot, *New York Times* bestselling author of *Black AF History*

"*Isaac's Song* is the lullaby we all need and the healing balm for generations to come. Isaac's life journey detangles with precise and mesmerizing language. Passages seem to melt together in a luscious, page-turning reading experience that one must consciously slow down to fully absorb. This riveting and important novel offers as its refrain one of life's greatest lessons: true freedom and liberation can only be achieved through unadulterated self-love."

—Joyce White, author of *Ecology, Spirituality, and Cosmology in Edwidge Danticata*

DANIEL BLACK

A NOVEL

ISAAC'S SONG

HANOVER
SQUARE
PRESS

HANOVER
SQUARE
PRESS™

ISBN-13: 978-1-335-09041-6

Isaac's Song

Hanover Square Press
22 Adelaide St. West, 41st Floor
Toronto, Ontario M5H 4E3, Canada
HanoverSqPress.com

Printed in U.S.A.

Recycling programs
for this product may
not exist in your area.

"To all LGBTQ folks whose parents didn't recognize the gift.
We did."

—The Ancestors

Also by Daniel Black

They Tell Me of a Home

The Sacred Place

Perfect Peace

Twelve Gates to the City

The Coming

Listen to the Lambs

Don't Cry for Me

Black on Black: On Our Resilience and Brilliance in America

The day my father died, a flock of red cardinals gathered in a tree outside my bedroom window. They chirped and shifted like fire. Mr. Charlie, Daddy's best friend, called with the news, and I listened with my eyes closed, trying not to tremble. He extended condolences, and I thanked him graciously. The birds continued their performance, tweeting and leaping with excitement.

When he hung up, I clutched the receiver to my chest as if it were Daddy's heart. I hadn't planned to cry, hadn't imagined I would crumble on this day. My father never meant much to me. We weren't close. We didn't speak often. I'd call him on his birthday if I remembered, but if I didn't, it didn't matter. We had built mutually exclusive lives that didn't allow—or invite—intimacy. Yet, much to my surprise, when I hung up the phone, I buried my face in a pillow and wept.

At the funeral home, I paused before viewing him, not wanting the image to linger in my mind, but then I exhaled and stared at Dad's still, ashy face. He lay in a dark brown suit I'd never seen, white shirt, and tie of the exact same muddy color. His fingernails were clean and clipped—something else I'd never seen—and his salt-and-pepper beard lay cropped and nicely shaped beneath high cheekbones. I thought he looked nice. Even the frown lines in his forehead were gone. It was his body, but not his spirit. There was no intensity, no urgency of expression, nothing that made me self-conscious. He was thinner than I remembered, but not puny. I was glad about that.

I touched Dad's arm and mumbled, "Travel easy, ole man."

Then I exited and collapsed. We'd never been friends. But he *was* my father.

We buried Dad in Arkansas, next to his brother, Uncle Esau, at the base of a big, pretty, ancient-looking oak tree in the community cemetery. Uncle Bobby Joe went with me. I told him he didn't have to, but he insisted. Said he wanted to go *the last mile of the way*. I wasn't sure what that meant, but he said Dad would know.

There was no formal funeral. Just old country folks in overalls and faded plaid dresses and hats gathered at the graveside. I didn't know any of them. I met Mr. John Davies, the old man Dad once told me about. Folks said he was ninety-somethin, but he didn't look a day over seventy. His high-pitched laughter made me smile.

When the hearse arrived, menfolk met it at the cemetery entrance and carried Dad's casket fifty yards to the burial site.

I had expected only a few people, since he'd moved to Kansas City long ago, but as the men bore him proudly, the crowd grew until there must've been thirty people singing, off-key, "Nearer My God to Thee."

I guess Uncle Bobby Joe had arranged for men Dad's age, childhood friends presumably, to carry him home. They wouldn't have had it any other way. I didn't protest. It was a beautiful sight, actually, a band of rustic, seasoned black men, three on each side, bearing my father like a king, while the rest of the crowd finished the hymn. I didn't know the song, but I loved the ritual. There was requirement in it, process that had to be done if Dad was to be at rest. At one point, those elders looked like ancestors marching down that little shady lane, and all I could do was shake my head. I didn't know what Dad meant to them, what they meant to him, what this little town had once been. But they knew. And they meant to send him off right.

After the burial, I joined Uncle Bobby Joe in the hearse, wearing my dusty black Giorgio Armani suit and matching pointed-toe shoes, wondering if Dad was in Heaven. Or anywhere at all.

Weeks later, I found myself in a therapist's office. I had lost ten pounds and hardly slept at all. I couldn't focus or talk without choking up. My mother had died years earlier, and I'd thought nothing else could affect me. She was the person I adored, the one I thought I couldn't live without. Not my father. But apparently that wasn't true.

The therapist asked what my father meant to me, and I had no answer. "Obviously you love him," she said.

"Obviously?" I murmured. "I'm not so sure."

"Well, you can be sure now."

"But that's the thing: I can't figure out why I'm so emotional. My father and I weren't close."

"What does that have to do with love?"

She saw my confusion.

"You can feel deeply for someone, especially a parent, and

be totally estranged from them. Being friends is not a requirement for having feelings. The heart decides who to love—
not the head."

I began to share the ways Dad had wounded me.

"That might be true," she said, "but it wouldn't keep you
from loving him. That's what I want to know—what you feel
about him. Not what he did to you."

We went back and forth, but she wouldn't let me blame him
for my troubles.

"You're too smart to be imprisoned by your father's short-
comings. That's a cop-out, Isaac." I had all the ingredients
for success, she said—college degree, good job, good health,
strong history. "We don't create our baggage, Isaac, but we
can unpack it. Everyone has agency, whether they use it or
not. Nothing has ever happened to you that's greater than your
power to heal it. Blaming others is merely an excuse to avoid
activating your own personal strength. It'll never work. No
one cares to heal you as much as you need it because that's your
job. How smart is it to get mad at a mountain?" I've never forgotten that question. It shifted my whole perspective. "Either
climb it or go around it, but don't spend a lifetime waiting for
it to move. Only a fool does that."

Well, I'd been a fool.

I explained to her how hurtful my father had been, how
his verbal and physical abuse had ruined my self-worth, and
she stared at me, indifferent. "No, it didn't. Self-worth is just
that—what you think about yourself. He might've shown
you the shallow nature of *his* self-worth, but yours can only
be shaped by you."

I didn't agree. "Parents wound children all the time," I

retorted, "then expect them to just get over it. But that hurt seeps deep down and settles in the soul. It's hell getting it out."

She nodded. "You're right. It's hard. But *you* have to get it out—not your father, not anybody else. Only you can do that."

I began to pace. "How? How do I do that?"

She leaned forward onto the desk. "Ask yourself this question: What did pain teach you?" Her blank stare dissolved my self-pity. "Until you can answer that, you're lost. And the answer is not a critique of someone else's behavior. It's the discovery of what you stepped over or threw away on your journey, trying to protect yourself."

I didn't like her just then. She yielded no room for my victimhood.

Now she stood, with complete authority, and asked, "Did your father try to destroy you?"

I rolled my eyes as hard as I could. "What? What do you mean? Of course not. I never said that."

"Then stop acting like he did. Stop hiding behind his limitations."

We argued like this awhile.

"I'm not trying to avoid anything!" I shouted. "I'm trying to get free!"

"Well, Isaac, freedom doesn't live behind other people's faults."

"I just want to hold them accountable!"

"And they *should* be held accountable! But that's not *your* freedom. It's *theirs*."

I was stunned.

"If your father apologized to you right now, you wouldn't be freer. *He* would."

I chewed my bottom lip and trembled.

"Apologies don't heal the wounded. They're for the perpetrator."

"I don't understand." Actually, I did, but I didn't want to.

"If someone shoots you, for instance, an apology doesn't mend the wound. If *you* don't tend it, it'll fester and kill *you*—not the one who shot you. The error is to think that revenge participates in healing. It doesn't. Most of us could've been healed years ago—if we'd stopped waiting for a wounded person to do it. When you cut your finger, the body goes to work immediately, without your permission, to heal itself. It doesn't care who committed the act. It has the power to restore, so that's what it does. No need being mad at the knife. Perhaps it was too sharp. If so, get rid of it. Or be more careful next time. But how imprisoning is it to spend a lifetime screaming at the knife?"

That was me. But the realization pissed me off. I had wanted my father to do something, to own all the ways he had offended me. I believed then that my issues would disappear. My therapist ruined that theory.

"You need to walk back through your life, Isaac. Every inch of it. And discover the pieces of yourself you threw away. You need those pieces now."

"Ma'am? That's what I came to you for! Aren't you the healer?"

She roared. "You're the only healer you'll ever have." Her laughter felt sarcastic, but I kept listening. "My job is to help you discover that."

Again I asked, "What do I do?"

She moved from behind the desk and stood before me. "Get

a legal pad and write your story. Start from the beginning. Tell it just as you recall, however difficult. Don't sweeten the painful, and don't sour the joyful. As you write, you'll discover what you missed. Then you'll have the ingredients for healing. Take your time. It's a slow, arduous process, but freedom lies at the end of it."

So I went home and started writing.

Day 1

My earliest memory is of my mother's voice. It was a high-pitched, honeyed song, a bird's morning melody. It carried authority, the way I imagined God might sound. Every night, when she read to me, I nestled in her lap and dozed off before the story ended. I tried to keep my eyes open, but her musical tone lulled me to sleep. It was intoxicating, hypnotic, and I couldn't fight it. Even when she reprimanded me, which was fairly often, her voice never lost its syrupy cadence. I listened to her chatting on the phone sometimes, cackling from one octave to another, and I'd smile and cover my mouth with glee. Her laughter, ringing through the air like a cornered hyena's, was even higher than her speaking voice. When she really got going, talking and laughing simultaneously, the whole house trembled with joy. When she died, silence settled in and almost killed me.

My father's voice was less notable. It wasn't deep and resonant like one might assume. It was actually pretty midrange—a strong alto—with unmistakable Southern black inflections. The minute he opened his mouth, the rural, uneducated South poured forth. Subjects and verbs rarely agreed. Mispronounced and made-up words composed the bulk of his vocabulary, and sometimes I had to think really hard before capturing the fullness of what he'd said. If he possessed any insecurity at all, it was his sketchy intellect. He envied my education, my pristine enunciation, which my mother guaranteed, and more than once I exposed his intellectual fragility unapologetically. I am sorry for that now.

My parents came from different worlds that merged in rural Arkansas in the early 1960s. My mother, a native Midwesterner, was visiting the south for the summer, a tradition among black people at the time that kept kids safe and supervised while out of school. My father, a country man in every sense of the word, was born in the backwoods of that Arkansas settlement and regretted ever having left. Theirs is the typical love story: teenagers meet at a church picnic and are immediately smitten. I can see why. Both were attractive people—far more than the average. Each shared their own version of who said what to whom and how the first kiss happened. I grew up dreaming of that kind of love. My parents weren't people who touched or kissed in public, but they were committed to each other. They meant to provide a wholesome, prosperous life for me, and they did that.

My mother's love was a given—my father's, a surprise. His main goal was teaching me how to work. Before starting school, I had chores around the house. Taking out the trash, sweeping the garage, making my bed. These had to be done daily. Saturday was even more strenuous. Raking the yard or shoveling snow—yes, at five years old!—or washing the car or whatever. There was always something to do. I never slept late. Ever. While friends watched cartoons and ate Froot Loops and Apple Jacks, I dusted furniture and cleaned the main bathroom. All before noon. Daddy's greatest fear was raising a lazy son. He would've beaten me first, which he didn't mind doing.

Once, my grandma Pearl, my mother's mother, got me a little blue race car for my birthday. I didn't like it. I wanted a red one and said as much. I think my tone was sharp and sassy, and that's what made Dad grab me and spank me right in the middle of her living room. He spanked hard too. His calloused, rough hands resembled sandpaper, and his strike hit quick and sharp as a hammer. My bottom tingled. From then on, I accepted any gift people gave me, regardless of how I felt about it.

Dad did the disciplining, but Mom reinforced it. She was sweet, but she meant what she said. Mom and I talked like old friends sometimes, laughing and whispering around my father, but when I overstepped, she was quick to correct me. "Stay in a child's place!" she would shout into my watery eyes after squeezing my arms. I soon learned what to say and what not to say. She believed in a sharp demarcation between children and elders. I had to say "yes ma'am" and "no sir" to all adults. If they were grown, they were to be respected. There were no exceptions.

Mom spanked harder than Dad—the few times she spanked me. One of them occurred when I was four years old. She'd told me never to play with matches or light the stove. I'd gotten hungry one day and decided I could make my own grilled cheese sandwich. I pushed a chair to the gas range, lit one of the eyes, and sat a skillet upon it. I did it just as I'd seen her do. The bread was browning nicely when she entered and screamed, "Isaac!" She covered her mouth and froze. I was proud of myself, so I smiled and, like a real chef, flipped the sandwich with a spatula. She thawed and screeched, "Boy, have you lost your mind?"

She yanked me from the chair and smacked me all over.

"Didn't I tell you not to touch this stove?" I tried to explain that I understood her edict to be for my three-year-old self, but of course she wouldn't hear it. All she saw, I think, was the house in flames and me in the middle of it, and she kept slapping my little butt until I couldn't sit down. I thought later she'd cry and apologize, but she didn't. She came to my room that evening, stern and tight-lipped. "Good night, Isaac," is all she said. "Aren't you gonna read me a story, Mom?" She peered directly into my somber eyes and said, "There will be no story tonight. You will go to bed immediately. I don't wanna hear a peep out of you."

She closed the door without kissing me. That's what I remember. When I got older, she told me that image—of me at the stove—haunted her the rest of her life. I never realized loving me could hurt so bad.

Day 2

I thought my father didn't like me. Unlike my mother, he never kissed me or read to me or hugged me. I wanted his attention, his applause to match his praise of the Kansas City Chiefs. *They* excited him. He'd sit before the TV on Monday nights, cheering and cursing, until his beloved team made a touchdown. Then he'd leap into the air, screaming, "Rachel! Rachel! Come see this!" Usually, Mom ignored him. He never called for me.

Occasionally, I'd watch from the hallway though. I learned team names like the Dallas Cowboys and the Cincinnati Bengals. I also learned about MVPs like Tony Dorsett and Drew Pearson. Sometimes I leaned against the wall for hours, hoping Daddy might beckon me forward, but he never did. Still, I watched, especially during playoff and Super Bowl season, trying to figure out the overall thrill of the game. Or perhaps

I hoped to learn exactly what made my daddy happy. I'm not sure I discovered either.

What I discovered was that I didn't like most boy things. Including football. And the color blue. Daddy painted my room blue, and I hated it. I asked if it could be yellow, and he said, "Hell naw. That ain't no boy's color." I said, "I like it," and he said, "Not in this house you don't," so it stayed blue a mighty long time. He bought toy soldiers and play guns, none of which I played with, and when he asked what I wanted, I said stuffed animals and books. He stared, undoubtedly wondering how he'd conceived a son like me. For years, the look of rejection lingered in his eyes.

It was my mother who nurtured me. She taught me, first, the joy of reading. She'd ease my finger across words and pictures that created worlds for me. Sometimes, after I got pretty good, I'd read to her, and she'd smile and nod when I pronounced difficult words correctly or read complex passages smoothly. Once I started reading, I never stopped. I traveled the universe in my mind. I learned about cultures, people, and traditions I'd never heard of. Books were my life.

Mom used to say, "You can live in the imagination when you can't live anywhere else."

My favorite childhood book was *The Snowy Day*. It's about a little black boy named Peter who wakes to winter's first snow. He goes outside and marvels at his own footprints, then lies in the snow and makes angels. One night Mom read it to me, and when I woke the next morning, snow covered everything.

I jumped from bed, screaming with joy. Mom laughed at

my excitement. We put on warm clothes and boots and went outside and made a snowman and had a snowball fight and made angels all over the yard. Dad was already at work. Our fun usually began when he left.

Mom hated the lack of children's books for black kids in the '70s. We used to go to bookstores and walk around, perusing the children's section, until Mom, aggravated and upset, dragged me away, cussing about stupid, narrow-minded white folks. Then, one night, I asked for a story, and she sat with me and started turning pages of an invisible book she called *Isaac's Song*. She created a whole narrative about a brilliant black boy who had every gift in the world. He was smart, creative, musical, and mystical. He could time travel and read people's minds. Mom held her hands in the position of a book and turned unseen pages for hours. Her descriptions materialized in my head until I saw the images before me: the extra large print, the colorful illustrations, the little black boy with smooth, brown skin and a head full of beautiful, nappy hair. For months, I didn't realize the story was about me.

I told Mom, "I like the story of the boy with my name." She hollered, shook her head, and said, "It's you, honey. The story is about you. It's your song." I halted, mesmerized. Every night until I started school, I begged Mom to read more of that story until she'd certainly conceived a whole novel. She never repeated anything. Sometimes she even acted out parts. I asked if Dad had heard the story. She said, "No. He doesn't like to read."

At six or seven, I started writing my own stories. One, I recall, was about a little black girl who wanted to be a princess. She lived in a poor village in Africa. Her folks were peasants who farmed the land and owned very little. She was pretty, but she thought she was ugly. One day, a black leopard approached and asked, "Why are you sad, my child?"

She said, "Because I will never be a queen."

The leopard asked, "Why not?"

She said, "Because my father is poor, and I am not beautiful."

The leopard frowned. "No one is more beautiful than you."

The girl, whom I never named, was hurt and offended, believing the leopard to be mocking her. She ran into the forest and a tree asked, "Why are you crying, little girl?"

And she said, "Because I want to be a queen, but my father is not a chief and many other girls are far more beautiful than me."

The tree lowered its branches and wrapped them around the fragile child. She cried and cried, but nothing the tree said appeased her. It sent her to the water. "Go," it encouraged, "to the brook and explain your problem. I'm sure it can help you."

The girl obeyed, bending and bowing at the banks of the little river. She put her ear to the flow and whined, "Oh wise water, can you help me?"

The water whispered, "What is your dilemma, my child?"

She explained, and the water burbled, "Your father is a good man. Your mother has taught you well. Now, your future is your problem. You will be whatever you decide."

"But I cannot be a queen if my father is poor. Princesses come from royalty."

The water warned, "Royalty is in the heart, my child. You are what you think you are. No one can make you beautiful or ugly—if you do not agree. Many queens have taken the throne without rich fathers. And many beautiful women have forsaken the throne because they could not see themselves. Come now and look at yourself through your own eyes."

She stared into the clear, gray stream, and suddenly there

was a beautiful little girl with a crown of jewels resting upon thick cornrows.

I don't remember exactly how the story ended, but I think she marched back to her village, walking upright and proud. The king's son married her, and on the day of the wedding, she realized she was already a queen.

Or something like that. The princess reminded me of the little black girl across the street. Her name was Jamie. She seemed sad most of the time, playing hopscotch and jacks alone on the sidewalk. Many days, I wanted to play with her, but my father would've killed me, so I watched her laugh and talk with invisible friends instead, having constructed a whole fantasy world all by herself. She was short, with stubby plaits, a flat, round face, and a lazy left eye. Like the princess, she thought she was ugly. Adults did too. I could tell because they paid her no mind. I wouldn't have called her cute, but I believed she deserved love. I don't know what happened to Jamie. I couldn't change her circumstances, but I could dream for her. Maybe she became a princess too.

Day 3

My father wasn't always mean. Perhaps in my memory I've misrepresented him. Sometimes, he was quite gracious actually. As a kid, I misunderstood this and took his kindness as responsibility.

Christmas of 1972, I woke eager to see if Santa had granted my wish. I'd told Mom, much to her surprise, that I wanted a red tricycle with bells on the handlebars. She told me it was too expensive, but she'd ask my father about it.

Later that night, I heard their conversation.

"Just 'cause he ask *don't* mean he oughta have it," my father mumbled.

"I know, but if that's the only thing we get him, maybe we can afford it."

"Maybe. I'd have to work a li'l overtime though."

They paused for a good while.

"When I was a boy, we didn't get no toys for Christmas. We saw em in the Sears catalog, and we wanted em, but our folks wouldn't spend good money on nothin like that. They gave us socks and candy canes and fruit."

"Fruit? For Christmas?"

"Damn right. And we was glad to get it."

I knew I'd never see that red tricycle. So, honestly, I stopped thinking about it. That is, until I saw Santa Claus at the Indian Springs Mall over in Kansas. I told him what I wanted, and I believed he could get it. So, by Christmas morning, my hopes were renewed. Boxes of various sizes stood beneath the tree, but none big enough to contain a tricycle. Still, I held out hope.

At daybreak, when my parents began to stir, I ran into the living room, anxious to see a large square box. It was not there. I tried not to act disappointed. My folks seemed oblivious to my desire. They handed me small packages, and I opened them as graciously as I could. They unwrapped gifts from each other and handed me more items from Grandma Pearl and some of my aunts.

Soon, we cleared discarded wrapping paper and ate breakfast at the little oval table in the kitchen nook. Mom and Dad exchanged small talk while I sulked through scrambled eggs, bacon, and grits. I knew if I cried, I'd be in trouble, so I asked to be excused and escaped beneath my bed. I fell asleep under there. I did that quite often. Mom found me, hours later, and told me to put on some clothes and come get lunch. When I rounded the corner into the living room, there was the tricycle, with a huge red ribbon, standing like a stallion before the lighted tree.

I couldn't believe my eyes. I think Mom heard me gasp.

She peeked over her shoulder, smirking playfully. "You have your father to thank for that." I tiptoed forward, still in disbelief, my mouth hanging open. "He paid good money, Isaac." I knew what she was saying. At least I thought I did.

I touched it lightly, smoothing my hand across the handlebars and the triangular leather seat. I looked at Mom; she looked at me. "He's in the garage," she said and resumed fixing lunch.

I dashed in that direction but hesitated at the door. What would I say? I felt selfish and spoiled. But I had to thank him. I owed him that.

When I entered the garage, he was bent over beneath the hood of the car.

"Dad?"

"Yeah?" he said without looking up.

I couldn't talk. My throat went dry. He slammed the hood and wiped his hands with a rust-red shop towel. "You're welcome," he said, staring at me.

I turned and reentered the house. I had wanted to say more, meant to say more, but nothing came out. Momma's suspicious glance made me nervous. Yet when I sat on the tricycle, my joy bubbled over.

Dad came in and said, "Give her a spin. Let's see what you can do!"

I frowned. "Right here?"

"Yes, right here!"

Momma hollered, in a playful tone, "Don't break nothin in my house!" and I knew, from that day, that Santa was real.

I spent hours pedaling wildly from the living room to the

kitchen, down the hallway and back, with Dad chasing after me. I've never had so much fun. I also never knew how much that tricycle cost. I never told Dad thank you.

Day 4

The following Christmas, Dad came through again. I was in third grade. Most of my peers were middle-class white kids. We were the gifted and talented ones, the accelerated students who teachers thought could learn at a faster pace. Jessica Carr and I were the only black kids in my room, and she never spoke. At first, I thought she was literally mute, then one day she whispered something totally brilliant, and I gawked with surprise. She was the smartest student in the class, hands down. No one outscored her on standardized tests. She was just socially awkward, so she didn't shine in a crowd.

Come December, my classmates and I wanted to decorate our room for Christmas. Some brought tinsel, some wreaths; others made red-and-white stockings, and a few baked holiday cookies. I sat numb, not wanting to spend my father's money, but wanting desperately to be part of the holiday celebration. Miss Vance asked kindly, "Is there anything you can bring, Isaac?" Everyone paused and looked at me. I had to say something. "Yes ma'am. I'll bring the tree." Why I said that I don't know, but I was immediately horrified. Kids clapped and cheered, so I couldn't take it back.

That evening, I sat at dinner with a bowed head.

"You all right, baby?" Mom asked.

"Yes ma'am. Just…tired."

I asked to be excused after a few bites and went to my room. Mom came in after a while, and I told her what happened. She said I shouldn't have volunteered something I couldn't do, but I knew that already.

"I'll see if I can get a little artificial one," she said, sympathetically. "It'll do fine."

I smiled, thankful that at least I'd have something.

On the day of the party, I looked for Mom around 10:00 a.m., the time we agreed upon, but she didn't come. By 11:00, I got worried. Students were antsy and anxious with no tree to hang their ornaments on. I asked Miss Vance if I could go to the office and call home, and she wrote me a hall pass. Just when I stepped toward the door, it swung wide and kids screamed, "Oh wow! Look! A real, live tree!" I didn't see anyone at first. All I saw were branches of the biggest, forest green Christmas tree I'd ever seen. Even Miss Vance exclaimed, "Oh Isaac! Just look at that beauty!"

Then I saw Dad's smiling eyes. He squeezed the massive tree through the door and cut the rope from around it. It splayed into form like magic. The tree was perfectly shaped and went from floor to ceiling. The smell of fresh pine consumed the room, and kids danced and screeched with glee. I stared in shock and amazement. Dad huffed and puffed as if the tree was the heaviest thing he'd ever carried.

"Mr. Swinton, we can't thank you enough," Miss Vance said.

He sighed and wiped his brow. "Oh yes ma'am. Mighty glad to do it. Anything for these kids...and my boy."

Dad wrestled that gigantic evergreen into a wooden base that held it perfectly upright. Students rushed me with affirmations, but my joy was tinged with shame.

When Dad finished, he stepped back and nodded, proud of his effort. Children began to hang homemade ornaments all over it, while I drowned in guilt and embarrassment. I'd gone to Mom. I hadn't even asked for Dad's help.

Miss Vance quieted the class. "Aren't you going to thank Mr. Swinton, young people?"

Everyone cheered, "Thank you, Mr. Swinton! It's the prettiest tree ever!"

"Awww, it wunnit no problem," Dad declared. "Gotta get to work now though. Y'all have a good day and a very Merry Christmas." And he left.

Someone discovered that Dad forgot his small tool set, so I grabbed it and started toward the door when suddenly he reentered. He stared at me kindly, then took the bag and winked at me. I sighed and smiled.

There was nothing more to say.

At my next appointment, the therapist asked, "Did you start writing?"

I answered reluctantly, "Yes, I did."

She clapped as if for a toddler. "Very good! What did you learn so far?"

I shrugged. "I don't know. I've only written a few pages."

She nodded. She was a pretty, topaz black woman, heavyset with large bulbous maroonish lips and quarter-size eyes that gleamed beneath long, fake lashes. Her breasts, like soldiers prepared for battle, stood at attention. She must've been fifty, although she could've passed for forty.

"Where did you start? In your story, I mean?"

I studied her face, trying to discern the undercurrent of the question, but couldn't figure it out. "At the beginning. As far back as I could remember."

She nodded but was thinking something else. "Don't just tell what happened. Tell me how you felt about things. Feelings are memories too."

"But feelings aren't accurate."

"Neither are facts. We think they are, but they're not. History isn't what happened. It's how we remember what happened. It's never objective. It's not supposed to be. That's journalism. History is a record of how humans feel about things as they move through time."

"Then how do you write an accurate history?"

"By writing an honest one."

Day 5

By age eight, I knew I was different. Not strange or weird, but different. Kids at school laughed at me, mocking my dramatic expression and my bouncy, twisty walk. Teachers liked me because I was smart. Most adults whispered and stared, wondering why some man hadn't straightened me out. Sometimes women called me "sweetie" or "baby," in that insulting sort of way, frowning their disgust as if I were intentionally effeminate. The few men who engaged me did so with exaggerated physicality: a slap on the shoulder, a jerk of the hand, a deepening of their voice as if it might deepen mine.

I tried not to be so girly, but I couldn't help it. The person I admired most was a girl. I loved everything about my mother. Before I turned ten, I vowed to be just like her.

I paid for that resolution. First with my father. If he hated anything, he hated a soft, expressive boy. I wasn't always soft—I was actually rather bold at times—but I was definitely dramatic. I cried and danced and hugged and sang with very little inhibition. Mom encouraged it. She said I'd be an artist one day if I didn't give up on myself. Dad wanted me to tone it down. Maybe he didn't dislike me, but he wanted a son who'd have a family one day. He wasn't sure about me. I wasn't either. Even Mom, who loved my free expression, worried about how others would treat me in the future.

Dad worked hard to alter who he thought I was. Or who he thought I was becoming. All my shirts were blue or brown or maroon. I remember Mom buying me a pink sweater—it was more red than pink—but Dad wouldn't have it. He came in my room and took it out of the drawer without saying a word. He never even looked at me. Mom told me not to worry. She'd get me another sweater. I didn't want another sweater. I wanted the one she'd bought. Dad confronted me.

"No boy in my house is wearing nothin like that. Do you understand me?"

He stood in the doorway between my room and the hallway. His threatening presence consumed the entire space.

"Why not?" I asked softly.

He took one step forward. "Some things is for boys, some for girls. God made the world that way. If you let things get mixed up, you'll have nothin but confusion."

"Yessir," was all I could say.

"When you get grown and get your own place, you can do what you like. But as long as you live here, you will do as I say. Am I clear?"

He didn't wait for an answer. From that day on, he guarded

my behavior like a truant officer. He examined me every morning before school to make sure I was presentable. He and Mom were not on one accord, but she wouldn't challenge him in front of me. Their arguments, however, became more intense over time.

Mom entered her bedroom one morning and found me dressed in Dad's old work clothes. His dingy blue post office shirt hung limp and long over my narrow shoulders, and his heavy laceless brogans swallowed my feet. I shivered, afraid I was in trouble. Instead, Mom hung her head and cried. She'd heard me, she said, standing outside the door.

"Boy, ain't I done told you to get outta that bed? I'll lay this belt 'cross yo rump if I have to!"

I started striking the bed as if it were a worn, dusty rug.

"You think I'm gon have a lazy, no-count bum in my house? I'll kill you first!"

I snatched covers from the bed and continued pounding until I stopped, exhausted.

"Now git yoself up and git ready for school. Dem teachers bet not have to call me!"

I never knew why Dad said that. No teacher ever called about my behavior.

"When you git home this evening, put on yo play clothes and straighten up that garage. Better be done by the time I get here."

Suddenly I turned and there was Mom, staring at me. My head bowed in shame. She said only, "Get cleaned up for supper," and left.

★ ★ ★

I dressed in her clothes too. I wanted to be beautiful like she was. I didn't know boys couldn't be beautiful. I sat at her vanity and made up my face with lipstick, powdered rouge, and eyeliner. It was a night Mom volunteered at the shelter, so I knew she'd be away. Dad usually left me to my own devices after dinner, so I didn't fear being caught.

He was watching *Hawaii Five-O* when I tiptoed into the living room in a pair of Mom's black pumps and a black-and-white polka-dot dress dragging behind me. This was before the sweater incident. I thought he'd get a kick out of my outfit. Mom's long, white pearl necklace draped my neck, and red, rose-shaped clip-on earrings hung heavily from my tender lobes. When he turned and saw me, he stood slowly, gawking and blinking at something so repulsive he couldn't believe his eyes. They were on fire, his eyes, blazing with rage and wrath. I sensed shock and terror in his demeanor, so I started crying. I knew I'd done something terribly wrong.

He grabbed my fragile little shoulders and shook me until the earrings tumbled to the floor.

"Is you done lost yo mind, boy!" he yelled.

I shook my head but didn't speak.

"You ain't got no business doin no shit like this! What's wrong with you?"

Suddenly my left cheek burned and trembled. I didn't realize, for several seconds, I'd been slapped. The room tilted and swayed. Dad thought I wanted to be a girl, but I didn't. I wanted him to love me, and I thought that if I were beautiful maybe he would.

"Take that shit off!" he demanded after a brief eternity. "And I mean now!"

I slid the dress from my shoulders, and it gathered in a pool of fabric at my feet. The necklace broke in the process, and pearls, like my fragile hope for Daddy's applause, burst free across the living room floor. His mouth quivered as I gathered what beads my trembling hands could find.

Through clenched teeth, he enunciated slowly, "Now get in there and clean that goddamn mess from yo face!"

I rushed to the bathroom and scrubbed my face raw. I'd never heard of makeup remover, so I rubbed soap into my eyes until they burned like fire. Anything was worth calming his anger.

"Get back in here, boy!" he yelled after a few minutes. I raced back to him. "What the hell's wrong with you? Huh?"

I had no answer. My pride in the costume chilled to a silent shame.

"Boys don't do that! Don't you know that?"

I mumbled, "Yessir," but apparently I didn't.

"Then why'd you do it?"

I shrugged. He shoved me into Mom's reading chair.

"You ain't no girl!"

I knew that, but I knew he was saying something more.

"You a boy! And you gon be a boy in this house."

I murmured, "Yessir!"

"What would yo li'l friends at school say if they saw you? Huh? Do you know how they'd laugh at you?"

I didn't care what they thought. I cared what he thought. Yet, for the moment, I stared at the floor and prayed he wouldn't hit me again.

"Did yo momma tell you this was okay?"

"No sir. I never done it before."

"And you bet not ever do it again! Do you hear me?"

"Yessir."

"You said what?" he shouted.

I screamed, "Yessir!" like a frightened army private.

"Now go to your room!"

I went and crawled beneath the bed and whimpered until I fell asleep. Mom found me the next morning. I told her what happened, and she confronted him. They argued until she took me to school.

"He's a baby, Jacob!"

"He ain't no baby, woman! He's a boy! And he ain't got no business in no women's clothes."

"He was just playin, honey. You're making too much of this!"

"No, I'm not!"

"Yes, you are!"

"I ain't gon have no chile like that in my house."

"*Your* house?"

"That's right. You heard me."

"I thought it was my house too!"

"You know what I mean!"

"I know what you said!"

"Take it like you want, but ain't no son o mine gon be prancin round in his momma's clothes like no damn sissy!"

"Jacob! Watch your mouth!"

"I ain't watchin nothin! I don't care if he hears me. Matter of fact, I hope he does!"

"You'll scar him for life, man!"

"I can live with that. What I can't live with is a son *like that!*"

I clamped my palms over my ears until things simmered down. Not until later that evening did I notice the bruise above Mom's left eye.

From that day on, Dad and I would never be friends.

Day 6

One time, Dad made me stand in the rain for hours. I was ten or so. He'd bought me a blue bike from the Swap and Shop. I was surprised because I hadn't asked for it. It was used, but it was nice. He took off the training wheels and threw them away. "Isaac," he summoned. "Meet me in the garage." I laid aside *The Lorax* by Dr. Seuss and stepped into my black-and-white Converse.

"You got to know how to ride a bike," he said as I stepped into the dark space. He lifted the loud, squeaky garage door and sunlight poured in.

I followed as he wheeled the bike to the sidewalk.

"All you gotta do is balance your weight," he instructed, holding the bike perfectly still. "Grab the handlebars tight. That's how you guide it. Pedal with your feet. If you fall, get up and try again."

I got on reluctantly, unsure of myself.

Dad began pushing the bike forward. "You gotta pedal, boy!"

So I started pedaling.

"Don't be scared."

Gripping the handlebars and the back of the seat, he started running.

"All right! You on yo own now!" he called and surged the bike forward.

I heard my teeth rattle. Fear kept telling me I'd fall, but I meant to defy it. At first, I glided along smoothly, proud of myself, but I forgot to pedal, so, within twenty or thirty yards, I crashed to the ground. Pain ran from my left foot up my leg and into my thigh.

I got back on and fell again. This time, I couldn't help but cry. My leg hurt so bad I thought I had broken it. But I couldn't walk the bike home. I had to ride it. I fell several more times around the neighborhood, trying to figure out how to balance the bicycle and pedal at the same time. Finally, with tears and bubbles of snot, I got on and gripped the bars tight enough to choke them, and pedaled as if trying to escape this world. Somehow I floated forward, upright and into the wind.

"Yes! Yes!" I yelled.

Dad saw me and nodded. Then went inside.

It began to rain, so I jumped off the bike and left it in the front yard. I was proud of myself, but I wanted the whole ordeal to be over.

I guess Dad saw the bike in the yard and got upset. "Boy! Get in here!"

I bolted into the living room.

"Where'd you put that bicycle?" he asked, staring through the screen door and into the storm.

Immediately, I knew what I had done. "I'll go put it in the garage," I said quickly and turned to get my shoes.

"No…no, you won't," he remarked sarcastically. "Don't put it in the garage. Leave it right where it is."

I didn't understand.

He turned and sneered, "Get your shoes and go stand with it."

"Sir?"

"You heard me. Put your shoes on and go stand right where you left it."

"But it's raining, Daddy."

"Sure is. You shoulda thought of that when you threw it down in the yard. Now go out there and stand with it."

Mom had been in the back, washing clothes or something. When she heard what he demanded, she told me to get the bike and bring it inside.

"No!" Dad shouted. "Don't touch it. Leave it right where it is! You don't preciate nothin I do for you, so I'ma teach you how it feels to be disrespected."

"He'll get sick, Jacob. He's sorry. He won't do it again."

"He ain't sorry! That's the problem!"

Mom protested further, but to no avail. His feelings were hurt, but he couldn't say that. He had to reprimand me to get an ounce of satisfaction. His mind was made up. "Now git out there and stand next to that bicycle until I call you back in."

Mom gave me an umbrella, but he snatched it away. "You

don't need that! Just stand there. Rain won't kill you. It might teach you something though."

I paused at the door in a black bubble jacket, worn blue jeans, and a gray skullcap. Dad opened the screen, inviting me into the torrential downpour. "Go on!" he insisted.

"This is ridiculous, Jacob! He's just a boy!"

"That's right! And my job, not yours, is to make him a man."

I stepped into the rain. Droplets landed cold and heavy all over me. My body chilled instantly. It was dark and windy. Dad stood at the door, staring at me and the bike, daring me, presumably, to come back inside prematurely. Within minutes I was soaked and shivering.

I must've stood in that storm an hour. At least it felt that long. Dad never moved from the door. I'm sure he thought he was teaching me something about manhood. And he was. Believe me, he was.

Day 7

Some of my warmest childhood memories happened at my grandmother's house, on Forty-Fifth and Terrace. Like my mother, she was a reader and an exceptionally smart woman. She was pretty, too, with long, thick gray and black hair that framed a dark reddish-brown, russet complexion. I never knew my grandfather, my mother's father, because he died before I was born, but I felt like I knew him. Black-and-white photos hung on every wall of Grandma's little two-bedroom house, showing Granddaddy in military uniform and fishing gear—the two things he loved. He was a tall man, six foot three, they said, and super quiet. Hardly said a sentence or two all day. Died in World War II. Grandma showed me the flag the government gave in his honor. It went to Mom when Grandma died, then I found it in a trunk when Mom passed. I don't know who'll get it after me.

★ ★ ★

I liked going to Grandma's because her cooking beat Mom's. Mom wasn't much of a cook. She said if she'd had her way, she would've hired a black maid to clean and cook for us. She wanted to spend more time at the women's shelter and go back to school. She should've. Sometimes, you could sense her carrying the weight of unfulfilled dreams.

My grandmother was a different story. She was happy all the time and converted joy into food. Any day of the week, one could find roast, barbeque chicken, dressing, macaroni and cheese, and greens on her stove. She always had greens. That's how I learned the difference between mustards, collards, and turnips. Sometimes she mixed them. However she cooked them, they were scrumptious.

Sundays were the big day at her house. My great aunts, her sisters, often stopped by with cousins my age, and we'd play in the street until dinner time. My grandmother went to Metropolitan Missionary Baptist Church, the one on Twenty-Third and Linwood, absolutely every Sunday, and nothing happened in her house until she returned. I'd go with her occasionally, but I didn't really care for church, so most Sundays, Mom and I sat on her porch until she returned. Dad came a few times, but Sundays were his other football day, so Mom brought him a foil-covered plate to avoid having to cook herself.

We'd turn Grandma's small dining table made for four into a picnic table made for eight. Some would fix plates and, after the blessing, sit in the living room. On Thanksgiving, we'd put two small tables and fold-up chairs in the tight space and eat til we couldn't move. It probably wasn't healthy, but it sure tasted good.

On Sundays, she'd tell me and my cousins about the ole days. The way they worked and struggled and believed in God. I loved her antics, her emphases, her pride in making something out of nothing.

"We was poor, but we had *dignity*!" She overarticulated proudly. "We worked for everything we got. We didn't owe nobody nothin. And we didn't blame white folks for our troubles. They was probably responsible, but still we didn't waste time foolin with em. All we wanted was opportunities. We didn't care nothin bout being equal. Hell, who were they to be equal to?"

My cousins and I chuckled, but Grandma wasn't playing.

She added, "Once upon a time, you couldn't beat black folks' work ethic. That's why white folks worked so hard to hold us back. 'Cause if they didn't, we woulda took over this entire country. They knew it, and we did too. Now, though, you can't hardly find reliable black help. Everybody lookin for shortcuts and schemes and ways to make money without working." She shook her head slowly. "It ain't gon never work. You young people get that through your head. It ain't gon never work!"

We glanced each other's faces and hoped, in our hearts, she'd move to another subject.

She did. She told us about her oldest brother, our great uncle Lee Junior, who was lynched.

"Down South?" I asked.

"Hell naw! Right over in Springfield!"

We grumbled our disbelief and shifted in our seats. "I thought lynchings were in Alabama and Georgia!" I said.

Grandma wiped floured hands on an apron and scoffed,

"Honey, lynchings were all over this country. Didn't nobody want colored folks. Nobody nowhere!" She saw our incredulity. "My daddy and momma was slaves in Springfield."

"What!" we cried. "Slaves? Our great-grandparents?"

"That's right!" she shouted pompously.

My cousin Jeffrey said, "I didn't know we had slaves in our family!"

"Sho we did. Most black people did. And they was right here in Missouri." She said it with an indignant authority that we wouldn't have dared challenge. We couldn't believe our ears.

"They were the best, the hardest-working people on this earth. They were children when slavery ended, but they remembered what it was like. They told us all kinds o stories."

"Like what?" we asked.

Grandma took the head seat at the table. "Like when my granddaddy ran to freedom."

Our eyes burst with amazement.

"Folks didn't never see him again. Guess he made it!"

She nudged me and Jeffrey. We chuckled.

"They said he could outrun lightning."

"Lightning?" somebody shouted. "Can't nobody outrun lightning."

"They said he could. Said he could run in the rain and never get wet."

Now we knew Grandma was joking.

"I ain't lyin! My daddy said his daddy outran a train one time. Slave master bet he couldn't catch it and jump on. It was roarin down the tracks with a trail o black smoke behind it. Daddy said Massa laid nickels and dimes on the ground to challenge him. Supposedly my granddaddy took off across an open field and disappeared next to the train. People didn't know if he caught it or not. Not til he walked back, later that evening, from the next train stop."

Grandma watched wonder color our faces.

"But Massa didn't give him the money on the ground. Said my granddaddy was his property, so he didn't owe him nothin."

We shook our heads.

"Didn't matter though," Grandma continued. "Granddaddy knew how fast he was. Within a week, he was gone. And he didn't come back this time."

"What happened to him?"

"Don't know. Daddy said he promised to come back for the rest o em, but he never did. They believe he made it though. Didn't nobody find him or drag him back."

Now I wanted to know my great-great-grandfather and hear his story. I asked Grandma, "What was his name?"

She beamed and said, "Hannibal. Hannibal Johnson."

I always wondered what really happened to him. Surely he didn't get free and leave his family behind. But if he did get free, why didn't he come back? Of course we'll never know. I decided to believe he got free but couldn't get back for whatever reason. Now I see how people finish their elders' stories. I would have to do the same for my folks one day.

Day 8

One rainy Sunday afternoon, when no one else came over, Grandma sat at the dining table, polishing her cherished silver tea set. Granddaddy had given it to her for one of their anniversaries, and she shined it regularly, as if buffing the old man's heart.

"Had this a long time," she sang, nostalgically. "Real, one hundred percent silver!"

I reached to touch it, and she slapped my hand playfully though she wasn't playing.

"Everybody's gotta have something they treasure. Keeps memories fresh and alive."

"I don't have anything," I said innocuously. "At least not yet."

"Keepa livin. You will. Usually comes when you love somebody."

I risked saying, "You think I'll love somebody one day, Grandma?"

She smiled but continued polishing a cup. "Of course you will, baby." Then she paused and stared at me intensely. "But love yourself first!"

It was a demand, a plea, as if she feared I'd forget.

"Ma'am?" I said, frowning. "What do you mean?"

She nodded and repeated, "Whatever you are—" that's when her eyes bulged "—love yourself." She kissed my forehead and returned to her treasure.

I was confused.

"God don't make mistakes, baby. The question ain't what other folks think about you. It's what you think about yoself!"

She'd caught me off guard.

I looked at her and asked, "What do you think about me?"

She faced me once again and blinked awhile before saying, "I think you my precious grandson and I wouldn't have you any other way."

It was as specific as she could get.

"I'm gon tell you somethin else too." Her tone became authoritative as if she feared I'd resist. "Yo daddy might be hard on you, but he means you well. This world is a hard place."

She nodded, dismantling my rejection before I could offer it.

"I know you can't see it now, but one day you gon thank him for what he taught you."

"It ain't today," I murmured.

"It ain't got to be today. Another day is comin." She collected the silver pieces and returned them to a suitcase-like container. "And watch yo mouth. Remember who you talkin to."

I sighed. "Sorry, Grandma. I just don't think Dad likes me."

"He raisin you, ain't he? He like you enough."
She wouldn't entertain my pity.
"Just be yoself. He'll figure out who you are one day."

It stormed during my next therapy appointment. I'd thought about canceling, but ultimately decided not to.

Before she could ask anything, I volunteered, "Okay. Dad wasn't a monster."

She nodded. "How'd you get to that?"

"I don't know. Just thought about what he did versus what he meant to do."

She closed her eyes a long while, then, staring into the storm, asked, "What do you think he meant?"

"Well, I think he meant to make sure I was strong enough to withstand the world's opposition to me."

"And why would the world oppose you?"

"Because I'm...you know..."

"No, I don't. What are you?" She walked to the front of the desk and leaned on it.

I huffed, irritated. "I've told you this already. I'm a man who…likes men."

"Why are you so uneasy saying it?"

"I'm not uneasy. I just don't announce it."

"Why not?"

"Because straight men don't announce their sexual identity. Why should I?"

"Because you're proud of it. *If* you're proud of it."

I'd never thought about that. I didn't know I *should* be proud of it. I'd thought of it as something I had no power over and therefore should simply accept.

"Well, I don't know that it's something to be proud of. It just is."

"Would you announce your blackness if you could hide it?"

I walked to the window. "That's not fair. Race and sexuality aren't the same thing."

"No, they're not. But your pride about them could be. Maybe your struggle, your whole life, has been asking others to celebrate what you cannot, and your father had no respect for that. I could be wrong, but he sounds like a man who honored confidence."

"That's true. But he also dishonored difference."

She glared at me. "Someone else does too."

Day 9

I actually liked myself as a kid. I could do almost anything: draw, sing, dance, write. I was the lead in practically every elementary school production. Mom always came; Dad rarely did.

In fifth grade, I starred in *Little Orphan Andy*. The drama teacher made an offshoot of *Little Orphan Annie*, since no girl in the cast could outsing me. I was so excited. I ran home the day I got the lead and told Mom all about it. She was excited, too, but suggested we not tell my father.

"We'll surprise him," she said, smiling a sinister grin.

I didn't realize until after the play that Mom feared Dad's reaction. She knew I'd be in a red wig and an outfit he didn't approve of. But she didn't dissuade me. She told me to practice hard and be the best Andy they'd ever seen.

That's what I did. Every day after school I hid away in

my bedroom and stretched my range by belting, "'Tomorrow, tomorrow, I love ya tomorrow!'" Mom would stand outside my door sometimes—I saw her shadowed feet—listening until I finished. She never said anything, which was the greatest compliment.

The day of the play, the cast stayed after school to do last-minute prep. I didn't know if Dad was coming or not, and that made me nervous. But I was ready.

By five thirty, the auditorium was pretty full. Every couple of minutes, I peeked from behind the thick red curtain to see if my folks had arrived. Just before six, I saw Mom and Grandma take seats in the fourth row from the front. Dad wasn't with them.

Curtains opened and the crowd went wild. It was my time. A few other characters went on first, and that's when I saw Dad take an aisle seat behind Mom and Grandma. He was in his post office uniform, so I knew he'd come straight from work. I prayed my anxiety wouldn't get the best of me.

I stepped on stage and spoke a few lines, then began to sing. Mom could hardly sit still. A glance at Dad's mortified face released butterflies in my stomach. His brow was so furrowed I didn't think it would ever smooth. The only way to redeem myself, I believed, was to sing my butt off. When I started the signature number, the crowd began to sing along. That helped, but it also crowded my moment, so I twisted and twirled to the edge of the stage, more dramatic than I'd practiced, and continued, "'Just thinkin about, tomorrow!'" Dad's forehead fell into his right palm. I was losing the battle. Mom was standing by now. "'Clears away the cobwebs and the sorrow,'" I sang, moving back and forth, lifting my arms to the Heavens for help. "'When I'm stuck with a day that's gray and lonely.'" Out of desperation, I ran to the center of the stage and tossed my head back, Diana Ross style, and wailed "'Tomorrow, tomorrow, I love ya tomorrow!'" and Dad rushed out. Mom applauded loudly. Grandma clapped but didn't stand.

Dad waited for us out front. He leaned against the car, smoking a cigarette. A few parents congratulated him, but he barely smiled.

"You were just marvelous, baby!" Mom said as we approached the car.

"You certainly can sing," Grandma said evenly.

Dad studied me from head to toe. He took the last drag of the cigarette and flicked the butt to the ground and smashed it with his heel.

"What possessed you," he began, "to let these crackers make a fool outta you like that?"

I didn't know what to say.

"Do you know what you looked like?"

"Jacob," Mom scolded.

Dad snapped at her. "They turned my boy into a damn freak with a red-ass wig on his head."

Grandma didn't say anything. It took me years to realize she agreed.

"Let's just go home, Jacob. Isaac's tired. He has school tomorrow."

"Oh yes," Dad mocked, "tomorrow, tomorrow!" He didn't know the rest of the words—thank God—but he wasn't finished with me yet.

"Ain't I taught you nothin? You didn't know better than to do some shit like that?"

"It's just a play, Dad."

My indifference fueled his fury. "It's not! It's not just a play. It's some racist-ass white folks who needed a black child who could sing they racist-ass song!"

I couldn't imagine what was racist about "Tomorrow," but Jesus the Christ couldn't have made me ask.

"And, Isaac! You're eleven years old. Why would you let somebody put a damn red ball of fire on yo head and—" his voice got louder "—make you dance around like a jackass?"

I was too defeated to argue, but since Dad waited for me to speak, I said, "I don't know. It's just what they told me to do. I didn't think the wig was that big o deal."

Dad clapped like thunder. "It was, boy! Is you crazy? A black boy with a fire-red nappy wig? What the hell is that?"

I'd not thought of it like that before.

"You ever seen a black boy wit a naturally red afro before? Huh?"

I shook my head.

"Exactly. And then you prancin and skippin round like some…" Dad shook his head and held his tongue.

Grandma sat in the back seat with her arms folded across her heavy chest. Mom kept trying to make Dad be quiet, to get in the car, but he couldn't move until he expunged the rage in his heart. I prepared to be smacked senseless, but, instead, Dad walked off a bit and lit another cigarette. Silence shrouded all of us for a while, then Dad, walking briskly, returned and said to me, "Get in the car. Let's go."

We dropped Grandma home without a word. Before pulling into our driveway, Dad said, "You might be talented, and you might be smart, but you ain't got no common sense at all."

We exited together as Mom said, "I'm proud of him, myself. I think he did a good job."

Dad cackled and said, "That's the problem."

He signed me up for Little League baseball. I remember the gleam in his eyes when he beheld me in the blue-and-white uniform and matching cap. He danced a soft shuffle around the living room, telling Mom how great I'd be. "You mark my word," he announced confidently. "This boy here gon be a hero one day. Bet he got a arm like Satchel Paige!"

Mom wasn't delighted, but she wasn't opposed either. "You need some physical activity, honey," she told me. "Do you a lotta good."

I started playing for the Kansas City Cubs Junior League team. We practiced every Saturday morning at 9:00 a.m. Dad was up at seven, calling me forth like Jesus called Lazarus, and even after we finished, he conducted one-on-one personal trainings. He meant for me to pitch. I meant to go somewhere and read.

As usual, he got his way. When I pitched the first game, we won 9–3. Still, I hated everything about baseball. I despised competition and thoughtless physical contact. I hated that I was expected to celebrate when someone struck out. I detested the way coaches screamed at us, as if millions of dollars were on the line, and I loathed the immaturity of parents who treated every game like the World Series. My father was one of them. Every few minutes, he shouted instructions at me, along with the coach, and truthfully I tried my best

to ignore both of them, but it wasn't always possible. Sometimes, when the coach called a time-out and approached the
pitcher's mound, Dad came running behind him.

My most embarrassing moment was when he whipped me
in the middle of a game. I'd had enough of baseball. I simply didn't want to be there, and I couldn't have cared less if
we won or lost. During the fourth or fifth inning, I started
throwing balls so wild they went over the umpire's head and
between the catcher's bent legs. I saw Dad stand, but I paid
him no mind. I really didn't care. I just wanted to go home.

The coach paused the game and asked if I was okay. I
shrugged with apathy, and Dad made his way to the mound.

"What's the problem, boy?" he inquired threateningly.

"Nothing," I huffed.

"Then why you throwin balls like you sowin seed?"

From some unknown place came the words, "'Cause I
don't wanna be here!"

I think my tone, as much as my attitude, pushed him over
the edge. "I don't give a damn what you want! You gon finish this game, and you gon pitch it like you got some sense!
Do you hear me?"

Rolling my eyes unleashed his fullest anger. He unthreaded
his belt from his pants and started beating me.

"Who the hell you think you talkin to?"

I collapsed to the ground, more for drama than from pain.
The coach grabbed Daddy's arm and begged him to calm
down. "You can't do that here, Mr. Swinton. It's not allowed."

"I can do whatever I want with my own child!"

The coach stood between us, prepared to negotiate a truce,

but Dad wanted only a victory. "If he don't do nothin else, he gon finish this game!"

I believed Dad would beat me again if I didn't comply. I somehow pulled myself together and pitched through the ninth inning. We lost, of course, and I never played again. Dad refused to speak to me for days after that. At the time I was a fatherless son.

Day 10

I don't quite remember how old I was the first time I found Mom passed out. I was still in elementary school though. I'd gotten home a bit earlier than usual because it began to snow. Dad picked me up and dropped me off on his lunch break. I ran into the house, yelling, "Mom! Mom!" but she didn't answer. An eerie silence lingered, and, for some reason, I began to tiptoe quietly. Something was amiss. I felt it in the air. "Mom?" I whispered. Her bedroom door swayed slightly, so I pushed it and walked in.

She lay curled upon the floor, mumbling to herself. Her hair looked like a fallen beehive, and her ragged housedress exposed far too much breast. I knelt beside her and touched her shoulder. The scent of alcohol arrested my nostrils.

I knew she drank a bit. I'd heard Dad warn her about it. But I'd never seen her in this state.

"Get up, Mom," I cried as I jabbed her arm. "Get up!"

She startled a bit and looked at me. I became angry.

"Mom! Get up!"

"Okay, baby. I'm getting up," she murmured.

I took her arm and lifted with all my strength. She was too drunk to walk, but I managed to sit her on the bed. I'm not sure if I cried from anger or sorrow, but I lay down with her and rubbed her forehead til she went to sleep. It's the day my childhood ended.

I went to the kitchen and boiled water for tea. When I re-entered her bedroom, she was sitting up, leaning against the headboard. She was still disheveled, but much of her consciousness had returned. She sipped the tea slowly, avoiding direct eye contact with me. I stood next to the bed, refusing to sit.

"Listen, baby," she began. "Let me explain."

"I know what happened, Momma." I had more shame than compassion. "Just drink the tea please."

I took the empty cup and spoon back to the kitchen and washed them over and over. I didn't know what to feel, what to think, what to say. I was ashamed of my mother for the first time in my life. It wouldn't be the last.

Her redeeming quality was the ability to hide her struggle. She only drank at home and then only when she thought Dad and I would be away. It wasn't a perfect plan, of course. We caught her more than a few times, and, ultimately, I think it's why Dad left. She told me, when I was about sixteen, that she never wanted a traditional life. She wanted to write poetry and travel the world.

"Why didn't you?" I asked.

"Because I got pregnant with you."

I didn't hear blame; I heard responsibility.

"When I looked into your precious little eyes, I knew I could never leave you."

"Why didn't you at least go to college?"

"I told you. Because I got pregnant."

"Plenty o people go to college who got kids."

"Are they women?"

I didn't know any, so I yielded.

"It's all right. I don't have a bad life. It's just not the life I wanted." She shrugged. "But I wanted you."

I took a risk. "And I guess you wanted Dad. You married him."

Mom's head fell back as she bellowed with laughter. "You're right, you're right. I married him. Nobody made me."

I waited for what she wasn't saying.

"I did what women were expected to do. That was my fault."

"Do you regret it?"

She didn't want to answer, but she gambled anyway. "Sometimes."

I always thought of her drinking as her way of surviving the life she didn't want. That wasn't an excuse, but it gave me sympathy. Most times, she seemed fine, but sometimes I found liquor bottles hidden throughout the house: in cabinets, laundry baskets, beneath beds, in her purse and coat pockets. Once Dad left, her drinking intensified, and, at one point, I thought she'd have to get professional help. She insisted she'd do better, though, and she did—for a while.

But I'm ahead of the story.

Day 11

Once Dad accepted he'd get no athlete out of me, I started playing piano. He asked how serious I was, and I said very, and he said, "If I buy a piano, you gon play it!" and I said, "Yessir. I will." So he bought it.

It took six months to get it off lay-a-way. When I came home from school and saw the piano in the living room, I covered my mouth and screamed. Mom looked from the kitchen and smiled. "You mighty blessed, young man. All you gotta do now is learn to play it. Your daddy ain't gon compromise bout that!" She paused then added, "And he shouldn't!"

I started lessons and, by eighth grade, could play pretty well. Sometimes I hated practicing, but Jacob Swinton insisted. "If you don't do nothin else in this world, you gon play that damn piano," he repeated weekly. So, whether I liked it or not, I went to lessons regularly and, day by day, got a little

better. After Dad moved out—I think I was twelve or so—
he still stopped by to make sure I kept my end of the bargain.

One Saturday afternoon, I had a recital at the teacher's
home. When Dad showed up, I froze. It wasn't that I didn't
want him there. I'd always wanted him there, but his presence made my hands sweat and quiver. I think he was the
only man in the audience, and I couldn't relax or focus. Mom
saw my distress and told me to calm down. "He's just your
father," she said.

Two white girls performed before me, playing flawless ren-
ditions of Bach, then the teacher stood and said, "And now,
ladies and gentlemen, I present to you Isaac Swinton." I was
the only black kid, as usual, so I shuffled to the bench and
sat heavily as the crowd applauded with expectation. Suddenly, the gray tie tightened around my neck, and my black
suit coat, which I'd outgrown, bunched beneath my arms.
But I had to go on. I positioned my hands and began to play.
Midway through, my mind went blank. I forgot everything.
I couldn't remember one note. The crowd gasped. I closed
my eyes and begged for my memory to return, but it didn't.
After sitting motionless, I got up and ran out. No one said
anything. No one but Dad.

I stood on the front steps, humiliated. He came out and
joined me, smoking a cigarette. "I ain't never played de piano,"
he said, "so I don't know what it take to do it, but I know one
thing: you ain't no quitter. I didn't raise no quitter."

"I just...forgot everything, Dad. My mind went blank."

"No, it didn't. *Your* mind ain't never blank. You think and
read too much for that."

"Maybe I'm scared."

"Scared o what?"

I shrugged. I couldn't tell him the truth, that he made me nervous. "I don't know."

"Well, when a man tries his best, he oughta be at peace." He paused. "Did you try your best?"

I thought about it. "I think so."

"No, you didn't. If you'd tried your best, you woulda succeeded. That's always true. Don't never forget that. You a Swinton, boy. We don't half do nothin. If we do somethin, we do it right or leave it alone. Simple as that."

I looked at him, finally, and he smirked. We stayed on the steps a few more minutes until he went back inside. I followed shortly, and my piano teacher asked if I wanted to try again. I nodded.

The crowd waited. I positioned my hands above the keys, exhaled, and prayed. Dad and Mom stared at me.

Once again, I began to play Haydn's *Surprise Symphony*. All the notes came back to me. I felt the movement, sensed the intensity and beauty of the piece, and played as if I'd composed it. I had practiced it many times, but now I was playing the emotions. My fingers trembled with memory far beyond my years. There was no sound from the audience. Only hope that I wouldn't betray my talent, and I didn't.

At the end, I sat on the piano bench, panting. The last note lingered for an eternity, and when I lifted my hands, Dad stood and clapped slowly. White mothers gawked and blinked as if something special had occurred. I felt it—the spiritual ecstasy that comes when you know you've done something awesome—and I beamed with satisfaction. Dad kept clapping, forcing others to join in, until most were on their feet, praising a little black boy for a soulful rendition of a classical tune.

On our way home, Dad mocked some of the other performances, saying many of those white kids needed to find new hobbies. "They ain't got no *style*," he said, "no *pizazz*." Mom and I cackled. Dad asked when I might get to play some black music, and I said I didn't know. "That'll come soon enough," Mom added and reached over the seat to touch my knee.

Dad pulled into the driveway and parked but didn't exit. Mom and I wondered what was wrong. Suddenly, he turned, with excited eyes, and shouted, "Shit, boy! You played that damn song!"

"Jacob!" Mom scolded playfully.

I laughed. I never forgot that. I also never forgot that I'm a Swinton.

When the therapist walked in, I was already pacing.

Startled, she paused at the door and said, "You okay, Isaac?"

I couldn't be still. Memories had rearranged my consciousness, and I didn't know what to do with unacknowledged truths. "This is too much," I said, shaking my head. "I can't do it."

She proceeded to the desk, smiling as if I'd said something wonderful. "What have you discovered?"

"Too much!" I said. "Nothing is what I thought it was."

"Ump. Ain't that the truth!"

"What do you mean?"

She waved her comment away. "That's for another time. This is about you. Guess you've been writing, huh?"

I nodded. "And I don't think I can continue. It's too difficult to process." I took my usual seat. "I get so frustrated as

I remember because my memory and my feelings don't always align."

"That's the point. And which do you trust?"

I jumped up. "I don't know! Is one more reliable than the other?"

"I don't think so. I always tell clients to put them together until they agree. Truth is somewhere between what we feel and what really happened. Neither of those is truth alone."

I took a deep breath and said, "My mom wasn't always the angel I made her out to be."

The therapist nodded, hoping I'd say more.

"But she was still amazing."

"Of course she was. Why can't she be both?"

I sighed. "Because I need her perfect in my memory. It makes the contrast with Dad more exact."

"If you made Mom what you needed, perhaps you did the same with Dad."

I'd never considered that. "Maybe."

"Your memory might not honor either of them correctly."

We locked eyes and wouldn't let go.

"It's worth thinking about. Just keep writing and you'll discover who they—and you—really are."

Day 12

I never stopped writing stories. While playing baseball and piano, I wrote about all sorts of things. There was a writing contest during the summer of my twelfth birthday. It was advertised in the *Kansas City Times*. Submissions could only be twelve hundred words or no more than five pages. Very little room, I thought, to tell a good story, but I wanted to try.

Dad was renting a room from someone off of Seventy-Sixth and Brooklyn. He couldn't take Mom's drinking anymore. I didn't think I'd miss him, but I did. He'd kept structure in my life, and when he left, things sort of fell apart. He came by to mow the grass and do other maintenance things, but it wasn't the same. I guess it wasn't supposed to be.

I thought to ask him about my newest story because he wasn't a classic reader. I figured if he could follow along and like it then most people would. But every time he stopped

by, he and Mom got into it about something, and I never got
the chance. Mom read it, though, and said it was the best I'd
written, so I felt pretty confident.

The story featured a black boy whose parents die in a car
accident. It opened with him, at ten years old, sitting with
his grandparents at a double funeral. He imagines his parents
walking, hand in hand, to the throne of God and being asked
several questions:

"Did you love each other fully and only?"

And they respond, "Yes, God. We did."

And God asks, "Did you give your son your best?"

And they respond, "Yes, God. We did."

And God invites them into Heaven, where they see rela-
tives and old friends again, but they have no joy without their
son. God notices their despair and asks what they desire, and
they say, "To return to the living realm."

God says, "That is not possible. No person has ever come
to Heaven and returned—much less wanted to."

The couple begs to be the first, but God won't hear of it.
They approach Him every day, but to no avail. Eventually,
God offers them an idea.

"There is no way for you to return," He says, "but, if your
misery cannot be allayed, your son can come to you."

They frown and ask, "How? How can he come here without—"

"He can't. He would have to die as well."

They study each other's perplexed face, never having considered the obvious.

"Can it be painless?" the mother asks.

"I cannot tell you that."

"Can there be no sadness?" the father wonders.

"I cannot tell you that either. You cannot control living things in order to satisfy the hopes of your heart. You would simply have to endure whatever comes."

The parents ask for time to think things over. God grants it, and they begin to ask others in Heaven the nature of their transition. Some say they came easily, slipped right into eternity in their sleep. They'd do it again, they declare. Others say they were in pain for months, begging God to take them, and God wouldn't. Said it wasn't their time yet, and no one can come to Heaven until it's their time. The glory of the place erased their pain, sure enough, but they wouldn't do it again. Or wish it on their worst enemy. A few advised that the couple relax and let God be God. "Eternity is a long time," they said. "You'll enjoy your boy soon enough up here. Let him live first."

Yet without him, their misery only multiplied.

They contemplated for weeks until finally reaching a decision. Carefully, cautiously, they approached the throne and asked for God. He appeared in all His glory.

"Yes?"

"We've thought about your proposal, Lord, and we have our answer."

God sat easily in the royal chair. His caramel brown skin glistened against a full white beard and jet-black robe.

"What is your decision?"

They bowed before Him and, in unison, said, "Bring him to us."

God shakes His head and asks, "Are you sure about this?"

They nod.

God shrugs and says, "Very well then. You shall have him with you in Paradise."

They rejoice and tell others their son is coming. Within

a few days, they see him in the distance, shuffling toward Heaven's gate. Hand in hand, they run to meet him, but there is no joy in his countenance.

"Gabriel!" his father calls, with outstretched arms.

The boy stands unemotive, his head bowed. Confused and dismayed, the parents look at each other, then the despondent child.

"What is it, son?" his distressed mother cries. "We're back together again! Isn't this what we wanted?"

The boy lifts a sorrowful head and says, "It's what you wanted, Mother. You and Father. I missed you terribly, of course. I cried many days. But I wanted to live. To know love. To grow. To discover what I believed. To figure out why I was born. To have children and tell them about you. You took all of that from me."

The parents looked at God and apologized. God said, "Paradise is not the absence of pain. It's the presence of joy with it. Heaven teaches you that pain and joy are one and the same. You must have both to fully appreciate the kingdom. Your son is not prepared to live here."

"What should we do?" they asked, bewildered. "You said no one can ever go back."

"That is correct," God said. "Gabriel must stay. And now he will know sorrow for all of eternity."

The child mourned forever the life he never had.

I waited weeks for a response from the competition committee. It came on a Friday afternoon, when Mom lay in bed, trying to sober. I opened the official-looking letter and read that I'd won. They described my writing as "creative" and "beautiful" and "soulful." I reread the letter fifteen times before returning it to the envelope. Mom was in no condition to celebrate, and Dad was nowhere to be found. So I sat at the piano and played "It Is Well with My Soul" and shed tears of joy all by myself.

Day 13

When I turned thirteen, I started dancing. Actually, I'd been dancing unofficially for years, standing before the TV during *Soul Train* and mimicking Baryshnikov's arabesques, pirouettes, and pliés. I never studied ballet formally—even Mom wouldn't have had that—but I admired the beauty and technique of the form. I loved the body as an instrument, speaking what the voice could not, and I wanted to master the craft. So, instead of ballet, I did modern dance at a studio down off of Fifteenth and Main although, at home, I practiced splits and toe-touches, and tried, with all my might, to stretch my legs into the six-o'clock position. Dancing proved more physical than anything I'd ever done, but it invited my freedom, so I embraced it. I had no reservations when I danced. I didn't monitor my feelings in my movements. I just reached and swayed and kicked and bent, allowing my body to say all the things I could never say.

Dad didn't know. Not at first. Mom said she'd tell him later, when I got a little mastery under my belt. Fine with me. Yet, when he found out, he didn't respond like I thought he would.

We sat at the dining table, like we always did for dinner. Dad had moved out for good, but he ate with us if he happened to be around or if he had something important to say to me. Mom had made meatloaf, which she did pretty well, and mashed potatoes and broccoli. They chatted about arbitrary things, mostly for my sake, I think, then Dad said, "Heard you dancin now." No transition, no tension. Just an announcement.

I bowed my head, prepared for the guillotine. "Yessir."

"What kinda dancin you doin? Tap? I like tap."

I glanced up quickly and met Mom's eyes. They told me to go easy. "No sir, it's not tap. It's modern."

Dad's lips pooched outward. Lines in his forehead deepened like freshly plowed earth. "What kinda dancin is that?"

His question contained no malice, so I sighed slightly and said, "It's what background dancers might do for Michael Jackson or Prince." That didn't seem to help, so I added, "It's also what most contemporary dance companies do. Where they use the body to tell stories and interpret history. Stuff like that."

He nodded but still didn't understand. I was grateful for the try.

"I like the Nicholas Brothers. Ever heard of them?"

I had. I couldn't believe he had. Dad saw my surprise.

"I ain't stupid. I don't read like you and yo momma, but I can preciate good art when I see it."

Mom, too, gaped with amazement. "You've seen the Nicholas Brothers?"

Dad tried not to be offended. "Not in person, but on TV. They were on *The Ed Sullivan Show* one time when I still lived down home."

"Y'all had TVs in the country?"

Mom spit a bit of Coke onto the tabletop. Dad stared at me and smiled. "Actually, we didn't, but some of the folks in Blackwell did. I'd watch it sometimes if I was at a friend's house."

Mom repeated, "And you saw the Nicholas Brothers?"

Dad was getting pissed. "Hell yeah, I saw the Nicholas Brothers. How you think I know their name? And why is that so hard to believe?"

I had an answer, but I definitely couldn't say it. Instead, I brought the conversation back to center. "I like them, too, but that's not the kind of dancing I do. Mine is more expressive maybe."

Dad nodded and continued eating. Mom refused to look at me. I knew the conversation wasn't over.

"I know some other dancers too," Dad volunteered. Our initial shock returned. "Like Sammy Davis Jr. and Gregory Hines. I don't know a lot about em, but I seen em on TV since we been in this house."

I felt bad. So did Mom. Dad didn't hate expression. He hated sissified drama. Like *Little Orphan Andy.*

He faced me and asked, "What you like bout dancin?"

I'd never thought of a formal reason. "It's just...fun, I guess." I didn't know what else to say. "I get to express myself without explaining myself."

He nodded. "Do it pay good?"

"I don't know. I'm not a professional yet."

"You know any menfolk what do it for a livin?"

I didn't know anyone personally, so I shook my head.

"You think you can have a family, dancin?"

I almost said I didn't want a family, but I knew that wouldn't have gone over well, so I said, "Maybe. I've not thought about it. I'm still young."

"You old enough!" he shouted. I jerked. "You a young man now."

I frowned.

"That's right! When I was yo age, I was doin a man's day!" He cackled with reprimand. I didn't understand the reference. "At twelve years old, I could hook up mules, drive em all day, and take em back to the barn, all by sundown, all by myself." Pride rumbled in his voice. I wondered why he was telling me this, what this had to do with dancing. "Yep. You's a young man now. Gotta get ready."

My mistake was asking, "Get ready for what?"

He stopped eating and looked at me as if I had missed the entire conversation. "For a family, boy. Whatchu think?"

I had so much to say, but Mom's pleading eyes stopped me. Dad didn't know me at all.

"Man's gotta provide, boy. That's his job. Bible says so."

I didn't argue. I had never read the Bible and didn't intend to.

"That means he gotta work."

"Dancing *is* work," I mumbled.

"What'd you say?"

"I said, dancing is work, sir."

He shrugged. "Well, if it is, I sho hope somebody pay you to do it."

"Me too," I said.

"But if not, you gotta figure out somethin else to do. You can dance on the side." He stood, sat his empty plate in the sink, and thanked Mom for the meal.

"I'll see y'all later," he said and escaped through the front door.

Mom and I continued eating in silence. When I finished, I, too, sat my plate in the sink and headed toward my room. "He's paying for it, baby. He oughta know," Mom said, looking through the kitchen window.

I paused and turned. "He doesn't think boys should dance, Mom. Not the way I dance."

Mom sighed. "That's fine. He'll grow to appreciate it. If he don't, that'll be on him. Just do it well, honey. Excellence makes a way for itself."

Suddenly, I spread my arms wide and twirled with delight, kicking my right foot high above my head. Mom gazed, impressed beyond expectation. I chasséd down the hall and into an uncertain future.

Day 14

My teenager years were an experiment in identity construction. I was unsure of everything: my convictions, my thoughts about God, my thoughts about myself. I wanted someone to love but couldn't admit who I loved. I spent years trying to be regular, to fit in, and still never did.

I started by running for eighth grade student council president. Quiet as I was at home, I was outgoing and popular at school. All the kids knew me. They called me Swint.

A white boy named James Willingham opposed me, on the slogan Reliable, Resourceful, Responsible. He wasn't as popular as me, so I thought I could beat him and his corny motto. I took the slogan All Diamonds Shine. That was corny, too, but I liked it at the time. So did many other kids.

We campaigned for weeks, making promises we couldn't keep. I was black; he was white. Yet race wasn't an issue. I had as much white support as black. Maybe more. Where we differed was class. He came from wealthy parents who could afford anything he desired. I hailed from working-class folks who struggled to make ends meet. He played every sport the school offered and was good at them. He was also handsome, which helped a great deal. I think I was jealous although I didn't know it then. I wasn't bad looking, but I certainly didn't share his appeal. My strength was my personality, which connected me to all sorts of students. That's how I intended to win.

We gave campaign speeches at a midday school assembly. I had worked on mine for weeks. Mom read it and said it was good, and I trusted her. I can't remember it word for word, but I spoke about the importance of differences among people. How a community is stronger when composed of folks from various backgrounds. "Can you imagine," I asked fellow students, "how beautiful Heaven must be? People from every race, country, religion, and gender all loving and respecting each other as God walks among them? Doesn't matter if you're rich or poor. Money's no good in Heaven!" Kids leaped and roared with thunderous applause. I went on to say something like, "We can have Heaven right here! If we're bold enough to stand together, regardless of our differences, and fight for change. If other generations did it, we can too! Let's not be afraid!" I declared, "Let's change this school then change the world!" Every student stomped his feet and shouted with excitement. Even teachers cheered. I was proud of myself—not because of my campaign, but because, for the first time in my life, I spoke boldly about something I believed in, regardless of the consequences.

James's speech was pretty standard, full of famous quotes most kids had never heard, but they applauded anyway. When the day ended, a white boy named Henry Adams caught me in the hallway and asked if we could talk. I said sure. He was tall with long, brown, hippie hair and sky blue eyes. I didn't know him well, but we'd shared some of the same classes. He was generally quiet and reserved although he made good grades.

We met on the lawn, beneath a beautiful magnolia tree that spread its limbs like a protective mother hen. It was warm, early May, as I recall, with flowers blooming and wind stirring softly. He sat, so I did the same.

"Your speech was incredible!" he said, fidgeting with delight.

"Thanks. I worked on it a long time."

"It shows! You said some really powerful stuff."

I nodded, unsure of what else to say.

"Most kids aren't as bold as you."

I frowned a bit. "What do you mean?"

He stared a moment, presumably reconsidering what he'd wanted to say, then said it anyway. "We're cut from the same cloth, I think. You and I. Aren't we?"

Dad's face crystalized in my mind. "I'm not sure what you mean."

"Aren't you gay?"

At first, I said nothing. But there was no malice in his question, no implied judgment. He simply wanted to know. I'd asked myself the question a thousand times, yet I'd been too afraid to answer it. I'd seen at school the way sissified boys got bullied, and I'd heard on TV jokes about sensitive, overly expressive men. They were all gay, I assumed. Yet, in that moment, without fear of my parents' wrath, I blurted a truth I'd never admitted aloud.

"Um...yes. Yes, I am." I blinked repeatedly, wondering the cost of my truth.

He smiled. "Good. I was hoping so!"

I had never admitted this. Freedom didn't feel so free.

"There are quite a few of us around here. Boys *and* girls."

He touched my arm kindly, and I stiffened with fear. "Please don't tell anyone."

His smile faded. "Oh no way, man. No way. We gotta stick together. Cover each other. Know what I mean?"

We remained friends a long time. He went to Yale when I went to Lincoln, and he started a gay student union there. Went on to law school and clerked for one of the Supreme Court justices. Has his own practice in New York City now. We check in occasionally, but I wouldn't say we're friends. I'd thought about law school once, but since I don't believe in the American judicial system, I abandoned the idea. Yet, when we were kids, Henry helped me more than he knew.

I came home and told Mom. She always asked about my day, and I believed she'd love me regardless of who or what I was. Yet her blank expression arrested me. "What did you say?"

That's when I knew something was wrong, but I had already said it, so I had to repeat it: "I think I'm gay, Mom."

"Don't you ever say that again!" she shouted. "You're not!"

I gasped. If anyone knew me, it was Mom. She'd been my confidante, my cheerleader all my life. Her response stunned me. In fact, it hurt. The fury in her eyes made me regret saying anything.

"You're just…different from other boys. That's all."

I didn't understand her objection. Yet I'd spoken too much truth to lie now. "No, it's not. I'm not *just* different. I'm something else altogether."

She pounded the kitchen counter. "No, you're not! I didn't raise you like that."

"I didn't say you did! It's just who I am."

"No, it's not!"

"Mom! Why do you keep saying that? It's not your fault. Or anyone's."

She paced back and forth. "I don't want that for you! I want you to have a family of your own one day."

"Can't gay men have families? I mean, I know they can't have babies the old-fashioned way, but can't they adopt or somethin?"

"I want you to have a *real* family, Isaac!"

"What? Every family's a real one, Mom!"

Slap!

The kitchen went silent. Mom covered her mouth and quivered. Shocked, I stood there, rubbing my cheek, until I shuffled to my room. That's when she called Dad. I heard her crying, telling him what a horrible mother she'd been. She didn't tell him what I said. She just kept repeating, "He needs you, Jacob. He needs you." Dad was the last person I thought I needed.

He had moved out for good. Mom told me it was over between them. I should've been sad, but, really, I was relieved. A life with just me and Mom sounded glorious—until that fateful day.

Dad rushed over and burst through the front door. "What's

wrong over here?" he shouted. Mom met him in the living
room and, presumably, told him everything. He didn't seem
shocked or surprised.

"What do you want me to do?" he asked with a tone of
frustration.

"He's your son!" Mom screeched. "You're his father! Talk
to him."

"What do you want me to say?" Dad asked helplessly.

"I don't know!" Mom cried. "But you're a man, and this is
a man's issue."

Dad cackled sarcastically, "Oh now you think he needs a
man? I been sayin this all his life, and now, when he gets in
trouble, you want me to do something magical?"

Mom didn't respond.

"Where is he?" Dad mumbled irritably.

"You know where he is," she said.

That's when Dad came into my room and asked me that
awful question: *Do you wanna be a sissy?* I crumbled onto
the bed and swallowed clumps of humiliation. Believing he
might hurt me, I flat out lied. No boy *wants* to be a sissy. Yet
why couldn't boys act like girls? What was wrong with girls?
I wondered. When they acted like boys no one seemed to
mind. People called them tomboys, as if their behavior reflected something virtuous. Was femininity less divine than
masculinity? And who had decided that? I had lots of questions, but no answers and no allies, so I surrendered. I even
convinced myself that Henry Adams had coerced that con-
fession out of me. I was *not* that way. I couldn't believe I had
said it. Why had that white boy made me say it?

I spent weeks trying to be something other than what I

was. I took centerfold photos from Mom's *Jet* magazines and plastered them all over my bedroom walls. The women were gorgeous, but I wanted nothing to do with them. Still, this was what boys did, so I did it. I asked Mom if she'd buy me some of those hideous football bedspreads and curtains, and she gladly complied. I threw away my stuffed animals and painted the room a deeper, royal blue. Mom said, "This is what a boy's room oughta look like!" When Dad saw it, he sighed as if to say *Finally*. My parents were happy with me, so I smiled and went along, but I was miserable. Nothing in that room reflected me. I'd turned into what they dreamed I'd be.

The therapist asked, "Why was your mother's response so surprising?"

"Because she knew me. She knew what I was. And I thought she loved me."

"What were you?"

I frowned. I hated when she played these games. "What are you talkin about?"

"I'm talking about you. What are you saying your mother knew?"

My head fell backward onto the sofa as my eyes rolled. "She knew I was gay! That's what she knew!"

"How would she have known that? You didn't even know!"

"But she knew. She was my mother. All mothers know."

"Think about it, Isaac. The only way your mother could've known your sexual identity is by doing what other people do, and that is to make assumptions. That's why her response surprised you—because she didn't do that."

I had to remain silent to keep from crying.

"If she thought you were gay, she probably would've confronted you. This seems logical based on her reaction to your announcement. But she didn't assume you to be gay *just because* you were artistic, sensitive, and effeminate. She couldn't have known for sure until you told her."

I understood what she meant. I'd just never considered it.

"It seems your father, quote unquote, *knew*. The announcement didn't startle him."

"That's true."

"So why are you more frustrated with him than your mother?"

I shrugged. "I don't know. I guess because I never questioned my mother's love. Even that day."

"Why not if she slapped you?"

"Because her love for me was already well established!" I stood and chewed my inner cheeks. Something about my thinking wasn't making sense. For a while, I studied the office walls, complete with paintings of floral pastures and rural bucolic sunsets. The room was orderly to the point of feeling sterile. Plants were fake, and the tannish-brown, shapeless furniture was obviously cheap.

"Some of the truths you discover, Isaac, are going to conflict with what you feel in your heart. Still, don't back away from them. This is what you're looking for. Not simply what you feel, but how you came to feel it. It comes to make us reconsider what we *think* we know."

I sighed. "Then Mom's anger might've been because I hadn't been honest with her when *I* knew."

"Perhaps. That's a real possibility. But you shouldn't be angry with yourself for that. You were a child. You didn't have the strength to carry that kind of truth at the time. Or probably even understand the complexities of what it meant to be gay. Not unless you were well-read on the subject. And unusually fearless."

She looked at me and waited.

I skipped the implied question and said, "And Dad did what I did. He assumed I was gay and said nothing."

"That's right."

Her assurance exposed my fragility. I felt small and pitiful.

"Isaac, the question here is whether you knew who you were. I don't mean did you conclude something based on what you thought others thought, but if you knew, down in your soul, who and what you were. That's the question."

"If you're asking me whether I knew I was attracted to boys, the answer is yes. I knew that."

"And is that your identity? Is that who you are? Is that what you want others to know about you?"

"It's part of it!"

"Great. What are the other parts?"

Day 15

The summer I turned fourteen, Dad took me to Arkansas.
I'd always wanted to go because he talked so much about it.
I felt like I knew Granddaddy and Uncle Esau and Grandma.
They were mythical figures in my mind, but I thought that if
I went "down home," as he called it, they might come to life.
Since I was little, he had spoken of the land, the people, the
place like a magical paradise, and I wanted to see it for myself.

I remember getting in the car at some insane hour of the
morning and waking up in the country, just an hour or so
from Blackwell. It seemed like a whole different world. Both
sides of the interstate were covered with trees and bushes so
green they looked artificial. I didn't see a building for miles.
You'd think this would've bored a city kid like me, but it
didn't. Something felt sacred about the South, something natural and easy and untainted. It lacked the stress of Kansas City,

and I liked that. I lowered the window and smelled a sweet fragrance, which Dad said was honeysuckle. I didn't know what that was, but it reminded me of a floral bouquet.

I kept asking how close we were to Blackwell, and he laughed at my anticipation. He seemed different down there. Something about home changed him. Or restored him. A glimmer of joy twitched in his eye, and I realized a man can be out of place, out of context, in this world. I liked Dad during that trip.

We exited the freeway, finally, and turned onto rough, graveled roads. I saw cows, barns, deer, goats, horses, and dogs running about freely. Dust billowed behind us like dirty clouds. Dad took a left at a fork in the road and, when we rounded the bend, I saw a breathtaking scene: open fields of swaying green grass, trees tall and upright like proud soldiers, squirrels and rabbits bouncing about, and wildflowers waving in bloom. Pride colored Dad's voice and countenance—"Here it is!" he announced—returning him to the childhood he re-vered. I'd never seen his eyes dance with wonder and delight.

He jumped from the car, so I followed and learned all sorts of things only a country boy would know. Like the fact that cows stand from their hind legs first. And most food is eaten only in its season. And flowers are picked after they seed so there'll be more next year. And gardens need morning sun more than evening sun. I got a whole education in country living and loved every minute of it.

Dad shared pieces of our family history that made me proud. He told me my great-grandfather, Wilson Swinton, migrated from South Carolina, after slavery, and bought five hundred acres in the center of Arkansas. That seemed enough land for an entire city! He and his sons then trapped game and sold wild meat and furs for a living. They also broke and trained mules for farming and other domestic needs. "We were a proud, hardworking people," he said.

The more Dad talked, the clearer I saw my ancestors. They weren't rich, but they were creative and resilient. "Dark black people," Dad emphasized. "No white blood in em!" He seemed proud of that. I was happy to be part of the bloodline. "Swintons was tall, thin, quiet folks. Not much for conversation. But you couldn't outwork em!" There they were, in my imagination, chopping wood, washing clothes, and tending the lawn. Something about that legacy made me smile.

We spent the day walking the land, from the old shack in which Dad was born, to the river and across fields and forests. Everywhere we went, Dad had a story.

The one I remember most was about a cousin named Isadore. They said his ancestors were straight from Africa. He was a juju man, a conjurer who could manipulate invisible things. Dad said he had a wife and five kids, four girls and a boy. His father and my great-grandpa Wilson were brothers who came from slavery together. They lived scattered about on the land, farming for themselves and raising their own cotton. They didn't work for white folks. They refused. According to Dad, Isadore put a spell on a white man who cheated him out of his cotton crop one year. Cousin Isadore couldn't read, but he could count, and he knew the man had swindled him. When Isadore confronted him about it, the man got angry and accused Isadore of questioning his character. All of a sudden, Dad said, Isadore smiled and walked away.

Within a week, both the man's sons had fallen ill. Everybody knew what had happened. Even the white man knew. Cousin Isadore's reputation was well-known. The white man came to Isadore, begging him to reverse the spell and restore his boys' lives, but Isadore Swinton wouldn't do it. The man even apologized and paid Isadore the money he had withheld from him, but, again, Isadore was unmoved.

"He stood on that porch lookin straight over that man's head like he wasn't even there!"

"A white man?" I said, surprised.

"Shit, yeah!" Dad declared. "We had some power, sometimes. This was one of those times."

The white man stomped away, so furious he could hardly see. When, a few days later, his boys died, folks told Isadore there'd be trouble, but Isadore didn't care.

The white man gathered up all the white men he could find and came to the land in the middle of the night. Cousin Isadore was sitting in the dark, waiting for him.

"Some say Isadore shot first, others say the white man did, but either way it go, there was a battle on Swinton land in the midnight hour. Just as white men came together, black men, too, stood as one in the night, shooting from every direction. All in all, twelve white men were killed but no black men."

"None?" I sneered.

"None! Not one."

"White folks didn't know what to do. Things calmed after a while. Most black folks thought it was pretty much over with. We didn't hear nothin for a long time. Then, one day, right before Christmas, Isadore come home, and his house was a ball of fire. Folks didn't try to put it out. There was no use. Granddaddy said folks stood around and watched it burn, glad wunnit nobody in it."

Dad looked at me. I knew there was more to the story. I wasn't sure I wanted to hear it, but I was too intrigued not to.

Isadore waited anxiously for his wife and kids to return from town, but, as the sun went down, they didn't show up. He summoned a group of armed black men to help him search for them, but no one had seen his family. By sunrise, everyone knew something bad had happened. Isadore was out of his mind. Practically everyone in Blackwell gathered before the burnt shack. Soon, the white man and five or six others come up the road on horses, smiling.

"Good morning to y'all," he said with a sinister grin. "I had a feeling you'd be here."

Everyone stood still. Most closed their eyes.

"Did you find your gift?" he asked.

It took several men to hold cousin Isadore back. Someone said, "We don't know what you mean, suh."

The white man acted surprised. "No? Oh my goodness. I guess you don't."

No one could've guessed what that man had done. Women grabbed children and held them close. Menfolks tried to be strong for Isadore, but many of them trembled and shook their heads.

"I wanted to leave you a gift, it bein Christmas and all," he said, chuckling while staring hatred into Isadore's eyes. "So me and some of my boys come out here early yesterdee afternoon, while you men were in the fields, and we wrapped your lovely little wife and children with rope and string and

put red ribbons all over em, and then we decided to make the
whole house red since that's such a pretty Christmas color."

Isadore collapsed and beat the earth.

"You didn't find them inside?" he mocked. "They was all
in a circle, right in front of the fireplace, waitin for Santa to
come. Guess you couldn't hear em screamin with Christmas
stockings in their mouths. Mighta gon up in flames before
you ever got here."

Shrieks and cries echoed among the trees. Isadore tossed
on the ground, yelling, "NO! NO!" frightening everything
in the forest.

"That's the only time I ever seen black men cry," Dad said.
"I was a li'l boy, but I remember that."

I didn't look at him. Something felt disrespectful about it.
But I asked, "What happened to cousin Isadore?"

Dad cleared his throat. "Spent the rest of his life in a rockin
chair in front of that charred pile. Wouldn't let nobody touch
it. Some days he'd speak, some he wouldn't. Cried a lot.
Couldn't believe he stood there doin nothin while his family burned inside."

"But he didn't know."

"Course he didn't," Dad sighed, "but that didn't matter. He
blamed hisself for startin the whole thing. Thought he was bein
a man. That don't always turn out the way you think it will."

When we left the next day, I understood my father better.
I saw what he was made of, what kind of life had produced
him, and I respected him for that. He was brilliant in so many
ways. It was the first time I believed my love of knowledge
might've come from him.

The trip inspired me to do a family tree. I wanted to see exactly where I fit into our lineage. I wanted to know names, dates, and stories of those whose blood informed my blood. I wanted to gather all the knowledge I could as an inheritance to my children—if I ever had any. Arkansas made me dream a future—and a past—I had never conceived in Kansas City.

Day 16

I'd wanted to ask Dad about his parents, his mother and father, but clearly he was avoiding the conversation, so I let him. I'd asked Mom once, and she said she didn't know. All she knew was that they had died young. She told me not to ask him about it, but to let him tell me in his own time. That time never came. I suppose this is the way of trauma. We file hurt and pain away in dark parts of the soul, never knowing it finds its own way out, disguised as something else altogether. We protect it with silence, but we don't heal it that way. We simply hand it to the next generation.

I'm trying not to participate in that, but I'm afraid I already have.

"So you got your storytelling skills from your father?" the therapist asked.

I shrugged. "I don't know. Guess I could've. I always thought I got them from my mother. She was the reader."

"Sure, but you don't have to read to tell stories. Storytelling is a gift. Reading is a skill."

I contemplated that a long time.

"The ability to entertain people by weaving together a narrative is a natural-born art. Most people can't do it, even those who think they can."

"Then I'm not a storyteller. I'm a writer. I can create stories on paper, but I'm no good at telling them off the top of my head."

"I see. That's a good distinction to know, I believe."

I felt a sense of disappointment. I'd wanted to master every creative expression, but alas I surrendered. I'd wrestle my ego later. For now, I wiped sweat from my brow and wondered if the air conditioner was broken.

"Both my folks were storytellers. Just in different ways."

She nodded. "So creativity is in your blood."

"Guess so."

I'd not wanted to give Dad credit for anything artistic in me, but seems I had no choice.

She remained silent awhile, forcing me to swallow truths I had denied. Then she changed the subject. "What do you do for a living?"

"I worked for Microsoft as a computer programmer until I quit a little while ago."

Her brow furrowed. "Why?"

"Why what?"

"Why did you work there? That doesn't seem like your kind of job."

I tried to cackle past the contradiction. "Dumb and desperate, I guess. Majored in Computer Science in college 'cause I thought I could make money."

"Was the money worth it?"

"Definitely not. BUT," I hollered, "I can't be broke."

"Who's asking you to be? Plenty of artistic people make plenty of money."

"I wasn't sure I could."

"Maybe that's what you're frustrated about. The fact that you had the world within your grasp and let it go."

"Maybe."

"Must be a horrible feeling."

"Dang! Can you not do that?"

"I'm sorry. I didn't mean to aggravate a sore wound. I just see your sadness."

I stormed out and into the hallway, where I melted to the floor. She didn't call after me or come get me. Eventually I stood and walked away. Just like that. Just as I'd done to my dream all those years ago.

Day 17

After the Arkansas trip, I hoped Dad and I might start over. He'd been kind and warm down there, something I'd rarely experienced. I saw a side of him I didn't know. So I painted a portrait of the countryside in Blackwell for a school art exhibition. I'd always drawn a little, and I was pretty good at it. I'd never painted before, but I believed I could.

Images of the land lingered in my mind. Every day after school, I sketched out the portrait, just as I remembered it. I invited Dad to the show, hoping to surprise him. Of course Mom would be there.

The evening of the exhibition, anxious parents flooded the school gymnasium. They buzzed and marveled at various paintings, especially one of a beautiful black woman in red. Her hair stood up like a crown, and an elegant white pearl necklace lay easily upon her chest. The portrait was so real it seemed alive.

The other picture folks admired was mine. A crowd stood before it, shaking their heads and murmuring about color, dimension, and depth. I'd put the shack in the distance, letting trees, birds, and flowers have center stage. I liked it, but I hadn't thought it was *that* good.

When Dad arrived and saw it, he shuddered. I hid, some distance away, watching him lick his lips and blink with disbelief. He looked around, perhaps for me, perhaps to see if anyone noticed his response. A sweet old lady, probably someone's grandmother, touched his back softly, and I think he wiped a tear away. She offered a handkerchief, but he shook his head and smiled. That was my cue to enter.

"You like it, Dad?" I asked as I approached.

He turned abruptly, too startled to speak. After a few precious seconds, he said, "My God, boy. I didn't know you could do this."

"Yessir. Me either."

For the first time I could remember, he put his left arm around my shoulders and planted his right hand over my heart. I didn't breathe one breath.

"If I was as talented as you, Isaac, I'd be a rich man."

Other parents agreed. They complimented Mom and Dad on raising such a gifted kid, but both rejected the credit.

"He came here with this," Dad said. "Trust me. I didn't have nothin to do with it."

"Me either!" Mom added, waving excitedly. "If it's creative, he can do it. Always been that way. Always!"

I basked in their pride. Friends gawked, asking why I hadn't painted before. I had no real answer. The principal joined in, asserting that perhaps I should consider art school one day.

Everyone thought I was special that evening, including me. My art teacher asked what I'd do with the portrait, and I told her I didn't know.

"Certainly hang on to it," she said. "From the looks of things, you might be famous one day."

On the way home, Dad repeated the question: "What *are* you gonna do with that picture, boy?"

I shrugged lightly. "I don't know. Hang it up somewhere, I guess."

Once Dad dropped us off, Mom pulled me aside and said, "He asked you because he wants it."

I frowned. "What? You think so? How do you know?"

She entered the house without saying more. I watched his rear lights disappear around the dark corner.

The next day, he, acting weird and awkward, came by the house after work. I heard his footsteps outside my door although, at first, he didn't come in. I wondered what he was thinking, why he hesitated so long. I didn't move either. Imagine that—father and son frozen on either side of the door because we couldn't decide what to say to each other. Yet I resolved to remain still until he made the first move. If he didn't come in, I wouldn't invite him.

Suddenly he knocked loudly. That's how I knew something troubled him. He'd never knocked before.

"Come in," I said, trying to sound surprised.

Dad opened the door carefully. "Whatcha say, boy?" he slurred, then closed the door and leaned upon it.

"I'm cool, Dad. You okay?"

"Oh yeah. Fine. Still thinkin bout that picture. You somethin else, you know?"

"Gee, thanks. Preciate it."

He tried to smile but managed only a stubborn smirk. "We had a good time down home, didn't we?"

"Yessir. I like it down there. It's peaceful and…beautiful."

"Yep. That's where I grew up."

Of course I knew that, so I waited for him to go on.

"Never thought I'd see it in a painting."

Again, I hesitated, not sure what to say. "Well, hope I did it justice. I'm no Monet. That's for sure!"

"You are to me."

I studied the floor, he looked elsewhere, and silence settled between us. "Guess I'll be goin," he finally said and turned to grab the knob.

Just then, I said, "Dad?"

He paused without turning. "Yes?"

"You can have the painting if you want it."

He halted a brief moment. I thought he might say something else, but he didn't. Days later, the painting was gone.

Day 18

By high school, I had dabbled with all the creative arts: writing, singing, painting, dancing, music. I loved writing best. Something about language freed me and invited my self-expression without shame or alteration. I wrote poems and short stories—really bad stuff—that no one in their right mind would've published, but at least I wasn't afraid to try. Words fascinated me, how they changed meaning by changing place in a sentence. Sometimes I rearranged words simply to see what new idea might come forth. Other times, I played around with specific words, especially verbs, because I liked how images shifted in my mind when I considered the slightest variation in vocabulary. Mrs. Kuntz, my eleventh grade English teacher, said one day, "There are no true synonyms." I never forgot that. She was right. I loved slight differences between near synonyms, the way certain words sharpened the meanings of others. I discovered this the day I wrote a story about a man who deemed himself unlovable.

His name was John Wright.

I liked the story, but I think I overrepresented his body. I put too much emphasis on his weight, which, although central to the plot, wasn't the point of the story.

John was a large man who could barely walk from the bed to the bathroom without exhaustion. He lived alone, on disability, and was grateful most days not to be seen. Chauncey, his only friend, dropped off groceries every few weeks and brought in his mail. They didn't talk much. Not like they once did when they frequented bars and clubs in their youth, before John tripled his weight. He'd always been thick, but he once had enough shape for people to see the difference. It wasn't until his mother died that John processed grief as hunger. He could never get full, regardless of what he ate, and Chauncey's admonitions fell on deaf ears. By the time John understood his relationship to food as a problem, he carried over four hundred pounds.

On Easter Sunday morning, Chauncey rushed John to the hospital because he couldn't walk back to the car from sunrise service. He went into cardiac arrest, and doctors told him that if he didn't lose weight soon, he'd be dead in a year. That didn't trouble John. What disturbed him was the death of his mother—the only person, he believed, who saw him for who he was. So John ate to allay his misery.

His last wish was a sensual, sincere human touch. Feeling sorry for his friend, Chauncey told him of a sex ring he'd heard of where a person could purchase their desires. John contacted them, and sure enough, someone agreed to the terms. No sex, no kissing, no nakedness. Just touching neutral zones. John had hoped for a little more, but he'd take what he could get.

When the day came, John struggled to the shower, sweating every step of the way. He hadn't had a visitor in years. His room was rank and musty, like an overused locker room. He couldn't replace the mattress—he'd spent his last dime—but he could change the sheets. Well, *he* couldn't but someone could. The landlord ended up doing it, charging John extra for having to vacuum and sanitize the place.

The date, as John thought of him, would arrive at 8:00 p.m., they agreed. John wrestled into a pair of khaki pants and a gray-and-black-striped dashiki. By 7:30, he was ready.

The guy arrived a bit late, 8:10 or so, and banged as if frustrated.

"Come in," John called kindly, unable to meet him at the door.

The guy saw John, squatted in the middle of the sagging bed, and shook his head.

"What's your name?" John asked.

He sighed, continuing to marvel with disbelief. "My name ain't important. Let's just get this over with."

"Have a seat there. Please."

The man refused. "I don't mean no harm, dude, but when you said thick and husky, you lied. You passed that a long time ago."

"I didn't mean to deceive you. We don't have to do anything that makes you uncomfortable."

"We won't! I promise you that!"

John felt the insult but refused to entertain it. "I'm John."

The guy didn't respond.

"What do you do for a living?"

Rolling his eyes, the man said, "I do this. Okay?"

"Okay."

"Obviously you don't do anything."

John swallowed hard. "No need to be hurtful. I've paid for your time, so you don't lose anything."

He shrugged and took the seat.

John tried to make casual conversation, but the guy refused. "Can we just do whatever we're gonna do, so I can go?"

"I'm trying to do it. All I wanted was...well...company. Someone to talk to and perhaps... I don't know—"

"What?" His expression reeked of loathing. It was precisely what John didn't want.

"You can go if you like. I don't wanna feel bad on my birthday."

The guy's countenance softened a bit. "Fine. Happy Birthday."

"Thanks."

For the next forty-five minutes, John faced the wall and spoke about his life and struggles. The man sat there, without as much as a grunt. The fact that he didn't leave encouraged John to go on. With the hour almost spent, John risked what he'd hoped for.

"Even if you don't talk, could you at least hold my hand? Please?"

The guy frowned and sighed heavily, as if someone had asked for his very heart.

Reluctantly, he extended his right hand. When John took it, John's hand dwarfed the man's so completely it disappeared.

John's eyes closed and he mumbled, "Yes. Oh yes."

The man stared at John's ecstasy, totally unaware of the

depth of his need. John couldn't constrain his weeping. The man almost let go, tried to pry his fingers away, but John squeezed them for dear life. He was in another world now, a place where his humanity wasn't debated. He saw himself, in his mind's eye, laughing with children and sharing ideas about politics with argumentative old men. John remembered bygone days, at half his size, and now in his dream, he saw himself again, wearing a tight forty-inch waist, walking with confidence long gone. The man saw or sensed none of this. He simply wanted to go.

At 9:00 p.m. exactly, he yanked his hand from John's and said, "All right. Time's up."

"Not quite," John pleaded. "I paid for an hour. You arrived at 8:10."

The man's patience waned. "Fine! What else do you want?"

John looked downward, and whispered, "Can you smile?"

"What?"

"Can you ignore what I look like and smile at me? Like you would someone you find beautiful?"

The guy cackled at John's desperate request, but John's sincerity trumped the man's sarcasm.

"It won't cost you anything," John said. "But it would do me a world of good."

The man feigned a fake smile. John winced and said, "No. Not that. Make it genuine if you can."

The guy would've laughed again except John's teary eyes stopped him.

"You serious, man?" he said.

John couldn't speak so he nodded. Finally, the guy looked at him, in all his pity and despair, in all his self-loathing and incomprehensible desperation, and, from his heart, he smiled, and John smiled and, together, they talked like men who dreamed what neither would ever have.

I submitted the story to another writing competition. Mom said it was incredible, but too mature for my age. Still, I liked it. It explored the depths and dimensions of the human soul, and that's what I meant to get at. I titled the story "Touch Me," which was pretty ironic, I thought. Again, I think I overemphasized John's weight, describing it in such detail that it got in the way of the overall plot. Needless to say, I didn't win, but I got an honorable mention plus priceless feedback that grew my writing skills. I think this was the moment I began to consider myself a bona fide writer.

I gave poems as Christmas gifts that year. It was 1978 or 9. Most people, except my cousin Jeffrey, threw them away, I'm sure. He called and said, "Hey, man! Preciate the poem. It's cool. Had to read it a few times to get it, but I dig it." His encouragement inspired me to write what I thought was my best piece yet. It went something like this:

There shall come a day, an hour
When love shall be unlimited,
Untainted, unreserved but never unknown…
Every man shall be free to be,
Every woman shall sing her own song.
And the gates of Hell shall not prevail.

No life shall be ashamed of itself.
Every living thing unveiled in naked truth,
All energy shared. Loneliness made illegal,
Racism the butt of every joke. Religions

Abandoned for insight and intelligence.
Jesus painted rainbow bright.
Healing ripe for the picking.

I didn't care what anyone thought. I had found my voice.
I wrote poems from then til now. Most are probably trash,
but I never intended to publish. Nothing ever freed me like
the liberty of language. Words beckon me to recognize parts
of myself I used to be ashamed of. I have countless journals
of poems and writings that reveal the nature of my journey.
It's been a difficult trip, but here I am.

"You got a cure for self-betrayal?" I asked the therapist at our next meeting.

She closed her eyes and nodded. "I wish."

I glanced downward and noticed, for the first time, a dark brown stain on the cream-colored carpet. Someone had tried to conceal it with the sofa, but edges reached out, like fingers in a horror movie.

"I should've been a writer all these years. There's nothing I love more."

She wasn't listening. Her mind was elsewhere, lost in something personal and painful, it seemed, that my truth definitely triggered.

"Don't beat yourself up, Isaac. We all do it—to one degree or another."

I couldn't resist the urge. "What was your betrayal?"

She smiled across regret and said, "This is your time. It's not about me."

"I know. But I'd like to know. Maybe your story could help me."

She shifted uncomfortably and said, "All right. I'll tell you. I won't give details, but I will answer your question."

She retired the notepad and pen to the coffee table between us. "I married someone I shouldn't have. I knew it all along."

"Did you love him?"

"I absolutely did!"

"Then what was the problem?"

"I didn't require him to love me."

Our hearts met in the ether and embraced like old friends.

Day 19

A turning point happened for me in tenth grade. I was fifteen or so and as fast as anyone on the school track team, or so I thought. I knew this simply by watching them. They were fast, but I believed I was faster. One of the track stars, a boy named Calvin Mutt, called me a faggot—a word I abhor—and I shivered with fury and shame. I challenged the bastard and his buddies to a race, and they accepted.

"You?" one of them shouted. "You race *us*?"

I nodded.

"Can you run?"

I didn't answer.

One added, "Bet he run like a girl!"

We agreed to meet after school on the track field. Apparently, they had told others, for when we arrived, fifty students stood nearby, anxiously awaiting the outcome.

I believed I could beat them. I was thin and in pretty good shape, so I felt confident.

All three boys and I agreed to the hundred-yard dash. One of them was a distance runner, but he still believed he could take me.

I looked around and saw several kids supporting me. A few waved thumbs high in the air and chanted my name. Others smiled as if to say, *Run those fuckers in the ground!*

A boy I didn't know stood at the finish line with both hands raised. If I lost, I'd be the laughing stock of Central High School. If I won, I'd be a hero—perhaps.

We spread across the start line and waited several silent seconds until the boy downfield shouted, "On your mark!"

We bowed and positioned our hands on the solid white line. Our legs lingered behind us in L-shaped anticipation.

"Get set!"

Please don't let me lose, Lord.

"Go!"

Those boys shot forward like bullets. I was last out of the blocks, but I had the most to lose, so I clenched my teeth and accelerated the way Harriet must've run to freedom. After forty yards, I had passed one of them. The others sprinted slightly ahead of me. With each desperate breath, I closed the gap until, nearing the finish, I thanked God I wouldn't be embarrassed.

Kids cheered when, simultaneously, two boys and I dashed past the hundred-yard line. I couldn't tell if I had won, but I knew I hadn't lost, and that was good enough for me.

"Damn, Swint! Shit! You can run!"

"You smoked they asses!"

"They can't say nothin now!"

The boy at the finish line declared a tie. I didn't haggle. Everyone saw me start out from behind, so a tie meant I had outrun them. That was my logic.

When I got home, Dad and Mom were posted before the TV, though neither was watching it. I was surprised to see Dad. He hadn't been by in a while. Mom lingered in the pages of some romance novel, traveling a world she'd never see. Dad's head was shielded by pages of the *Kansas City Star*, although I knew he wasn't reading it. He looked at the "funnies," as he called cartoons, chuckling proudly whenever he thought he'd comprehended a complicated joke.

I burst through the front door.

Mom smiled, sensing something wonderful. Dad looked over those unspeakable reading glasses, the ones with the do-do brown frames and cracked lens, frustrated that I had interrupted a perfect, mutually constructed silence.

"I won."

Mom placed her novel on her lap. "You won what, baby?"

"A foot race."

Dad folded the paper, having heard something that piqued his interest.

"A few boys on the track team challenged me to a race."

"How many?" he asked.

"Three."

"And you beat them?" Mom declared more than she asked. "You beat them *all*?"

"Yep!"

I looked to Dad for affirmation, but he had none to give. "I was behind at first, but we were even at the finish line."

Mom stood and hugged me. "That's good, honey! You surprised yourself, huh?"

"Guess I did. I knew I was fast but not *that* fast!"

Dad repositioned the newspaper before him and said, though not uglily, "You didn't win, boy."

I frowned. "What do you mean? You weren't there. How do you know?"

Mom's eyes narrowed. "Isaac." Dad didn't look at me.

"'Cause you didn't beat them. You tied them."

I wiped joy and sweat from my brow.

"Dad, I was behind when we started. I caught up with them."

"That might be true, but that don't mean you won."

Mom stared from me to Dad and back again. She gave me the let-it-go smirk. Of course I didn't.

Dad and I argued until, defeated, I surrendered. "Fine. Whatever," I said, and stepped toward my room.

Before I got there, he asked, "*How* did you run?"

I turned and chewed my bottom lip. "Excuse me? What do you mean *how*?"

Mom sighed, "Jacob. Please."

"I mean *how*. Like…"

I knew what he meant, but nothing in the world would've made me answer that question.

"I ran like people run!"

The insult moistened my back and underarms. Soon, sweat streaked my temples.

"I hope you did. I hope you wunnit out there…"

"Out there *what*?"

"Stop it, you two. Just stop it."

"…embarrassing yourself."

"How could I embarrass myself if I won? Or almost won." I stared at him, daring him to say what he was implying.

"Well…" He shrugged. "It don't matter now."

My eyes must've blazed scarlet. "Yes, it does! If you got something to say, say it!"

"Isaac!" Mom shouted, afraid my tone would incite Dad's rage. "Go on to your room!"

"No, Mom! I won't go to my room! I'm gonna stand here and wait for Dad to say whatever he's trying to say."

Neither of us yielded. Dad stood and matched my gaze.

"I said what I wanted to say," he overenunciated slowly.

His warm breath brushed my face. Knowing I couldn't whip him—I never thought I could—I went to my room and slammed the door.

If Dad had said what he was thinking, we might've fought that day. He worried that I had sashayed down the track, twisting and twirling toward the finish line. Even though I had won, or tied from his perspective, his concern was whether I had run like a girl.

Well, I hadn't—I didn't think. But I wasn't sure, and that bothered me for days.

I couldn't get the possibility out of my head. There was only one way to know, and, finally, I faced it.

I approached a white boy from Geometry class who had been at the scrimmage. He was always reasonably kind, so I thought he'd tell me the truth. I also thought he'd be uninvested in my emotional response.

"Hey, David! Wait up," I called after class a few days later.

He turned and smiled. "Hey, Isaac. What's up?"

"I…um…wanna ask you something."

"Sure. What is it?"

"Remember the other day when I raced those boys down on the track field?"

"Yeah, man! You can really run!"

"I need to ask you something. It's sorta personal."

His innocence morphed into suspicious curiosity. "Sure. Anything."

I swallowed hard and tried to keep things light, but I'm sure my expression looked fake and insincere. "I was just wondering if you think…or if you thought…that I…uh…ran like a boy?" My voice cracked.

He shook his head and touched my shoulder. "Isaac, you ran fine. Don't worry about that."

Now I got worried. That was nice, but it wasn't an answer. "David, do you think I ran like a girl?"

Hearing desperation in my voice, he knew what was at stake. "I don't know. I can't say."

He tried to leave, but I clutched his arm. "Please, David. Don't spare my feelings. I just need the truth. Please."

David looked at me then looked away. "I don't like this, Isaac."

"I don't either. But I have to know."

He sighed and shrugged. "Some boys laughed at how you ran. Said your butt twisted and switched. I told them to cut it out, but they wouldn't. When you caught up with the others, they shut up."

I nodded.

"Don't pay that shit any mind, man. You have nothing to be ashamed of. You outran those stupid fuckers!"

"Thanks," I mumbled, and escaped to the gym.

I *had* run like a girl. I hadn't meant to. That's why those boys hadn't said anything afterward.

I had won, but I had lost too. Far more than I knew.

Day 20

I started dating girls that year. I was scared of boys intimately. Yes, I had considered what being gay might mean, but I had not weighed the cost of being out. I'd seen on the news and read in magazines and newspapers what people did to gay boys, so I thought I'd better learn how the whole romance thing worked with girls. I was no good at it though. Girls liked me, but I was awkward and uninvested. Yet I sincerely wanted companionship. However, most of them saw through me before a relationship could evolve. In my heart, I wasn't gay. I liked boys, but I wasn't willing to love them. Not openly. Not for the whole world to see. It wasn't worth my life. I'd seen a special on TV where doctors called homosexuality a disease, a mental illness, and some states even had facilities where families sent gay sons to be "corrected." That frightened me, and I didn't want anything to do with it. So I denied my truth until the idea of being with a boy disgusted me. Like it seemingly did most others in the world.

Marie, the girl Dad liked so much, was the first I brought home, though not the first I kissed. That title went to Jessica Winfield. She was pretty and thick, but not super popular with the boys. I approached her one afternoon and asked if she wanted to meet me in the gym locker room. She smiled and nodded. Around three forty-five, we met behind some large workout equipment and started kissing. Everything was okay until she slid her tongue in my mouth. It felt slimy, and I didn't like it. I pushed her away.

"What's the matter with you?" she asked softly. "You the one asked me to meet you here!"

"I know, but I don't like to kiss like that."

"Like what? That's the way you do it!"

"Not me. It's not the way I do it."

"Maybe because you don't know how to do it. Not with a girl."

I grimaced. "Excuse me?"

She cackled. "Come on, Isaac. You know what people say about you. I just wanted to see if it was true."

Too embarrassed to speak, I swallowed hard and waited.

"Guess it is," she sneered.

"No, it's not!" I shouted much too loudly.

But she was halfway out of the room. I followed.

"Please, Jessica! I'm sorry. I just…don't have a lotta experience with—"

She tossed over her shoulder, "It's okay, Isaac. Don't worry. I won't tell."

And she didn't. In fact, when I saw her the next day, she

spoke as if nothing had happened. We became friends. We even joked about that time, reenacting my revulsion, until both of us hollered. She was such a good person.

The next girl approached me. She was new to Kansas City, from Los Angeles, I believe. I remember the day she arrived. Boys whispered about some gorgeous new girl at school and wondered who would get her. When I saw her, she took my breath away. I wanted her because everyone wanted her, and I thought that if she wanted me, people's doubts might be quieted.

She really was a beauty. I knew I had to do something special to capture her heart, so I wrote her a poem. She liked it, and we started exchanging notes every day. I garnered the courage to take her to a movie. I don't recall which movie because all I wanted was to put my arm around her. When I did, during the last ten minutes of the show, she smiled and touched my thigh. I was glad not to have been rejected.

She never said she was my girlfriend, but I thought of her that way. Boys didn't congratulate or tease me about her; they glared instead, wondering, it seemed, why in the world a girl like Tracey Newton would want me. I only hoped they wouldn't tell her what they thought of me. If they did, I'd be ruined.

We kissed a few times, the way I liked to do it, then Tracey invited me to her house. I thought I'd meet her folks and let them get a sense of me, but they weren't home. She led me into her bedroom, and we talked awhile. Then, she started kissing me and unbuttoning my shirt. I didn't know what to do. I was too nervous to be aroused. What if her folks came home and caught us? I remembered the error I had made with Jessica, so

I played along, rubbing her back and tugging at her bra strap. She yielded easily, which turned me off. Still, within seconds, we stood before each other in nothing but our underwear. I wanted an erection, but it wouldn't come. I prayed intensely, while she embraced me and slid her fingers around the rim of my underwear, then lowered them slowly down my buttocks. I unsnapped her bra and removed her panties. I had never seen a naked girl before, but she seemed perfectly at ease with my body. She placed my hands on her breasts, which were warm, soft, and supple, as she kissed her way down my chest to my privates. When she took it in her mouth, I gasped and shivered. She moaned. I liked it, but I didn't like that she liked it. I thought a respectable girl wasn't supposed to like it. That's what Mom had said. So I couldn't get aroused.

I lifted her to eye level and said I had to go. She touched my privates again, but I pushed her hand away and lifted my underwear. She asked if anything was wrong; I said no. She asked if I thought she was sexy; I said yes. She asked why I wouldn't do it with her, and I said we should mean something to each other before that. I could tell she didn't agree. I could also tell she thought something was wrong with me.

I left abruptly. At dinner, Mom inquired of my day, and while I smiled sheepishly, trying to conceal my dilemma, I hated myself for being unable to perform. If I was a real boy, I could've gone all the way, I told myself, but apparently I wasn't. I had no choice but to consider, once again, that maybe I was *that way*. My body hadn't responded when I'd needed it to, so obviously I wasn't what I thought I was. Or what I wanted to be. Yet I couldn't accept that. My truth was far too heavy back then. I told myself I was just nervous.

If we'd been someplace else, I could've done it. If she'd been a respectable young lady and let me make the first move, everything would've been fine. Her aggression had turned me off, I decided, which would've been true of any young man. I had to try again.

The next day at school, she wouldn't speak to me. I sat next to her in the lunchroom, but she grabbed her tray and walked away. I tried to explain that the problem wasn't her, but she continued on as if I were invisible. Boys roared with laughter. They knew I had failed somehow, and they enjoyed mocking me. I didn't know what she said, but it was enough to incite unbridled jeering all over the school. I drowned in shame and self-pity. We never went out again, but I wasn't through with girls. Not yet.

I met Marie at a basketball game between our high schools. She sat alone in the bleachers, but I noticed her beautiful, full-moon afro and couldn't stop staring. Most black girls were wearing straight perms then, but Marie's large, rounded hair reminded me of Mom when she was younger. I was attracted to Marie—erection and all. This convinced me I could date her without disappointing her.

When the game ended, I bumped into her, literally, intentionally, at the exit. She turned quickly, and I said, "Oh I'm sorry. Forgive me."

She smiled the loveliest smile. I grinned like a Cheshire cat, as Dad might say, and she said, "No harm done."

I didn't know what to say next, but I had to say something. "I'm Isaac," I announced. "Isaac Swinton."

She chuckled and said, "Okay," and kept walking. I followed. I must've been sixteen by then.

"I'm a nice guy. Real respectful of women."

"Is that right?"

"Yes. That's right. And I'd like to get to know you."

She paused a bit and said, "How do you know you'd like to get to know me?"

"'Cause you pretty," I said. "And I bet you're special."

"Ha! That's what you say to every pretty girl, I'm sure!"

I got desperate. "No, I don't. You're the prettiest face I know."

Marie stopped and studied my eyes. "Thank you…Isaac Swinton. I'm Marie." She extended a strong, firm hand.

We shook and she sashayed away. "What's your last name?" I called after her.

Over her shoulder, she teased, "That's for me to know and you to find out!"

I found out: Washington. She was the daughter of Reverend Cleophas Washington, pastor of one of the largest black churches in Kansas City. But she wasn't stuck up or overly religious; she was sweet and thoughtful and smart, and I genuinely liked her. We met at the movies and school sports games for months before we kissed. When we did, it was great, but something was missing. I knew it and so did she.

"It's all right," she whispered sincerely. "We don't have to do that."

"But I want to! I really do. I think I'm just…"

She put her index finger over my lips. "You're wonderful, Isaac. That's what you are."

We continued spending time together. Her folks liked me; Dad and Mom liked her. What he didn't know was that we never touched sexually. Not once.

Yet we were extremely intimate. Many days, we held hands, laughing and sharing in Swope Park. I was more open with Marie than I'd been with anyone. She knew about me, she said, before I told her. She understood me. Gave me space to be myself. She was my soulmate—not my girlfriend. But since the world thought otherwise, we played along. It was a scheme we perpetuated in order to maintain each other's peace. Her father hoped she'd marry me. He told me so. I almost laughed in his face. Then I felt sorry for him.

I'm sorry I deceived Dad. It was the only way I knew to settle his fear of who I was. I knew it wouldn't last forever, but I thought it might cover me until I finished high school and left.

It didn't.

Marie asked me to the park one Friday evening and took my hand. We sat on a bench midway beneath two gorgeous maple trees. Streaks of sunlight penetrated leaves and limbs, showering us with just enough orange-red light to see each other's shadowed faces. She wasn't smiling. Soon I wouldn't be either.

"I can't do this anymore," she started, sighing with relief.

"Why not?"

Squirrels scampered between trees above us. They made such ruckus that Marie squealed.

"Did I do something wrong?" I asked.

"No, no. It has nothing to do with you. You'll always be my friend. At least I hope you will."

"Of course I will. I just don't understand why things have to change."

She exhaled. "I found someone. Someone I love."

Now I was sad. "Really? Wow. Okay."

"Please be happy for me."

"I am! I am!" I shouted, dropping her hand and standing.

"Sit down, Isaac. This is hard enough already."

I obeyed.

"We always knew this day could come. That one of us or both of us might find someone we actually *wanted* to love."

"I know, Marie, but not now. We have a good thing going!"

"We do," she said, "but it's not real. I mean, it is, but we're not in love. We love each other, but not romantically. I want that part too."

It was my turn to sigh. "Me too."

"You'll find someone one day," she assured, staring into my weepy eyes. "When you're not afraid of yourself."

I swallowed the critique and asked, "What's his name?"

She shook her head and paused. Then looked at me hard. "It's a girl."

I gasped, too shocked to speak.

"I didn't know either until recently. We met at school and became friends, and it went from there. I mean, I've always found girls pretty, but girls get to do that. She touched my hand one day, and I felt something magical."

I didn't know what to say.

"I always thought I'd marry a man and have his children and endure like most other women do."

"Is it endurance?"

"It is if it's not what you want."

"Are you sure this girl is what you want?"

"Yes. I guess we've both been lying to ourselves."

We cackled together.

"I really like her, Isaac. And I'm gonna be with her."

"What about your folks? What will they say?"

"They won't know. I'm not gonna be with her publicly. I ain't no fool."

"Then why can't we keep on as we've been doing?"

"Because I wanna share more of my intimate time with her." I resumed my seat. "Gosh, Marie. What am I gonna do?"

"We're still friends, Isaac. We'll still talk."

"But you can't be my play girlfriend anymore. You got a real one!"

She nodded. "That's right. No more playing. This is the real deal."

We sat for hours, dreaming imperfect futures and devising ways to survive the present. She could imagine marrying this girl, she said. I screamed. Who'd ever heard of such a thing? Yes, she might like a girl, I said, but God wouldn't approve. And if God wouldn't approve, how could she marry her? Who said God wouldn't approve, she asked? I was stunned. We got into a whole discussion about God and the Bible, and I left the park confused, but enlightened. I had never questioned God before; now all I had was questions.

Day 21

I wondered if I could have a family. Of course I couldn't legally marry a man, but I could make a home with one, couldn't I? I just needed someone who loved me and had a little imagination. Unfortunately, most black gay men wanted what straight men wanted—the facade of regularity. They hated effeminate men. So they hated me. They wanted real men, the ones whose public behavior didn't embarrass them. The ones who could dominate them and stand under pressure and make their grandma smile. They wanted men whose being wouldn't conflict with the church, men who reminded them of their fathers. I was none of these. I could be someone's best friend, but not his live-in lover.

I was just too girly. At sixteen, people frowned at and prayed for me, whispered about and cursed me behind my back, belittled and humiliated my hope of fatherhood. When I approached a black gay boy at school, thinking we might make a go of things, he told me that if he wanted a woman, he'd be with one. *What does that mean?* Then I figured it out: he equated effeminate guys with women. No one really believes a man is *naturally that way.* I mean, come on! A boy is a boy, right? God would never send him any other way.

This was what people believed. I believed it too. Most boys weren't like me, so I had no choice but to consider that I was the flawed one. This caused me to wonder if something had happened to boys like me. Some people believed we were all molested. That's why they looked at me with pity and sympathy. Others swore an absent father was the cause. Without a daddy, a boy was sure for failure. Well, none of this explained my situation. Dad was always present and strict with me. And, thank God, no adult had ever touched me.

My problem was that I couldn't change. And, much as I asked, God wouldn't change me. I didn't hate who I was; I hated that others hated it. It left me alone, without community, and that is a sad, devastating thing. I wanted a village. I wanted to belong.

I wanted to make a difference in others' lives. Yet, if I had died, few would've missed me. That meant my life had been in vain. I couldn't live with that. Somebody had to remember I came.

That's the day I turned my back on God. If He wouldn't change me, I had no choice but to be myself. Little did I know that would make all the difference.

I asked Dad, the summer of my senior year, who he thought wrote the Bible, and he said God, and I laughed. He grimaced, upset. I said the notion was ludicrous, and he got so angry he cursed. I didn't fear him anymore. I guess I was growing up.

He said the Bible was God's holy word, so no one else could've written it but Him. "It's perfect just the way it is," Dad declared. I smiled, shaking my head. "God literally sat down and wrote a book?" He said, "I don't know if He sat down, but, yes, He wrote a book! Ain't no book in the world like it!" His confidence became more and more absurd. I had read several books about how the Bible was assembled, after Marie sparked my curiosity, so his statements seemed ignorant in the truest sense of the word.

"Dad, God's not human. God doesn't write. In order to write, God would need a hand, pen, and paper. And if God *did* write, then God would be like us. And we'd be like God."

He stared with vehemence. I didn't intend to cower.

"Plus," I continued, "why wouldn't God have written His book in every language so every nation could read it? Why would God write only in Hebrew?"

"Hebrew?"

"Yep. The Bible was first written in Hebrew. And Aramaic. Most of it."

He swallowed hard. "I don't know about that. Musta been wrote in English too. At least the King James version."

"Oh Dad! Come on. Even you oughta know better than that!"

"Isaac," Mom warned from the kitchen. I pulled back a bit.

"The King James Bible is a translation. It's not original. No tellin what they put in there and what they left out."

His hands trembled; his lips quivered. I almost felt sorry for him.

"You ain't as smart as you think, boy. You might read books about God, but that don't mean you *know* God. There is a difference."

"Maybe you're right. But I know something else too: God didn't write the Bible. And those who did didn't love us."

He was outdone. "I don't low no blasphemin in my house, boy!"

Mom rushed between us. "Isaac! You are out of line! Cut it out." I saw my reflection in her red eyes, so I sighed and said, "Sorry, Dad. I didn't mean any disrespect."

He stood behind her, clenched fists and all, fully prepared to knock me out, but my apology calmed him slightly. "You might think you smarter n me, and you might be, but what you ain't gon do is talk to me any kinda way!"

"Yessir."

Mom returned to the kitchen. He took the sofa again, I took her chair. I should've shut up, but I didn't. I jumped right back in.

"I'm not blaspheming, Dad. I'm just saying the Bible belongs to a certain people and culture, and they're not ours."

"Jesus died for everybody."

"Actually, he didn't. Plus, Jesus and God aren't the same."

"Jesus is the son of God, so he's God in the flesh. That's what they taught us."

"Jesus is the son of God because he said so—not because God is his actual father."

"God *is* his father! Mary conceived as a virgin and birthed a savior. I believe that!"

I glanced at Mom around the corner. She motioned for me to let it go, but I had to say one more thing: "It wasn't God's sperm, Dad. God doesn't have sperm. It was probably Joseph's. Mary was too young to be pregnant, though, so they conceived a story to cover things up. That story, over time, became myth and made its way into the Bible. That's how folklore works."

He had had enough. "You can believe whatever you want, mister, but I'm gon believe in that Bible. It's done guided black people this far, so it's the best thing we got."

"Is it?" I sang. "There are a lotta other books we should be reading too."

"All right, Isaac," Mom warned again.

"No, no. Let him keep runnin his mouth. I'm gon pop him good in a minute."

I knew what I was doing, and I didn't care how insulted he felt.

"I'm not gon have no blasphemin in my house!" he repeated.

"I'm not blaspheming, Dad. I'm just saying God didn't write the Bible. I mean, let's be honest: God would've written something far more excellent!"

That's when he dashed forward and slapped the shit out of me.

"Jacob! No!" Mom cried, running into the living room. I had overstepped, and I knew it. I didn't care. His naked insecurity was its own reward.

He stood over me, daring me to react, but I knew better. Mom pulled his arm gently as he relented, mumbling threats the whole time. Once both were some distance away, I grumbled, "I don't even believe in God anymore."

Mom gasped and shook her head violently. Dad halted and said to the ceiling, "What did you say, boy?"

I wouldn't repeat it. I didn't want to die.

His mouth shuddered. "If you ever say anything like that again in this house, you will leave here! Do you understand me?"

I sighed without looking at him, then nodded.

"I said, do you understand me!"

"Yessir," I murmured as softly as possible.

He stormed out. Mom returned to the kitchen. I sat alone in the living room, proud that I hadn't surrendered. Mom said I was an arrogant fool, but for the first time, I had beat Dad at something, and no one in the world could take that joy from me.

It took him weeks to recover. Whenever he stopped by, I smiled as if nothing had happened. He despised my smug, haughty attitude, and he refused to engage it. We were good at avoiding each other. It was our pattern: disagree, fall out, silence. We never resolved anything. We simply stepped over it and moved on.

Day 22

We spoke again the day I told Dad I might attend Lincoln University. Mom said I had to tell him since he'd be paying at least some of the tuition.

"Smart as you is, you could go to any school in the country!"

"What's wrong with a black school?"

"I didn't say nothin was wrong with it, but you can go anywhere."

Dad wouldn't say what he meant. But I knew.

"You ain't thought about Yale or Harvard or none of them?"

I shook my head. "No sir. Why would I?"

"Umph!" he cackled, as if knowing something I didn't. "When you come outta them schools, you set for life."

"Not if you black," I said.

He didn't counter. Instead, he said, "Well, it's yo choice. You gotta make that decision on yo own. I can't help you with that." He tried one last time: "I'm just sayin you smart enough to go anywhere you want."

"And I think Lincoln is where I wanna go."

He sneered a bit. "I ain't never even heard o that school."

"I hadn't either, but the school counselor mentioned it to me, and I did a little research. It looks like a good school."

Dad rolled his eyes. He thought I was cheating myself.

"I just wanna see what an all-black learning environment feels like."

That won a few nods. He added, "Plenty o black girls there, I'm sure. You shouldn't have no excuse."

I didn't take the bait. I swam right around it. "I'm sure Lincoln's black professors are as good as any. Probably better."

Dad shrugged innocently. "A good student can thrive anywhere. I just thought you might go to one of the top schools 'cause *you can*."

A compliment lingered in his emphasis, but, at the time, I was too defensive to notice.

Mom didn't care where I went. She just wanted me to go. All she said was, "You're mighty blessed, Isaac. College is a dream most black kids never experience. Don't squander it. It can change your whole life."

She was right. It did.

But I had to get there first.

I was still determined not to be gay, but I was losing ground. No woman would stay with me. Even the *Jet* centerfolds, plastered across my walls, began to fall. The women were beautiful, but they couldn't help me. They seemed to turn away whenever I looked at them. I tried to masturbate in their presence, but that didn't work. I'm one who needs an emotional connection to have a sexual experience, and I couldn't imagine why any of them would want me. I have to feel wanted and needed and desired, and I knew, in my heart, those women didn't want me. Not a boy *like me*.

I was trying to like girls—but something always went wrong when we got naked. I soon realized I didn't want to penetrate them. I wanted to love them, to know them, to be in their company. Most wanted more, so, at some point, they found me out.

I dated a few other girls that year, but no one memorable. I was too miserable to relate to anyone. The lies, the constant manipulation, the self-deception—it was all too much. So, a month shy of my eighteenth birthday, I quit trying. I felt like a loser. I didn't care if the whole world knew what I was. The facade was too heavy to bear. I resolved to be myself, come what may. I didn't know what that would mean though. I had lied so long I wasn't sure I knew the truth. But I knew what I felt, and it wasn't self-love.

I tore those half-naked centerfolds from the wall. I couldn't believe I had hung them. I yanked that hideous football bedspread off my bed and snatched those matching curtains from the window. Mom heard the commotion and came running. She flung the door wide and gawked with horror.

"What are you doing! What's wrong, baby?"

I swirled in circles of joy and freedom. The curtain flew behind me like a cape.

"Isaac, honey! Stop it! Stop it!"

"No, Mom," I sang with delight. "I won't stop it. I won't!"

Books, paper, and clothes rained throughout the room. I screamed as my adrenaline burst forth. Mom began to sob. That's when I calmed and collapsed across the naked bed.

"I can't do it anymore, Mom! I just can't do it!"

"What is *it*, baby? What's troublin you?"

"I can't do it," I repeated. "I'll die first."

I think that frightened her. "You'll what? What are you talkin about?" Her eyes grew large. She walked over to the bed and sat next to me.

I lay there, panting.

"Answer me when I'm talking to you!" Her tone shifted from worry to frustration. "I said, answer me!"

Rolling over slowly, I said, "Mom, I'm done. My whole life I've been trying to be what you and Dad wanted, what my friends wanted, what I thought God wanted. But no more." My head shook fiercely. "I can't do it. I just can't. I'm miserable and sad, and I hate who I am!"

She touched me and continued crying.

"This is no way to live, Mom!"

She covered her face. "You right, baby. You right."

"I don't care what Dad says. Or thinks. I'm not doing it anymore."

She took my hand in hers. "Just be yourself, sweetie. I'm sorry for what we've done to you. I really, really am."

We cried together a long time. After a while, Mom rubbed my head the way she'd done when I was a little boy. I had missed that touch, that gesture of unconditional love. I put my head in her lap and she sang my lullaby:

Sweet little Isaac, my precious baby boy,
You're the sweetest li'l baby, my heavenly joy;
Nothing on this earth, I do declare,
Can harm or destroy you, I swear!

You're the only sweet chile I got,
My angel, my dreams, I love you a lot;
There's no chance you'll ever leave me,
Dance like the wind and just be!

The words were a little awkward, and Mom definitely
couldn't sing, but that song always healed me. I hadn't heard
it in years. She used to murmur it when I didn't feel good
or got my feelings hurt. I needed it that day more than ever.

That's the year I got to know Ricky Stanton. He was the
star quarterback at my high school—we were in the same
grade—but he was super cool and down-to-earth. We hadn't
ever really talked, except for mutual nods in the hallway. He
saw me one afternoon, in the football bleachers. I'd thought I
was hiding from the world, enjoying my own pity party, but
he stared a few seconds then invited himself forward.

He stood six-two or so and bore 220 pounds of sculpted
muscle. His low-cut fade, manicured goatee, and thick bushy
brows made me gawk with envy. That was enough to solidify
his beauty. Yet when he smiled those pearly straight teeth and
his mouth curled upward into parentheses, I had to look away.

Three or four levels beneath me, he called out, "Hey, man!
You okay?"

I nodded, praying he'd leave me alone, but he persisted.

"Why you chillin up there, all by yoself?"

When I didn't answer, he sensed my anguish and started
climbing.

"Can I help?"

He took a seat beside me.

"What's on your mind, brotha?"

Why I trusted him I don't know. His heart seemed genuine, so I sighed and said, "Just got a lot goin on. That's all."

He nodded. "I'm a great listener."

I turned and stared into his dark chocolate eyes. He didn't turn away. He wasn't nervous or uneasy. Just calm and composed, waiting for me to go on.

"I'm tired of trying to be what other people want."

"Hmmmm."

"It's so fucking exhausting and demeaning, fighting your own parents for the right to be yourself."

He nodded again, just to confirm he was listening. I think I trusted him because subconsciously I remembered how he'd helped me in ninth grade. Several boys stood at my locker, teasing me about my "funny walk." Ricky approached confidently and dispersed the crowd. He didn't actually say anything. He just stood nearby, a few lockers away, looking at the boys as if daring them to go on. They didn't try him. When they left, he did too.

"I'm not like other people. I've never been."

He touched my hand lightly and asked, "What *are* you like?"

I was afraid to say. I shrugged and sank back onto the bleachers behind us.

"Why not just be yourself?"

"'Cause it ain't that simple, man. Some people get smooth, easy lives and some get hard, complicated lives. I'm in the latter group."

Ricky shook his head slowly, staring across the football field.

"Naw. Nobody gets a smooth, easy life, man. Everybody's life is hard as hell. Trust me, I know."

I wondered how he knew. What difficulties could a high school jock possibly have?

"Since most people don't tell their business, other folks don't know, but I think everybody struggles. It's just the way things are. Would be a lot easier if we talked to each other and shared the load."

"Yeah, man. A lot easier."

I told him about Dad and Mom and the girlfriends. I even read him a new poem I had recently finished. He reached for my hand, and I surrendered it. I'd never held a grown man's hand before.

"Damn, that was beautiful, dude. The way you put words together. I would never think to say things that way. Sounds like the Bible or Shakespeare or something."

We chuckled. He continued holding my sweaty hand as he told me who he was. He loved football, he said, but he hated being thought of as a jock. Girls always wanted to spend time with him, but most of them were whiny and shallow.

"I guess that's what athletes want, but not me. It ain't what I want. Not by a long shot."

In my naivete, I blurted, "What do you want?"

And he said confidently, "Somebody like you."

I dropped his hand quickly and looked around, shocked. "Excuse me?"

He didn't blink; he didn't budge. "Yeah. That's what I want."

"You're...?"

"I guess so."

Neither of us said it. He assumed I was; I never considered he was.

"Did you always know?"

"Yeah."

"How? You're not…girly."

Ricky clapped playfully. "Ain't I, honey chile?"

I screamed. "That's not funny."

"It wasn't meant to be. I was tryin to show you how silly that is."

He drove me home and told me never to spend another hour trying to prove myself to anyone. Then he kissed my forehead and said good night.

I tiptoed into the house and went straight to bed but didn't sleep a wink.

Day 23

We started hanging out, mostly at his house. His parents either didn't know or didn't care about his sexuality, a fact which puzzled me greatly. All black parents cared back then. His father spoke with me as though never noticing my effeminate ways. His mother too. She called me *baby* and *honey* and *sweetie*, and I wondered why my family wasn't so embracing.

By the time Ricky and I became friends, I didn't know who I was or what I wanted. I was afraid to know. I thought I was in love with him, but he wasn't in love with me, so I denied it. I'd learned that trick over the years—how to deny my truth—as my primary survival tool. It worked only temporarily. The day I needed the truth and couldn't find it, I was in trouble. I thought God might help me, but God never said a word. I know I said I hated Him, but I didn't. I hated that He wouldn't change me. Or reprimand the world on my behalf. When I prayed, I imagined a bearded guy—probably a white man back then—with a smirked expression and an upturned nose, shunning my self-rejection as if to say, *I made you the way I wanted you.* I would thank God for that, twenty years later. But, at the time, we were avowed enemies.

For years, I hid behind Ricky's confidence. He refused to be ashamed. I wanted that assurance, but, with no allies, I lacked confidence that my truth wouldn't cost my life.

Still, I opened up to him. We became soulmates. I told him my desire to write or dance or do something creative one day. It was frightening, really, being that honest, that open, but the purging felt good. I even undressed in front of him without hesitation. He never once gestured toward me uninvited. In fact, a few times he denied me. I would've felt rejected except that he explained, "Touch me when you can touch yourself proudly." I understood. "I don't want to be part of your guilt."

We finally kissed on prom night. He brought me home— we were both a little tipsy—and, standing beneath the tree in the front yard, we hugged and said good night. He began to walk away then returned and kissed my lips softly. Stars glimmered more brightly than I'd ever seen before.

The day I redecorated my room, Mom warned that Dad wouldn't like it. I didn't care. I had had enough of trying to please him. I thought he might yell at me, but I didn't worry about that either. I was almost his height, and whatever he did to me, I believed I could survive. In a year or less, I'd be gone anyway, so, for the first time, I prioritized what I liked—regardless of anyone's opinion. The rearranging took all day, but when I finished, I was proud. My walls were covered with floral wallpaper: tulips, petunias, marigolds, lilies, daisies, pansies, all bloomed and brilliant with jubilant color. I loved flowers, their scent, their beauty, their silent majesty. My curtains and bedspread were light green, my favorite color. I suppose the room looked like a huge potted plant. When I finished, I fell backward upon the bed, pleased with myself and my courage.

Dad saw the room, several days later, and looked around with indifference. I leaned upward, surprised.

"You got some kinda talent, boy. Take most folks months to do this kinda work."

"Took me a long time too."

"Naw, it didn't."

I didn't want to argue, so I held my tongue.

"We grew some of these flowers down home. A few bloomed wild in the woods. I'd pick em and give em to your mother. Back when we was goin together."

I laughed at the phrase. Soon, we were deep in the woods of Arkansas, searching through his memory, picking pink, yellow, and white blooms. Eventually he sat next to me on the bed and told me how he and Mom met and how beautiful she'd been. Next day, I told her what he said. He knew I would.

I think he'd given up trying to change me. I was a young man, a year away from college, and he knew he had lost the battle for my identity. I knew he didn't agree with who I was, so I stopped trying to change him too. Our hearts drew a truce but never reached a treaty.

Nothing in my room was boyish, but that didn't seem to bother him. He even said, "Your favorite color is green too, huh?" I remember staring at him, skeptical of his calm, but he never registered an objection. It was the strangest thing. He sat there, looking around, ushering me through his past, like we were old buddies. The green of my bedspread, he said, reminded him of young corn sprouts in spring. He smiled. My eyes narrowed. Something was definitely amiss, and I waited to discover what it was.

Then I realized he really had surrendered. There was nothing more to fight about, nothing more to argue over. I was free now, in his mind, to be whatever I was. It didn't matter to him anymore. He was done.

"You actually like flowers, huh?"

"Yessir, I do."

He studied every wall. "I think I like em too. Boys in my time didn't think much about such things. We gave flowers to girls because girls were like flowers—pretty and...well... fragile, I guess. I'd never heard of a boy liking flowers. But—" he shrugged thoughtfully "—why not?"

Now I looked at the walls too.

"Guess a man oughta be able to preciate a beautiful thing."

"I think so. And—" I took a risk "—everything beautiful ain't fragile."

He paused. "You right. Some things beautiful is strong too."

I nodded. He faced me and asked, "What you wanna do with yo life, boy?"

It was the hardest question I'd ever pondered. Truth was, I didn't know. But I wasn't gonna tell him that.

I reached deep within and said, "I wanna do something that frees people from fear."

He stared as if I had three heads. "Not sure what that is though. Something in the arts, I guess. Writing probably. Dancing maybe."

"How can that free people from fear?"

"Well, I think art makes people imagine a world different from the one we live in. I wanna write stories that help people see themselves freer than they are now."

He nodded, but I could tell he didn't fully understand.

"The whole point of writing is to make readers think about people and things in new and creative ways. That's how you change the world."

He stood. "All right. Just hope you can pay yo bills while you doin it."

"Me too."

He walked out. I didn't know what he was thinking, but I believed he had changed. I definitely had.

Day 24

The day I graduated from Central High, the sun burst forth, blazing white and brilliant, at 6:02 a.m. Reddish-orange specks outlined its edges, but most of it glimmered a vivid yellowish white. I know because I watched it rise. I couldn't sleep the night before, so I sat up, waiting for the coming day.

Mom rose early, bustling about, humming and fussing, ordering me to get a shower then come to breakfast.

"Make sure you iron that robe, Isaac! We don't want any wrinkles!"

"Mom!"

"I'm just saying! You'll be on stage, and everybody'll be looking at you, and you don't want to be embarrassed. Just do it!"

We fussed about what I'd wear beneath the robe until I gave in and put on my good black suit. I couldn't believe this day had finally come. She entered the room just as I extended my arms through the sleeves of the robe. I then put on the mortarboard headdress. That's when she started crying.

She grabbed both my hands and said, "You're the most beautiful son a mother could have."

We sat arm in arm on my bed.

"I just don't know what I'm gonna do without you."

"You're not losing me, Mom. I'm just graduating high school."

I offered a handful of tissue. "I know. But you're my only child. It's hard to watch you leave the nest."

As much as I loved Mom, I refused to be sad that day. "You raised me well, Mom. Just be proud."

She blinked quickly and said, "Chile, don't pay me no mind! I'm just yo momma!"

We laughed as she zipped my robe and took a thousand pictures. Then Dad knocked on the front door.

He sported a suit I'd never seen—a new navy blue getup—with a white shirt and black tie. His shoes were the same black ankle-high boots he always wore. They didn't complement the suit, but I appreciated the effort.

"My, my," he teased. "You a grown man, boy." He clutched my shoulders as if he might hug me. I got misty too.

"Thanks for coming, Dad."

He scowled, offended. "What you thankin me for? I'm yo daddy. Where else would I be?"

I tried to massage the wound. "I mean, thanks for takin off work. I know that's not always easy."

"It ain't, but I wouldn't miss today for nothin in the world. My son is finishing school." He clapped slowly as the reality hit him.

My mouth went dry. He'd never called me *son*. I was always *boy*.

Staring off dreamily, he said, "Always wondered what it felt like to get a high school diploma."

I wasn't sure he was talking to me, but since there was no one else in the room, I assumed so.

"Grandma made me stay in school til the eighth grade. Then Granddaddy made me quit."

"Why?" I asked, trying to help him process something painful.

"'Cause I had to work. We was poor people back then, and poor colored people made children go to the field sooner'n they made them go to school. Eatin was more important than knowledge."

He never turned to face me. He spoke to something out in the world, something he saw clearly that I couldn't see at all.

"At first, I liked school and wanted to go. I remember learnin how to read and bein excited when I called words right." He cackled a bit. "But I missed so many days I got behind and never did catch up. That's when I started hatin school." He paused. "I was too embarrassed to ask for help, so most days I sat at my desk, struggling to understand the teacher's lesson. I was pretty good at figurin, but I never did get writin down too good. After a while, I gave up." He shrugged several times and shook his head. There was so much he hadn't said, and I wasn't sure I could bear it.

"I think I woulda been smart if I coulda gone regular. Never know, I guess, but I think so."

"You're smart, Dad." It was the dumbest thing I could've said. He knew I didn't believe that. Not then.

"Ha. Naw, them days gone. I missed that train, son."

I didn't know what to say. He continued staring through the window.

"You might be the first person on my side of the family to graduate from high school."

"Ever?"

"Since the day we got to this land."

That moved me. It seemed unbelievable. It was 1984.

"How is that possible, Dad?"

He chuckled sadly. "Easy. We was tryin to survive, son. We didn't know nothin bout no readin and writin. We wanted it, that's for sure, but we needed land and resources first. A few black children went to school all the time, but most didn't. The rest of us worked, right alongside our folks."

"You didn't *have* to go to school?"

"Shit, naw! This country didn't care nothin bout no colored chillen goin to school. They didn't know if we went or not. Most of us didn't. We was work mules, son. That's why they brought us here."

"Guess I'm pretty lucky, huh?"

That's when he turned. His eyes flashed red and moist as if he'd been crying.

"Luck ain't got nothin to do with it! Ain't you hearin what I'm sayin, boy?"

I closed my eyes. I had missed something.

"Every generation before you prayed for what you finally got. We wanted it too. Worked hard for it. But we didn't have the opportunity." It was the first time he stared directly into my eyes without looking away. "We gave you a gift, boy. You and all colored children in this country. And we paid dearly for it!" He was practically shouting. "Shit, you ain't lucky. But you mighty blessed!"

He marched past me and slapped my shoulder. I wouldn't get the fullness of his words until years later.

"Missed you at our last appointment," the therapist said. "What happened?"

"I don't know really. Something about writing my story has me all twisted up. Some days I'm good, but others I drown in self-pity. So much of what I thought just isn't true. It's like my memory grabbed what it wanted in order to justify my emotions. If I could blame Dad for all my troubles, I wouldn't have to bear shame about what I didn't do, how I dropped my own ball."

"It's hard, huh?"

"Yeah, it is."

I started my ritual walk around the room, frustrated that I couldn't see the end of my own story.

"Try to move away from needing anyone to blame, Isaac. That's our first default in this Western culture. Just assemble the pieces and let the story speak for itself. You don't need a hero. Or a villain. Just a complete story."

"But I see so many places where I messed up or missed the point. Like the day I graduated from high school. Dad was telling me something really important."

She closed her eyes and nodded.

"I was the first person on his side of the family to graduate from high school. Do you know how incredible that is?"

She didn't look at me, but she chuckled. "Yeah, I think I do."

"But not because I was smart."

She nodded, seeming to have arrived at my revelation.

"But because *they* were. They never lost hope, never stopped trying, never gave up the dream. It made sense that I was the one."

"Why?"

"Because Dad got to the eighth grade, so he prepared the way for me. I couldn't do anything but finish. He made sure I had no excuse."

"Plenty of black parents gave their all and still their children haven't finished high school."

I wanted her to look at me, but she wouldn't. Something in the ether absorbed her attention.

"I know, but Dad gave me something many parents, black or white, don't have."

"What is that?" she burbled.

I didn't want to say, but I had no choice. "Discipline."

"And you thought he didn't love you."

"I still think that sometimes. I know it's wrong. That's why I'm having such a hard time writing my story. Because my fruit and my wounds don't align. They don't add up."

She didn't say anything.

"It's like I made up a history. My memory doesn't support my frustrations. Not completely."

"It rarely does. We make people what we need them to be so our feelings make sense. Everyone does it."

I felt so confused. "I'm not as special as I thought I was. That's what I'm discovering. I'm not smarter than my parents were—either of them. I didn't go to college because I was smart. I went because my folks set me up to go. It never crossed my mind *not* to go, and that's what's smart—to raise a kid and point him in a direction that he has no choice but to follow." I paused. "All this time, I thought it was me."

She opened her eyes. "You're almost there now."

"Where?"

"Freedom Land."

Day 25

The day I went to Lincoln University, everything changed. No one looked at me funny or asked me to be something I wasn't. I stared at people, waiting for their sneers or mocking expressions, but they never came. I wasn't sure what to make of this. Black kids from all over the nation befriended me and embraced my *sissiness* as who I was. I spent freshman week looking over my shoulder, waiting for them to deride me, but it never happened. I'd stepped into a new world.

To celebrate, I started partying. I didn't do hard drugs or smoke weed, but I didn't judge those who did. My peers let me be, so I returned the favor. What I did do was drink. I'd never even tasted alcohol before college. Mom's struggle had left a bad taste in my mouth, but something about my new-found freedom made me drop all inhibitions. When I first got drunk, it was the most fun I'd ever had. There was a party in a frat house on campus, and some boys—some straight boys—invited me and a few other freshmen. I felt normal, special, included, so we went to the party and had a ball. I was loud and free and unashamed.

At first, I sipped lightly, but as the night wore on, I began to guzzle. They had vodka, rum, Coke, and beer, and I drank it all. I didn't hesitate or act shy. By midnight, I was messed up. That's what we called it. Everything ached the next day—my head, my stomach—but that didn't bother me. If that was the price of inclusion, I was glad to pay. No one scorned me because I was effeminate. No one asked if I liked girls or boys. No one wondered about my earrings. We just danced and drank the night away. Girls flirted with me, and a few boys did too. Other boys saw them but said nothing. Was this Heaven?

I think I went to every party that week. I pranced around, sipping alcohol and stumbling like a drunken fool. Yet I was having the time of my life. I met a girl named Marquetta who wanted to sleep with me, so I slept with her. Simple as that. It wasn't love. I didn't even know her, but I didn't have to. That's why I did it—there was nothing to prove, no one to convince that I *could* do it. And it was fun. We laughed about it later.

Once classes started, I was serious about my studies. I always took school seriously. I read books and encountered ideas that shaped a whole new consciousness in me. We read standards like *Antigone* and *Siddhartha*, which I had read many times, but the black texts blew me away. We'd not read those in high school, but at Lincoln, where most of my professors were black, they introduced books about people like me. I'd never heard of most of them. I felt ashamed, not knowing my people's literary tradition, but it didn't take long to learn. We started with James Baldwin's *The Fire Next Time*. I remember shaking my head at the meticulous language, the cadence, the beautifully rhythmic sentences. It was like reading a song. Baldwin warned of the price of racism in America, and he was right. Ignoring it has only made it worse.

His other books were equally mesmerizing. They weren't on the syllabus, but I read them anyway. You should've seen me, walking around campus with armloads of books, like a ravenous nerd. My book bag was packed, and sometimes I carried stacks in both hands. In every class I learned of some new writer or idea, and I wanted more. I wanted everything black I could get my hands on.

After Baldwin, I delved into Zora Neale Hurston. She had an insatiable love of black culture which made me proud. She wrote of rural black folkways and linguistic patterns and re-oriented my critique of *bad nigga speech*. She posed that what I'd been taught as errors in black idiomatic expression were actually complicated vernacular structures that demonstrated the inherent brilliance of a dispossessed people.

I learned to appreciate my history in ways white teachers never taught. Hurston explained how our African origins informed our present cultural ethos. Every new black author—Richard Wright, Paule Marshall, W. E. B. DuBois—got me one step closer to self-love. My ignorance melted

away. I know it sounds crazy, but, at Lincoln, I fell in love
with black people.

Many times, I thought of Dad. The way he spoke, his use
of extended adjectives, his belief in the Invisible. I'd once
thought he was stupid, but I'd been the stupid one. I thought
white folks were the standard of things, but he knew better. He didn't care what they thought. He loved black music
and storytelling and communalism because it's who we are.
I didn't understand that then. I read all those books and discovered what he already knew.

I made fun of things he said. Like "Get from out from
under that table, boy," or "Stop all that wallin on the flo!"
I hear his musical tongue in my head now, and I smile. I
hadn't grown up in the South, but he had, and everything
Hurston said about the black South was true. It was in his
mouth. Now I consider that perhaps my love of music came
from him. I'd forgotten that, on weekends, he'd sit by the
record player in the living room and listen to blues and gospel until he fell asleep. He didn't know that sometimes I lay
awake in my room, listening along with him. I even sat in
the hallway occasionally so I could hear better. I loved B. B.
King most. His coarse, raspy voice moved through the air
like the ocean's stormy tide. He seemed to know something
about rejection and loneliness. In the depth of his moaning,
I found healing.

I guess I'm saying that, once I started studying black culture, I understood Dad better. As a kid, I didn't know anything about oppression and disenfranchisement and the ways
white supremacy had limited his life. I thought he was just
mean and unhappy because he was too country to know bet-

ter. When I learned about black subjugation, I felt sorry for
him. And me. And all black people. For the ways American
society had constructed our fractures and guaranteed our tensions. Their scheme almost worked.

In my African American Lit class, we read *Song of Solomon*
by Toni Morrison. She won the Nobel Prize in Literature in
1993—the first black woman ever. And, man oh man. That
book left me in the clouds.

It's about a young, troubled black man who discovers that
he can fly. In fact, flying is his birthright. I don't mean in an
airplane. I mean his very black body. He realizes, from trac-
ing his family lineage, that he comes from people who could
lift their arms and take to the air. What moved me so was
that his difficult history didn't hinder his inheritance. That
was new to me—the notion that one's context doesn't define
one's possibilities. I had defined myself by the way Dad saw
me. Now I was growing my own set of eyes.

I think I believed that, by acquiring knowledge, I was de-
fying Dad. Every so often, I looked over my shoulder, thinking he was following me, hearing me, shaking his head even,
as new information corrected all the wrong things he'd said
to me.

But he never came. We had parents' weekend every year,
and I told Mom about it, hoping the two of them might
surprise me, but they didn't. I suppose I should admit that I
wanted Dad to come. To see me in my element, thriving aca-
demically and making friends with all sorts of kids. For the
first time in my life, I lived in confidence and assurance that
I wasn't a disappointment. I was where I was supposed to be.

★ ★ ★

On my way home for Christmas break of my junior year, I read Richard Wright's *The Outsider*. I stared through the Greyhound bus window, smiling about this tingling in my soul. I wasn't a boy anymore. I was a man.

Dad met me at the station.

"Where you git that grip from, boy?" he commented playfully as we tried to crush each other's hand. Then he added seriously, "You done found some strength somewhere, look like!"

I chuckled along and said, "Sure have, ole man. Sure have."

My boldness disturbed him. I could see the reservation in his piercing eyes. "So you a big man now?" he teased, grabbing one of my two large suitcases.

I grabbed the other. "I don't know about *big*," I said, "but I'm definitely a man."

He shrugged and touched my shoulder kindly as we walked to the car. After loading suitcases in the trunk, we got in and Dad asked, "Whatcha been learnin good lately? I magine in college you learn new stuff all the time."

"That's true. I took a class this semester called Social Problems in American Culture where we talked about the differences and similarities between race, class, and gender oppressions."

At first, he didn't say anything. Then he glanced over and said, "Well, what'd you learn about it?"

I didn't want to insult him by speaking over his head, but I also didn't want to insult him by assuming what he didn't know, so I simply said, "The thing that stuck with me was the ways black women suffer more oppressions than anyone in this society."

"Is that right?"

"Yeah," I mumbled and nodded. "They endure racial hatred, class stratification, and black patriarchy."

Dad frowned. "What's that?"

"It's domination and oppression from black men who think black women ought to serve them."

"Who thinks that?"

"Most of us."

Dad stared at me, and, without apprehension, I stared back.

"I think we ought to respect black women," he said.

"Dad, I'm not sure you think that."

His head turned so fast I heard the *swoosh*.

"What do you mean? Didn't I always respect your mother?"

"Not always," I said. "I didn't either."

My statement troubled him.

"When did I ever disrespect your mother?" he asked, defensively.

"Dad, let's not do this now. I just got home. Let's just enjoy—"

"No, answer my question. I wanna know. I'm a big boy. I can take it."

I sighed and, against my judgment, turned to face Dad as he stared forward. "Dad, you can't respect a woman you hit."

He blinked a long time, then swallowed hard and said, "You right." He nodded repeatedly. "You right."

I looked away.

"That was years ago. I haven't done it since then. And I wouldn't do it again. But I did it. Once."

"Once?"

"Maybe twice. But I guess that don't matter. Once is too often."

"Did you think it was right?"

He scowled. "I don't know if I thought it was right. I thought I had the right to do it. That's what they taught us."

"Who is 'they'?"

"Everybody. The world, the church. Granddaddy."

"Now we know the price of following the crowd."

"Ump," he grunted and blinked.

We stopped at Gates and Sons and got chopped-beef sandwiches. When we got back in the car, Dad asked, "How did you disrespect your mother?"

I had hoped he wouldn't ask. My sigh was long and sorrowful. "By thinking she should serve me."

"How is that disrespect?"

"Because I assumed she wanted to do it. I ate without washing a dish. I dropped clothes into the hamper without a thought. I took a shower every day without cleaning behind myself. Of course I did other chores, but I never honored hers. I just thought she was supposed to do it, so I never thought twice about it. When you were kind to me, I was appreciative. When she was kind to me, I didn't notice."

"But she was doing her role! Just like you and me."

"No, Dad. She was doing the role you and I and the world assigned. And she hated it."

We ate in silence. Then Dad drove home and parked in the driveway.

"I understand what you sayin. It's just hard to hear 'cause I come from a different world."

I nodded. "That's the point of knowledge—to merge worlds and generations so we see each other more clearly."

He got out, opened the trunk, and grabbed both bags. I tried to take one, but he winked and said, "Don't fight me. Let *me* grow this time."

Day 26

At Lincoln, I met the smartest person I've ever known. His name was Adam Stewart. He was a quiet guy, small framed, 135 pounds. Standing five-five or so, with tiny, narrow crescent eyes, he could've been mistaken for a twelve-year-old. Long, elegant lashes canopied half-moon eyes, leaving girls to wonder if the lashes were real. Some stared, with disbelieving awe, but Adam never paid them any mind. He simply blinked at the absurdity of the question and walked away. He was strange and weird and awkward, but brilliant beyond measure.

We took World Lit I together, second semester freshman year. He, withdrawn and shy like a stray cat, sat behind me without a sound. I didn't notice him til the semester was half-over. He coughed one day, and I looked around and saw those dreamy eyes and simply had to meet him. So I passed a note:

"Martin Hall, room 223." He showed up before midnight, knocking so softly I barely heard him. When I opened the door, he didn't say anything. With downcast eyes and clothes far too large for his thin frame, he came in and we talked—I talked—for hours. He wasn't one for conversation, but he loved listening. He was the only person I knew who could be perfectly invested in a conversation without ever opening his mouth. Perhaps that's why I loved him—because he demanded so little.

"Where you from?" I asked.

"Springfield, Missouri."

"You have siblings?"

"Yes. One. A sister."

"You close to your folks?"

He shook his head but continued staring at me. I saw pain in his eyes, so I changed the subject.

"Favorite book?"

Now he smiled. "Hard to say. Maybe *The Souls of Black Folk*. Maybe *Giovanni's Room*. You?"

I shrugged. "*The Fire Next Time* probably."

We chuckled like old men.

"You on scholarship?" I asked.

"Wouldn't be here without it."

I took a chance. "Girlfriend?"

His head bowed. "No."

He didn't ask, but I volunteered. "Me neither."

We sat still a moment, agreeing silently to abandon the question of our intimacies. I switched tone and asked, "Any movie bring you to tears?"

He answered quickly though softly, "Oh yeah! *Roots*."

Without thinking, I grabbed his hands and shouted, "Me

too! I love that miniseries! I watched it with my dad when I was little."

He didn't resist my clutch. Rather, he returned it, holding my hands far longer than I'd intended to hold his.

"My dad and I never did anything together. Not one solitary thing."

How could that be? "Did you not grow up with him?"

"I did."

"So...was he...always at work?"

"No. He just didn't prefer me."

"I have a hard time believing that."

"Do you?"

I sighed. "No, actually I don't. It's sorta my story too. My dad and I did things, but we had tough times too."

He nodded. "They don't know us. We came unannounced."

That's what I loved about Adam. He could say so much in a few words. Sometimes I talked for hours, and, in one sentence, he'd dwarf the entire exchange.

He had sickle cell, so he spent time in the hospital occasionally, but he was so brilliant he made A's regardless. His analysis left everyone spellbound, including the professor. I recall when he stood before the class and analyzed Langston Hughes's poem "Minstrel Man." Most of us had never heard of it. Adam read the poem in such an intensely quiet whisper that, subconsciously, our ears turned toward him, and our eyes narrowed:

Because my mouth
Is wide with laughter
And my throat
Is deep with song,

You do not think
I suffer after
I have held my pain
So long?
Because my mouth
Is wide with laughter,
You do not hear
My inner cry,
Because my feet
Are gay with dancing,
You do not know
I die.

When he finished, he stood in absolute silence, waiting for us to experience the full emotions of the text. No one moved or said a word. Then he explained, "The poem is a requiem to the death of black creativity. It is an obituary for the lives of singers, musicians, and poets who dare believe they share the authority to act and think. The beauty of the poem is its juxtapositions: laughter and suffering, song and pain, dancing and dying. Yet this is the black American dilemma—how to live in a nation committed to one's destruction? How to find joy in the midst of terror? How to do art when one has not been deemed human?" He paused several seconds. I stared at Adam because I'd never heard him speak publicly. And I'd rarely heard anything so profound.

Our professor shook her head and dismissed class. In the hallway, Adam was visibly unsettled.

"What's wrong, man?" I asked, confused. "That was incredible!"

He waved me off. "I don't care what I said." He hesitated. "I hate that everyone was looking at me."

"We stared in disbelief, dude!"

He shivered with humiliation. I couldn't think of much to say. I'm not sure I understood.

"People just won't let you be free," he said, after some time. "They wait for the chance to judge you. I feel it all the time. I'd rather be by myself in peace." We headed toward the café. "Now I understand God's invisibility," he slurred. I thought about that. All these years later, I'm still not sure I get it.

Day 27

There were openly gay students at Lincoln, but most weren't my friends because I wasn't fully out yet.

A guy named Willard Henry, who we called Will, pledged Kappa. He was clearly effeminate, but handsome as could be. That's probably why they took him—to make the pretty boys prettier. Anyway, the day of their probate, everyone gathered on the yard with great anticipation. We couldn't wait to see Will do his thing.

When the Kappa pledges emerged, everyone screamed and shouted Will's name. He never looked around. At first, we thought this simply part of the drama, but once they began to step, our enthusiasm waned. Something was wrong. Will exuded none of his usual vibrant personality. We frowned and whispered, wondering what had happened to him. In the middle of the performance, he started a song-and-dance routine laced with so much hypermasculinity that we covered our mouths and shrieked.

Somehow, his voice had dropped an octave, and his spirit had lost most of its marvelous flair. We hated it. He'd been a pillar of self-confidence on campus, far more assured than most other students. Yet the day he crossed into Kappa Land, he seemed to have traded his soul for red and white paraphernalia.

"I like pretty girls! Ones whose big asses swirl!" he sang and stepped in staccato rhythm.

Kappa candy canes tapped the sidewalk with rhythmic endorsement. I watched as Will surrendered his spirit to the group.

He strutted in his Kappa gear for weeks, and I felt sorry for him.

We ran into each other late one night when the campus was asleep. I'd been sitting outside reading under a lamppost when he walked by. He didn't notice me until he passed before me.

"Oh hey. What up, Swint?" he mumbled and walked on.

I jumped and followed him a few paces. "Will! What's goin on, man? What happened to you?"

He turned, clearly irritated. "Nothin happened to me. I'm fine." He took a few more steps.

I pressed the matter. "You're so different now. Before, you were bold and...um...unique and... I don't know. Yourself, I guess."

He swiveled angrily and said, "Swint, this whole fuckin campus is bullshit. Where were y'all when the world was laughin at me? Huh? I don't remember nobody protestin when people made fun o me. Then, all o sudden, when I become what everybody else is, people start trippin. Fuck this, man!"

He turned, once again, to leave.

"You were so...amazing, Will. Everybody wanted your freedom, man."

He rolled his eyes and shouted, "Did they? Did they really, Swint?"

"Yeah."

"Then why didn't y'all sit with me in the café or come by my room to study or chill with me in the library? Huh? If everybody loved Will, y'all sure did a good job of avoiding me."

"You were a lot, man. I ain't gon lie about that."

"Authenticity is always a lot. That's the problem. When I was myself, I was alone. Who wants that?"

"But did they *make* you do—"

"Nobody made me do nothin!" He stomped and flailed. "I was tired. Everywhere I went, people snapped and clapped for me as I defied the world, but then they went right along with it. They got asked to proms and out on dates. Plenty of folks wanted to sleep with me, but not to live with me. I had fucked enough. I wanted something everyone else had. I was tired of carrying people's hopes and dreams. So I dropped them." He shrugged and walked several feet away, then, over his shoulder, slung, effeminately, "I'll take a little bondage with my regularity."

I didn't respect that. Then, some years later, I turned around and did it.

The therapist asked, "Did you ever regret going to a black college?"

I frowned. "Absolutely not. Should I have?"

"Oh no. I'm not suggesting that. I just wondered if you ever considered what your life might've been like had you attended a major white university."

"Why would I think of that?"

"Because that's where most black kids go. And most of those schools don't teach what black schools teach."

"True. I have friends who went to white schools, and I always think they missed something."

"Like what?"

"Like a glimpse at an all-black world, one where every referent is within one's own culture. The music is black, the teachers are black, the books are black, the dance is black, the parties are black, and the stupidity is black too."

"What does that mean?"

"It means everything is our own doing, even our mistakes. Black colleges are far from perfect. They leave a lot to be desired. That's why graduating from one is an achievement. It's not easy, and it's not all fun. Black schools suffer from poor resources, but we also suffer from poor management. And it's not always true that the former produced the latter. The real problem, I think, is that we keep looking for our solutions from white schools. We're always comparing ourselves to them, trying to create their equivalent in black. That means we miss our own genius and creativity sometimes."

"Do you think you might've gotten a better education at a white school?"

"I don't think so. I doubt it very much. I've taken classes at University of Chicago, and they were no better than classes I had at Lincoln. In fact, I didn't enjoy them as much. Teachers at Chicago had knowledge, but very little spirit. Their analysis was shallow too."

"Really?"

"Absolutely. Where did you do undergrad?"

She smirked and said, "Oberlin."

"Oh cool. Did you like it there?"

She nodded. "I did. It was fine."

"Do you ever regret not having gone to a black school?"

"Sometimes. The pride HBCU graduates carry makes me envious. That sense of belonging seems precious and rare."

"It is!" I shouted. "Every black child in America should experience it, I think."

"I might agree with you. But I'm not sure it prepares them for the larger world."

"Of course it does. Do you say the same to white kids who go to white schools?"

She gasped. "You got me there."

"That's what we learn at black colleges—to see the world from our own center—like every other people on the planet."

She shook my hand. I leaned back in the chair, crossed my legs, and waited for the next question.

Day 28

During my last semester, I took a popular course titled Psychology of Sexuality. It was a fairly new elective, which, at first, I feared because of what others might think, but the course sounded interesting, so I tried it. Others spoke highly of it, and no one judged anyone for having taken it, so I took a seat in the front of the class and hoped to learn something about myself.

All semester we discussed the nuances of sexual identity and behavior and argued the biological components of sexuality. Some kids believed that certain people "end up gay" because of social factors like single motherhood and absent fathers. Almost everyone agreed that a child would be gay if they were sexually mishandled. Only a few believed people are born gay. I was one of them.

"God wouldn't do that to nobody!" a boy named Hiram

Henry declared one day in class. He was from Mississippi, and you heard it whenever he opened his mouth. "'Cause it's a sin. That's what it is."

"It's not about religion," Cassie George, a sassy girl from Los Angeles, refuted. "It's about a person's right to be whoever they say they are."

"You can't just *decide* to be something and be it!" Hiram rebuffed. "You gotta be what God made you!"

"This has nothing to do with God!" Cassie sneered. "And, anyway, why can't you be whatever you want to be? That's what identity is—the right to construct yourself."

"But you can't go against God! You gotta at least start with what God made!"

"Why!" she shouted. "You're born with a body, but not an identity. You get to create that yourself. It's your responsibility!"

They barked back and forth, until most of the class was divided into conservatives and liberals. It could've gotten ugly except that Dr. Jackson, our professor, warned us to remember our respect for one another as scholars. She also reminded us that our final research paper, which was thirty percent of our grade, was due in three weeks. We were free to choose our own topics.

I knew what I would research. I wanted to know if God really made people gay. Or if something went wrong in them. I look back now and laugh at myself. I was still trying to blame someone for who I was. God was as good as anybody. I claimed not to believe in God, but maybe I did. I believed in *something* supernatural, and I needed to know if my being was calculated or if my desires were merely a reaction to not having a nurturing father.

I tried to read the work of black scientists and theologians, but I couldn't find many. This was the late '80s. Black scientific scholarship around sexuality was scant at best. Writers such as Marlon Riggs, Essex Hemphill, and Audre Lorde were doing creative work to laud the legitimacy of black queerness, but I wanted scientific evidence, empirical proof that I hadn't chosen what even God, supposedly, despised. Perhaps I was asking for too much.

I started with James H. Cone's *Black Theology and Black Power.* Surely there was something in there that explained the complexity of black sexuality. After all, how could the text be liberatory if it didn't? I scoured the book but didn't find much. Then I combed through *The Cross and the Lynching Tree.* It compared Jesus's life and death to those of black cultural activists, showing how Christ too was once seen as an enemy of the state and thus destroyed for political—not religious—reasons. This was enlightening and informative, but it didn't answer my question.

I went to scientific journals and found knowledge that exploded my assumptions. Many researchers argued for the impact of chromosomal differences in human species as a marker of sexual orientation. They suggested that some people were simply born with XY variations, and that if one sibling was gay, another was likely to be gay because of the similarity in genetic composition. This blew my mind. I was an only child but the notion that my orientation might not be a preference, as most people thought, boosted my self-assurance. Other articles overwhelmed me with scientific jargon too thick to decipher. They spoke of monozygotes and dizygotes in twins and how the body's genetic pairing had everything to do with arousal zones via chemicals called dopamine and serotonin. All of this to say that we are born with something that plays a role in who we love.

I decided to believe I was sent the way I was, and God was waiting for me either to accept it or not.

"And do you stand firm in that decision?" the therapist asked. "That God sent you the way you are?"

"I thought I did. Until my father died."

"What's he got to do with this?"

"Everything." I looked away and sighed. "He made me feel so bad as a kid that I've been scared to just flat out accept myself. Even now, I think about what my father might think before I make decisions. His death didn't solve my dilemma; it intensified it. I wanted to buy a car recently, and all I could hear was Dad's voice, questioning why I needed a car if I already had one."

Surprisingly, she said, "I get that. I really do."

"But working through it is my job, right?" I offered sarcastically.

"Yes, it is. It's called agency. You become an agent of your own existence the minute you stop blaming others for what they did to you. Those who hurt us cannot heal us. That's our job."

I nodded but I hated what she was saying.

"So have you decided God is okay with you?"

Our eyes met in battle. "I try not to think about God much. Church and religion are sore spots in my life these days."

She cackled. "You're avoiding my question."

"I avoid my own too."

"And that's why we're here."

I stood. "I just decided to be me. That's all."

"Is that really all? I think you have to decide there's nothing wrong with you, and that you will have joy—regardless of what happened to you. As long as you're blaming your father, you'll never have peace. And you have to believe your being is not sinful."

"I don't think I'm sinful. That's not my struggle."

"Isn't it?"

"No. I gave up caring what church folks think a long time ago."

She shook her head. "You're missing the point. I'm not asking about religion or other people's beliefs. I'm asking if you—" she pointed directly between my eyes "—are clear that God loves you just the way you are."

"I said I don't care what God thinks!"

"Indifference isn't empowering, Isaac."

I almost walked out. She wasn't hearing me.

"How can you ever know if God loves you the way you are? God doesn't say much."

Her laughter echoed throughout the room. "Isn't that the truth!"

"And, anyway, according to the Bible—"

"Isaac, listen." She lowered her voice. "The Bible can't help you with this. *You* have to decide what God thinks of you. And once you decide, make that your truth."

I loved the idea, but I feared it too. She could tell.

"It's a scary notion, but it's the only way to peace."

Day 29

Adam was salutatorian although he refused the speech. I'm not sure anyone knew but me. No one from his family came, but it didn't seem to bother him. He was happier than I'd ever seen him. He was almost giddy.

He'd told me a few days earlier that he would take a job with a political think tank in St. Louis. It wasn't something I thought he'd ever do, but I was happy for him. He said that, from the way the people described it, they'd spend lots of silent time contemplating political systems and strategies and sell those ideas to high-level politicians and political machines across the country. Of course he'd have to talk sometimes, but at least he could think most of the time, and that's what he wanted. If it didn't work out, he'd do something else. I worried about him. Adam was unusually self-contained, and I couldn't imagine him thriving anywhere among people, but I didn't dissuade him.

Believe it or not, we were never lovers. We probably should've been. Yet neither of us could carry our truth back then. Not completely. Not yet.

I've never been closer to anyone. He lived with his heart wide-open, and it was beautiful—like the tail-spread of a peacock. Most missed him because he didn't say much, but I saw his fragile splendor and loved him deeply. He took that job in St. Louis, and I took Microsoft's offer in Chicago. We lost touch over time.

He came by the house one summer and got my number, he said. He called and told me about the life he'd made with some older guy he thought really loved him. I gathered that they'd hooked up after a one-night stand and Adam moved in. But the guy didn't love him. He wanted a sex toy, and, for a while, Adam submitted. I didn't know he was sick until he called and told me. I cried all the way to St. Louis, picked him up, and brought him home with me. He died, a few months later, lying next to me in bed. I loved that boy. I loved him more than I can say.

I buried him too—in a beautiful silver casket trimmed in black. He lay like a prince in a thousand-dollar Ralph Lauren suit. It didn't totally disguise his illness, but the boy looked good.

Those were devastating years in the gay community. Every hour, someone lost his life to AIDS, and, within that hour, someone else demeaned him. Many lay in funeral homes unclaimed, unloved, unburied until friends or agencies gathered the funds to put them away. Some had funerals where families lied about their lives and what ultimately killed them. No one declared our brothers "Sons of God" or "Kings of the Village."

That's not what they said. Most preachers begged God to forgive them, and, if He could or would, receive them into Eternity. What we all knew was that most Americans—black, white, or otherwise—saw our existence as abominable and wished death upon us shamelessly. If we wouldn't change, they seemed to say, we'd definitely pay.

After a few years, I stopped going to funerals and memorials. Not because I didn't care anymore or became numb to the countless lives buried without celebration or ceremony, but because my heart ached. It couldn't carry more grief. I was emotionally spent. I didn't have many friends to begin with, but I heard about those who did, and because they shared my story, I sobbed for every life, every soul unsung. After a while, I had no more tears. I couldn't weep, I couldn't talk about it, I couldn't feel sorry for all the gay children in the world. Not if I were going to thrive. And, for myself and them, I meant to thrive.

Often, when Adam and I talked in the dark in college, I talked about Dad. Adam spoke of his father, too, whom he didn't know very well, but wished he did. He said he wanted to know what having an *invested* father felt like. He said I was stable and levelheaded because of my father. I told him that couldn't be true, but he said I didn't have to agree. He *saw* the influence on me, sensed it in my confidence. I laughed and told him I didn't feel the least bit confident, but he said I definitely was. Said my tone gave it away. I spoke with authority most kids didn't have, as if someone had granted me permission to speak. To exist. I told him it was probably my mother, but he insisted it was my father.

"Mothers don't give sons that," he declared more loudly

than he'd ever spoken. "Mothers make boys thinkers. Fathers make boys bold."

I've always remembered that. I didn't want to give Dad credit for anything concerning my success, but as years passed, I saw what Adam meant. And he was right. It was definitely Dad.

Day 30

I moved into an apartment on the South Side of Chicago, right in the center of Hyde Park. It was a beautiful old building, on Fifty-Second and Harper, surrounded by restaurants and stores. I could walk for almost anything I needed. The only drawback was the winters. It wasn't merely cold; it was brutally freezing. I wore long johns, sweaters, hats, scarves, gloves, thick coats, and still I was cold all the time. Natives laughed at me, coming to Chicago with a simple peacoat and boots. To make matters worse, it didn't thaw until damn near May! How people lived in Chicago a lifetime I didn't know.

But in spring, the city bloomed into a kaleidoscope of lavender, pink, and red flowers, outlined by forest, olive, and lime green trees. Summers were hot as hell. Chicago was a city of extremes, although winters certainly lasted longest. I've grown to love it here, but every winter I threaten to leave.

When I first arrived, loneliness was my only companion. I didn't know anyone, and for the life of me, I couldn't find a black, sexually liberated community. Another gay boy named Leslie Hunter worked at my job, but he was a little too flaming for me. He was attractive, and, in some ways, that exposed my homophobia because had he been masculine, I would've definitely entertained something between us. Yet I avoided his effeminacy like a contagious virus. Still, we spoke occasionally, when we were alone, and he told me of a black church he thought I might like. He didn't know of my tumultuous relationship with God, and I didn't tell him. I'd gone to chapel only a few times at Lincoln and had very little respect for organized religion. But I liked gospel music, and he said the choir killed every Sunday, so I decided to go.

It was called Apostolic Church of God, located at Sixty-Third and Dorchester. It was a big church, bigger than any I'd attended, and it was loud and rowdy, with people running aisles and speaking in tongues. I liked the energy. Yet sometimes it was a bit much. It often felt more performative than sincere, but that's my judgment. People dressed meticulously in conservative dresses and heels and expensive three-piece suits.

The main thing I didn't like about the church was its debilitating theology. Everything was a sin. And women never shared the authority of men. I couldn't believe women submitted to such nonsense when they composed the majority of the church. Women and gay men. Some queers were obvious, some weren't, but many danced in stark invisibility. It sickened me, actually. I hadn't grown up in church, so my relationship to it wasn't complicated. I saw it for what it was, and I knew that, if there was a God, He wouldn't be caught dead in there.

Still, the music healed me. One Sunday, in the fall of 1988, the choir sang a song titled "There Is No Failure in God." I'm not sure I've ever cried like that. The soloist, a thin but tall woman, screeched into the mic with the highest natural voice soprano I'd ever heard. I felt her sincerity. She paced back and forth across the pulpit area, declaring the excellence of God, and all I could do was weep. Most of the congregation was devastated. Some lay on the floor, slain in the spirit; others walked between pews praising and thanking God for things they thought they didn't deserve. If church had been nothing but music, I could've stayed.

It's the doctrine that ran me away.

"A woman is a helpmate," the pastor said. "Not a leader. She can lead other women, but not men. That's out of divine order."

I think I laughed out loud. There was no way God believed that. They also taught that homosexuality is an abomination. I wasn't strong enough to disagree publicly, but I certainly shook my head. Guys couldn't wear earrings or perm their hair. They couldn't paint their nails or wear tight clothes. Because God apparently abhorred men who loved men.

During one sermon, the preacher declared with conviction, "God created Adam and Eve—NOT Adam and *Steve*!" The crowd jumped and roared with praise, even the gay ones. I laughed so hard people frowned. And I couldn't stop. That's when I knew I had to leave—the day I watched gay men agree to their own bondage. I exhausted myself trying to comprehend how black people had ended up in such a spiritually self-

degrading place. Unable to make sense of it, I walked out. A
few smirked as I passed, but I didn't care. When I got to the
exit, I could've sworn I heard God laughing too.

I never returned to that church. Or any other. But God
and I made up.

It's funny, really, how it happened.

I was having lunch one Saturday afternoon at Mellow Yellow Restaurant, around the corner from my apartment. It was
a bright, beautiful summer day. When I finished, I walked a
small distance down the sidewalk and noticed, on the ground,
a young birdling, having fallen from its nest. It flopped about,
side to side, naked and trembling. It looked weird, really,
with patched young pinfeathers and exposed blue-gray skin.
I stepped around it at first, then I turned back, fascinated by
its fight. I knew it would die soon if it didn't get a little help.
I looked up and saw the nest from which it had fallen, but it
was too high to reach. I thought about Dad and our trip to
the country, and I wondered what I could do.

I found small twigs and dry grass lying about and made a
makeshift nest. With strips of cloth from a nearby trash can,
I weaved together a structure that looked more like a black
grandmother's church hat than a bird's home, but I believed it
would work. I sat it between the intersection of a few limbs of
a young oak sapling. Then I scooped the shivering chick with
two pieces of cardboard and sat it in the improvised nest. There
was no guarantee it would survive. But the chick seemed to
calm after a moment. Then, something magical occurred: the
mother bird, a beautiful little red cardinal, appeared, circling
the makeshift nest frantically, then settling into it cautiously.

The nestling opened its mouth wide, pleading for food, but the mother had nothing to give. Her head twitched nervously, presumably searching for danger, then she flew away. I didn't know if she was gone forever or simply searching for a morsel for her baby. So I found a short stick and began digging around for worms. Finding none, I stopped several people and asked if a pet store existed nearby. No one knew. Yet when I turned back to the nest, the mother had returned with a bug or something in her mouth. I cackled with astonishment. She quickly deposited it into the beak of her baby, and once again flew away as the chick chirped for more.

I almost walked away, satisfied the chick would survive, but then I realized something: the whole thing had been orchestrated. I had to walk down this street and see the helpless chick and decide to assist so that the mother bird could find her nestling in the makeshift nest and continue raising it to adulthood. Its fall from the tree wasn't misfortune. That was part of its destiny. Just like walking down the sidewalk was part of mine. Our encounter was preordained. It had to be. The chick's need coincided with my sympathy at the appointed hour. And my help made the difference. Just as God's help had saved me. I'd fallen several times in life, but each time, I survived. Perhaps because someone had helped me. God—and my Dad.

I hadn't seen it before. He'd paid half of my tuition, so I had no student loan debt. He'd worked ten hours a day, so I always had everything I needed. Every year, at the end of summer, Mom would take me shopping for new school clothes. I loved her for that; I'd never loved him for making it possible. His was the invisible hand in my life, providing so excellently

I never even noticed. Just like the bird. It wouldn't remember what I'd done. Yet without my intervention, it probably would've died. Just like me without Dad.

I stood in this revelation a long time. God had assured my success. Just as He'd assured the vulnerable little bird's survival. I'd never seen God's intervention so clearly. The birdling didn't owe me anything. Neither did its mother. My joy from helping it along the way was its own reward. *This must be what God feels every day*, I told myself. *God uses human hands, but it's His design.*

Every day since, I've been mesmerized by what humans fail to see.

"Have you ever tried writing a novel?"

"No, but I've definitely thought about it."

"Why not? I bet you'd write a good one. Your insight plus your creativity would be magical on the page, don't you think?"

"I don't know about that. I think it's really hard. You gotta sustain one idea for hundreds of pages and make all the details connect. Plus, you gotta make symbols and metaphors work in the reader's mind so that they see the story as they're reading it. That's no small task."

"I'm sure! But I think you could do it. You've been writing short stories all your life."

"Yeah, but it's not the same. A novel is not just a long short story."

"Of course you're right, but if Langston Hughes and Maya

Angelou and whoever else could do it, you can too. You're creative by design. Others have to work at it."

"I work at it too."

"Hmmmm," she groaned, conceding the point, "but you have a gift, Isaac. I hear it when you talk. Sometimes I see it in your expressions. You're not afraid to feel, and I think that's the key to creation. Just keep writing your story. I think you'll discover that you're doing more than simply reconstructing memory. My guess is that you're also creating it."

Day 31

My job at Microsoft kept the bills paid but offered little joy. I worked long hours—sometimes twelve a day—and often had time at home only to shower and sleep. Colleagues were kind, but some were also subconsciously racist.

We had an office Christmas party my second year. They did it big—Microsoft did everything big—by hiring a decorator to transform the place into a winter wonderland. There was fake snow everywhere and multiple Christmas trees dripping with tinsel, garland, and flashing, colorful lights. Each employee was given a green, gold, red, or silver striped box with an unknown gift enclosed inside. Whatever it was, it was valuable. Michael Spornec, our regional manager, wouldn't have had it any other way.

From the moment we entered around 9:00 a.m., Christmas music blasted throughout the building. Large, elegant bowls of red punch, assorted finger sandwiches, and cups of cut fruit welcomed us to a relaxed atmosphere of holiday cheer and comradery. Mr. Spornec kept encouraging everyone to drink and have fun.

"It's Christmastime, folks!" he shouted as if we didn't know. We clapped half-heartedly.

Leslie and I, and a black girl from purchasing, looked around cautiously. We knew to walk easy when white folks started drinking, so we captured each other's eyes to make sure we knew where the black folks in the room were.

"Open your gift whenever you feel like it," Mr. Spornec announced. "We'll just spend the day enjoying each other and remembering why we do what we do." He guzzled more punch then added, "We have a surprise for you in an hour or so. But for now, enjoy each other's company and spend some time spreading love!"

We dispersed throughout the office, some standing near flashing trees and talking more than we had in two years, while others returned to their cubby areas and did the exact opposite of what Mr. Spornec requested.

The black woman, who I didn't know personally, made her way to me.

"Hi. I'm Jackie," she said, shaking my hand firmly.

"Hey. I'm Isaac. Isaac Swinton. I've seen your name on documents, but I didn't know you were—" of course I whispered it "—a sista."

"Well, I am," she whispered back, and we laughed together. We shared life stories for a while, then spoke of our uncertain relationship to Microsoft.

"Yeah, they'll pay you," I admitted, "but they want half your soul for it."

Her head nodded vigorously like those brown dashboard dogs of the '70s. "I started three years ago, but I'm telling you right now I won't be here three years from now. I promise you that. What department you in?"

"Computing. Just one floor up."

"Oh!" she mocked. "You up there with the big boys!"

"I wouldn't say that. It's just a job. Like everybody else got."

We talked awhile longer, then Mr. Spornec gathered us again. This time, there was a small stage and a microphone stand. He was obviously drunk.

"I thought we might have a little fun!" he slurred slightly. "I don't wanna put anyone on the spot, but I thought maybe Issac or Leslie might come up and lead us in a few Christmas songs."

Jackie covered her mouth and screeched, "I can't take these people!"

I couldn't believe what I had heard. Had he named me and the other black guy?

What really tripped me out was the way others cheered and applauded. I gawked, dumbfounded. Mr. Spornec waved me forward, but I didn't move. Neither did Leslie.

"I think they're shy, guys!" he teased and prodded. "Maybe they'll come if we shout a little louder."

NO! I wanted to scream above the festive mayhem.

A few white women understood the problem and looked at me sympathetically. Jackie couldn't stop shaking her head and shrieking into both palms. "Go on up there!" she prodded playfully. "Massa wants some holiday entertainment."

I couldn't laugh. This wasn't funny. All eyes rested on me and Leslie, but I was frozen with horror and disbelief.

I shouted, "I don't sing, Mr. Spornec," which, of course, wasn't true, but he didn't have the right to assume it.

"Can't you try?" he pleaded. "Come on! It's Christmas. You gotta know a few soulful tunes."

If he could've read my mind, he would've fired me. I've never been so furious. Leslie sulked in the back of the room, hoping, presumably, my refusal would save him, too, but it didn't.

"Leslie, how bout it? You probably grew up singin in the church, right?"

Jackie's eyes ballooned into full moons. Everyone heard her mocking laughter now, and most dropped their heads with shame. Only a few chanted, "Leslie! Isaac! Leslie! Isaac!" along with Mr. Spornec. Neither of us budged.

With immeasurable disappointment, Mr. Spornec finally conceded. "Okay. Fine. But I was trying to have a multicultural event. Can't say I didn't try!"

This was the nature of racism in the early '90s. It's worse now. At least bigots once thought to disguise their stupidity with smiles and fake kindness. Now they say dumb shit and discriminate against you without caring who knows.

Soft Christmas music resumed throughout the office. I blinked repeatedly as various colleagues touched my shoulder or whispered, "Fuckin asshole!" Leslie and I escaped to the men's room.

"Did that shit really just happen?" he asked both himself and me.

I was too mortified to respond. I leaned against the wall, trying to settle my breath. Leslie told me to let it go.

"You know who these muthafuckas are, man. This ain't no real surprise. We just never thought it would happen *to us*."

He was right. I'd read about racial microaggressions in the workplace, but never in my life had I believed I'd experience anything like that.

"We shoulda gon up there and really cooned, man. Embarrassed them into consciousness."

I hadn't said a word yet.

"But we need this job, so…"

That's when I said, "So…what?"

"So we gotta be cool. That's the bottom line. We ain't gotta love em, but we gotta live with em."

Do we? I wondered.

That's the day I started planning my exit.

Day 32

I called Mom the next day and told her what happened. She heard amazement in my voice, but I heard nothing in hers.

"Can you believe that?" I shouted.

She grunted. "Yes, I can."

I waited for rage, but it never came. She seemed, in fact, a bit put upon.

"These white folks are a trip!"

"No, not really. They're what they've always been."

I paused a second and said, "Am I missing something here?"

She cackled freely and offered, "Might be, sweetie."

I think I was offended, but I waited to hear her thoughts. "Well, what is it?"

"You bent all outta shape 'cause a white man acted white, 'cause he treated you the way they been treatin us for four hundred years."

"Mom! This is corporate America! Not some small town in rural Mississippi!"

She held the phone away from her mouth so her screeching wouldn't pierce my ear. "You must be crazy, honey! It's the same people! You don't know that?"

"No, I don't," I said defensively.

"Your father and I sheltered you too much. That was our fault. Now, you too naive for your own good."

"I should expect this kinda behavior? Is that what you tryin to say?"

"Absolutely! That's *precisely* what I'm sayin." Her emphasis arrested me. "You think white folks spose to be different *to you*?"

I knew not to answer.

"Why would they be? What you got that most black folks ain't got?"

Before I could retrieve it, the words escaped my mouth. "A degree."

Momma hollered so loudly I laughed at her laughter. "Chile, you got a lot to learn. Education ain't never protected black people from white folks' foolishness. DuBois had more education than you and they still called him 'boy.'"

I hadn't thought of that.

"Our people dreamed of knowledge, not because it would make white folks treat them better, but because it gave us opportunities to do better. Actually, you got off pretty easy."

"What? Momma!"

"You ain't swingin from no tree, are you?"

My mouth wouldn't close.

"Then you should give thanks. Of course what your boss

did was wrong. We know that. And I'm not sayin ignore it. But I am saying consider the context and understand that what you endured is what we all endured."

"Somebody white treated you like this?"

Once again, she bellowed. "The worse thing we did was not to tell y'all the truth. We thought we were protecting you, but actually we created a fragile, arrogant generation. That's our fault. We'll have to fix that later on. For now, let me say this: of course white folks treated me like trash. They treated all black people like trash."

I gasped and queried, "When, Mom?"

She said, "When I was in tenth grade, coming home late one Friday evening. Me and a girlfriend were walking down Paseo, between Forty-Sixth and Forty-Seventh Streets. We turned on Forty-Seventh, toward her house, when a carload of white boys pulled to the curb behind us. We didn't pay em no mind at first, but when they got out of the car and started whistling we got scared. It was just before sundown. We tried to walk faster, but they followed us, calling us names and telling us to stop. 'Hey, nigga gals! You come to us when we call you!'"

"Momma! What? You never told me this."

"Well, I should've. Maybe you'd understand things better if I did." She cleared her throat. "We stopped and told them we had to get home, or we'd be in trouble. We thought to run, but figured they'd only chase us and make us pay, so we turned and looked them in the eye, hoping our boldness would send them away. It didn't.

"An old black man was on his porch, watching everything. He ran inside. We knew he probably called the police, but we also knew they weren't coming anytime soon. It was rare for white boys to be in that part of town that time of the evening, but there they were. And we couldn't do anything about it.

"Anyway, they surrounded me and Margaret Ann—that was her name—and touched all over us before they got in their cars and drove away."

"Momma! Does Dad know about this?"

"Sure. I told him. What can he do?"

I gasped.

"You done missed the point, son. We was glad not to be raped and killed. All black folks done been mistreated by white folks in one way or another. We endured it and kept our mouths shut, hopin one day you'd be free of it. But you ain't never gon be free of it. Never. You gon have to succeed in the midst of it. Education don't exempt you from this. It makes you *prepared* for it. Least we thought it did."

"Well, it didn't, Momma."

"I see that. Our assumption was wrong." She paused. "But you understand now. And remember this: you have choices where we didn't. If you don't like the job, leave it. Somebody else'll pay you for your skills. But if they white, you gon get the same treatment. You can't get away from that long as you live in America."

I couldn't believe what I was hearing.

"You'll be mad about it and wanna get em back, but don't waste your time. Not unless you have to defend yourself. Now if they make you go there, whip they asses!"

We hollered. Momma said she had to run. "Just let white folks be themselves, sweetie. You're there because they need you. You wouldn't be there otherwise."

★ ★ ★

I called Dad later the same day. After he recovered from hearing my voice, I asked about his racial experiences, and he asked suspiciously, "Why you askin me this?"

"Because I'm having a hard time on my job and I'm trying to figure out how to survive it."

He sighed. "Just do yo work and be good at it. Don't worry bout what white folks do."

"But, Dad, that's not enough. I don't know how to stay there and work with them when they treat me like crap!"

"Just go on bout yo business! That's what you do. Whatever that man tells you to do, you do it."

"I already do that, Dad. That didn't keep them from treating me bad."

"What'd they do to you?" He sounded protective in a loving sort of way.

I almost felt warm inside. I didn't tell him what I told Mom. I simply said, "It's just racist stuff. That's all."

"Well, you'll survive it. We all do."

"That's what I wanna know. *How* you do?"

Dad gulped a drink of something and said, "You learn to outplay em at they own game. Don't fight em; outthink em. First time I had a run-in wit white folks I was bout eight years old. Me and Granddaddy was in town, handlin business. He said we needed to stop by the courthouse and pay taxes on our land. So we crossed the railroad tracks and entered the courthouse. Someone directed us to the tax assessor's office, where we waited a long time before being seen. We heard em laughin and talkin behind the door, but we didn't say nothin. We jes waitin for em to come out. It was over an hour though.

"When they come out, they asked us what we wanted, and Granddaddy pulled out a small wad of money and said he was there to pay the taxes on his land. The white man invited us into his office and had his secretary bring him a folder with our information in it. He opened it and said, 'That'll be fifty dollars, please.'

"Granddaddy frowned and said, 'Cuse me, sir, but there must be some kinda mistake. I come down here a few months ago and asked how much I'd owe this year when the taxes came due, and yo secretary there said it'd be thirty dollars.'

"He acted sympathetic and slurred, 'Oh you know how women are! Careless and all. She just made a mistake. I doubled-checked the figure. Yep! It's fifty dollars all right!'

"Granddaddy's large hands began to tremble. He searched his wallet and pockets for any other stray money, but of course he didn't have any. It had taken everything to gather thirty dollars. He was buying time, trying to figure out how not to lose our land.

'Sir, I don't have but thirty dollars.'

"The white man shook his head pitifully. 'I'm mighty sorry, sir, but that's not enough. It would cover some of yo land, but not all of it.'

"Granddaddy began to boil. His voice got deeper and thicker. 'This land been in my family since slavery days, sir. We always pay the taxes, and we pay em on time. Ain't never been late. Don't intend to start.'

'Well, Mr...um...'

'Swinton. Abraham Swinton.'

'Mr. Swanson, if you don't have fifty dollars, then you either gotta find it real fast or just sell us a few acres of the land to cover the taxes on the rest. You wouldn't even miss it, I tell ya!'

"I heard Granddaddy's teeth rattle. 'We don't sell the land, sir. None of it.'

"The white man tossed his hands in the air. 'Fine. Fine! Then you get twenty more dollars by 5:00 p.m. tomorrow, or we gon have to shave off a few acres of that land o yours.'

"Granddaddy wiped rivers of sweat from his chocolate-brown brow. 'Let's go, boy,' he said emphatically. To the white man, he said, 'Be back tomorrow. We'll have the money.'

"Outside the courthouse, Granddaddy mumbled, 'Mutha-fuckin crackers!' and marched so fast I could hardly keep up. By the time we got home, I was too tired to do anything but eat supper and go to bed. He told Grandma what happened, and she slammed pots around the kitchen, shouting for God to make a way outta no way. Next day, Granddaddy called for me to go to town again and we returned to the same office and the same sinister tax collector.

'Swanson!' he called, surprised to see us.

'Name's Swinton, sir. Abraham Swinton.'

'Okay, okay. Whatever. Let's not get testy. Did you get the money?'

"He anticipated Granddaddy's failure, but the old man reached into his pocket and pulled out a fresh, new fifty-dollar bill. The white man's blue eyes turned fire red.

'Very well.' He called for the secretary. 'Bring in the Swanson folder please.'

"She brought it and left. Granddaddy handed him the money. He opened the folder, scratched something with a pen, closed it, and tossed it onto his desk.

'Guess that'll hold you til next year.'

"Granddaddy motioned for us to go. Before we closed the door, the white man said, 'It'll cost you more next year. Inflation, ya know.'

"Granddaddy didn't say a word. We walked back to the mule and wagon and rode home in silence. I never knew how he got that fifty-dollar bill. I'm not sure I wanted to know. But I'm sure he practically gave his life for it."

"You never asked him?"

"Shit, naw, boy! You didn't ask a grown man bout his business back in them days."

I had inherited that belief.

"It just made me clear I wanted to leave. At least I thought I did. Til I got to Kansas City, and it was worse than Arkansas."

"Really? Kansas City?"

"Boy, when I first got to Kansas City, black folks had to be off the street by dark. Don't care how old they was."

Dad went on about the ways race had constricted black life in Missouri and Kansas, and how black folks had gotten around it. "That's how we survived," he said proudly. "We learned to dance with no music."

I told my therapist, "I think those conversations grew me up."

"How so?"

"I saw my mom and dad as people—regular, everyday black people—who work and struggle and hope for their kids. But I wasn't a kid anymore. I now had to carry my share of the load. And part of that load was pain. They didn't try to hide it anymore. It was simply part of bein black in America."

"Were you angry about it? The realization that you couldn't escape the pain?"

"I think I was at first, but then I discovered that our strength is greater than the pain, so I stopped thinking about it."

"Did you wanna hurt someone on behalf of black people?"

"Not only someone! Someones!"

She nodded. "That's logical and sensible—just illegal."

"Yeah, I know. I guess everybody black thinks about it at

some point. But it wouldn't help, so we drop the notion and go on about our business. But we never forget about it. Rage simmers in our minds day and night. If anybody or anything ever truly tips us off, they gon have a problem."

She chuckled.

"Do you think black parents did your generation a favor by protecting you so completely?"

"It's complicated," I said. "I wanna say no, but I see why they did it, and I see how it helped. We didn't have the same burden of race as they did, but in some ways, we ran in the wrong direction. We were freer, but we were blind."

"Hmmmm. In hindsight, which would you prefer?"

I took several deep breaths before saying, "I think I'd choose the burden of race over the freedom of ignorance."

"Why?"

"Because we've proven we can survive the burden of race. The jury's still out on the freedom of ignorance."

Day 33

I settled into Chicago just as the house music craze popped off. All over the city, people sponsored house parties to groove and grind to the energy of electronic, fast-paced 4/4 rhythms. Jackie was the social diva, so she invited me somewhere practically every weekend. We'd bonded over our attempt to survive at Microsoft, whispering and sending private emails about the microaggressions at work. She was smart, much smarter than me, and I loved how she put white folks in their place without insulting them. Or compromising her character.

These parties were so packed some folks couldn't get in. But they didn't mind. Many danced and drank right in others' backyards.

Dad had told me about honky-tonks, deep in the woods in the South, where poor black folks went on Friday and Saturday nights to relax and be unsurveilled. House parties in

Chicago in the '90s met a similar need, except we were ed-
ucated kids, trying to figure out why college degrees hadn't
saved us.

We grooved all night long. Even in the winter, we created
so much heat and sweat that folks had to go outside sometimes
to breathe. Parties were loud and wild, full of mixed drinks
and random flirtation, which I didn't mind at all. Some folks
became close friends. Like Darcy Taylor. She was a few years
older than me but acted like my momma. She and Jackie were
good buddies, so I fit right in. Together, we'd go to these
gatherings and dance the night away.

I'd leap the minute they started playing "Strike It Up."
People would scream all over the house and lift cups into the
air as bodies circled and swayed with the thunderous beat.
The rhythmic drums at the beginning of the song beck-
oned me like a hypnotized zombie to the center of the dance
floor. Darcy always came along. She was a shorty—five-one
or so—and on the thick side, and definitely a cutie pie in the
face. Pretty white teeth, deep dimples, thick, gorgeous hair,
and hefty breasts, which she displayed proudly. And loud as
could be.

"Get it, Swint!" she'd holler as we bent, twisted, and twirled
through half the houses on the South Side. Others laughed at
us, having made a name for ourselves, but we were dancing
for our lives. We just didn't know it. Darcy's jam was CeCe
Peniston's "Finally." Darcy knew every word and could sing
it in CeCe's range. People would clear space when the song
began, and Darcy would take the stage and kick, spin, and

toss her head back and forth until she went down in the splits, and we'd yell and stomp until all our worries vanished away.

One Saturday night, after a house party on the West Side, I went home and fell asleep on my little blue sofa. Early the next morning, Ricky, whom I hadn't heard from in a while, called. He was living with a partner in Omaha, Nebraska. Together, they were raising the man's two small boys. It was just the life Ricky wanted.

He shouted, "Turn on your TV, Isaac! Hurry!" He hung up. Dazed and half-conscious, I obeyed and listened to the breaking news:

"At 12:45 a.m. this morning, in Los Angeles, a black man named Rodney King was beaten within an inch of his life by LAPD officers. Mr. King led the officers on an eight-mile high-speed chase on the I-10 where he initially refused to pull over. Once he complied, the officers, led by Sergeant Stacey Koon, descended upon him, tasing and beating him mercilessly. King tried to run, but officers blocked that attempt, striking him on the head and body more than fifty-six times. King suffered a fractured leg, multiple facial fractures, and countless bruises and contusions. A nearby civilian, George Holliday, perched on a balcony across the street, caught the ordeal on a live video camera. This is one of the first times in history such behavior has been filmed in real time and stands as proof that America has a very real problem with people of color and the public justice system."

"What the fuck!" I mumbled, rubbing sleep from my eyes. Other commentators chimed in, and, within a few minutes, every station was reporting the story. I leaned forward from the edge of the sofa, trying to make sense of it all. Why had they beaten him like that? What had he done? Leslie and Jackie called, but I hung up quickly in order to hear more. By the time Darcy called, I was pissed off.

"Do you see this shit, girl?"

"I know, I know! I can't believe they beat him like a dog!"

"What did he do?"

"Do you have to do anything?"

"True, but what are they sayin he did?"

"Speeding, I think. And he didn't pull over fast enough."

"That gives them the right to beat the shit out of him?"

"Guess so. They ain't never needed no excuse. That's for sure. But damn!"

All the arresting officers were white. That only made matters worse. I watched the video repeatedly and heard the billy clubs land all over his body as he screeched and screamed for mercy. Certainly, I knew of police brutality, but I'd never seen it on national TV. They continued beating King until he collapsed. It reminded me of the way Kunta Kinte's master beat him, except that, now, there were four or five of them, extracting from a black man's flesh everything they needed to maintain their throne of white supremacy.

I called Ricky back. "This is some crazy shit, man!"

"Dude!" he shouted. "What the fuck's goin on?"

"I don't know! I just don't know."

"Do you see how they beat him?"

"Hell yeah, I see it. Can't help but see it!"

"Something's gotta give, bruh. For real. This gotta stop."

"How? How we gon stop it?"

"I don't know! But we gotta do something!"

"March in the streets? You think that's gon help?"

I didn't. "Naw, that method's gone. We need something new."

"Yep. Just let me know when you think of it."

I hung up and watched the video yet again. For what seemed like hours, they beat Rodney King until he lay perfectly still upon the asphalt. I thought he was dead. I mean, who could withstand those blows and live to tell it? But he wasn't dead. I still couldn't believe they beat him like that on public television! *They aren't ashamed?* I kept thinking. *They don't fear punishment? Who gets to do that?* My memory took me to the Middle Passage, when white crewmen threw enslaved Africans overboard simply because they were insubordinate or wouldn't eat. Then I thought of slave owners who, for four hundred years, beat enslaved Africans for standing idle or looking a white man in the eye. That led me to the Civil Rights Movement where public officials lashed nonviolent black bodies just because they could. I realized, finally, that the man they beat on TV was the man they lashed on the plantation and the man they hosed down during the '60s. To them, we were just a body—an abhorrent, black body—that demanded punishment because we didn't look like them. There was no difference between them and me. America made sure I knew it.

It all made sense now. Our blackness stood in opposition to

who they thought they were. Something about us made them believe we were a threat to their system. And they meant to remind us that we were under their control. They also meant to make sure we never believed we were as good as them. That was my problem. I knew I was.

I relaxed into the sofa, sighed, and shook my head. The world became clear before my very eyes. I wouldn't succumb to racism. Too much was at stake. America wouldn't count my destruction among its victories.

I followed the Rodney King incident like a detective. The police who beat him were charged with assault. The story dominated the news for weeks. Someone had caught everything on video, so there was no disputing the matter. Or so everyone thought. When police went to trial, they were found not guilty. *Not* guilty? How could that be? The world had seen the whole thing! We watched them beat Mr. King to a pulp. We saw it with our own eyes. Even white folks at work were seemingly horrified. I stood at my desk as I heard the verdict. They tried not to look at me, but they couldn't help it. Their pity was palpable, their shame inescapable. A few even stopped at my cubicle and whispered, "So sorry, Isaac." I stared back. Why were they sorry *for me*?

Then I laughed. They knew my black body could be next. They knew that, any minute, for any reason, public officials could find my behavior unacceptable and I might be beaten on some street somewhere, begging for mercy that never comes. They also felt sorry for me because they knew no one was coming to help me. Not even them.

I had a hard time talking to white folks that week. They wanted me to decry the riot because such behavior destroyed black communities, but they failed to understand the psychology of oppressed people and why they demolish their own property in the midst of social injustice. I wouldn't co-sign the sentiment that black people "just don't know how to act," and this made them wonder if I were one of them. Well, I was.

However, I had learned to be quiet. My own encounter with white authority had taught me how to grin and take my rage home. Ricky convinced me, instead, to write something about the ordeal, so I did. I titled it "You Can Beat Me, But You Can't Kill Me." I sent it to the *Chicago Tribune*, but never heard back. It was too militant, now that I think about it. But I couldn't very well soften the truth of what they'd done to Mr. King. Or thousands of other black men. In the article, I traced the beating of black men from slavery to the present. I highlighted what state troopers did to John Lewis and others in 1965 at the Edmund Pettus Bridge in Selma, Alabama. Of course authorities had beaten black bodies since our arrival, but to do so on national television seemed outrageous even for white people. But it wasn't. It just proved that they didn't fear reprisal. They assumed the nation would support them, and they were right.

It's really hard to explain how this fundamentally changed my perception of America. I hated this country back then. It cared absolutely nothing for me and my people, and that angered me because I knew enough black history to know that black blood fertilized the soil of this nation. Black women had breastfed white children for centuries, then, later, were raped by them; black men had bowed before and chauffeured white men while being called "boy" and "nigger" and other ungodly things. I recalled a slave narrative in which a black man was made to eat off the ground like a common dog. What kind of human makes another do that?

I now understood Nat Turner's wrath. He was my hero. He knew he was going to die, but he led a slave rebellion anyway. That was a bad brother! He refused to live like an animal, and I was proud of that. It's the same rage that later fueled Stokely Carmichael and Fannie Lou Hamer and Malcolm X in the '60s. You can't treat people like shit and expect them not to act. Somebody's gonna rebel. Yes, Nat Turner died, but he didn't fail. He took out sixty or so white people before they destroyed him.

This is what I wrote about in my article to the *Tribune*. No wonder they didn't publish it.

Well, I wasn't finished rebelling. I couldn't fight California police, but I could make my wrath known. For three days, I turned my stereo to its loudest volume and played Public Enemy's "Fight the Power." I had some pretty strong speakers, so people heard it throughout my complex. Neighbors complained, and I suppose they should've, because it was loud and intrusive. That's what I wanted. I played it during the evening and all times of the night. When police came, I turned it off and acted like I didn't know what they were talking about. Each time they left, I'd wait several minutes then blast it again. A few bold neighbors knocked on my door and confronted me, but I cursed them out and slammed the door in their faces.

Some were black; some were white. None of that mattered. I meant to disturb the peace, and I did.

A few days later, I turned it down. I had made the point. I relaxed with Tupac, A Tribe Called Quest, and a new group from Jersey called Poor Righteous Teachers. They had a hit called "Rock Dis Funky Joint" that I played almost every day. It had a smooth groove, sorta like the music of the '60s, but some really powerful, positive lyrics. That's what I liked about hip-hop back then. Rappers knew our history, our story, and weren't ashamed to tell it. Back in the '90s, hip-hop was the voice of frustrated, maligned black youth who had something to say to the world.

Later in 1991, after the Rodney King debacle, I heard a brilliant hip-hop album titled *2Pacalypse Now*. It was a classic from the beginning. One song has stayed with me a lifetime. When I first heard it, I was washing dishes, but I stopped and sat at my kitchen table and stared into nothing as Tupac told the story of a young girl who had a baby. What startled me was that she was practically a baby herself. I'd never heard of a twelve- or thirteen-year-old being pregnant. The real horror was who the father might be. I knew he was older than her. The whole image was incredibly disturbing.

Then I realized Tupac wasn't simply telling a story. He was implicating a community, the black community, that had allowed such reprehensible behavior. Of course, I'd grown up in relative safety and security. The most outrageous thing I'd ever heard of was a boy "borrowing" his father's car without permission. I thought that was the worst crime imaginable. I assumed all black people were like us—hardworking, refined,

God-fearing. But once I moved to Chicago, I met another kind of black people, and I wasn't always proud of them. Of course, I was among them, but, in my mind, I wasn't one of them. "Brenda's Got a Baby" showed me that something had happened to black people, something bad and recent, that most of us couldn't explain. But we saw the result.

I'm not sure why, but I felt responsible for that little black girl. I think I had finally become an adult—a conscientious citizen of the world who cared about things, especially black things. I didn't have sisters, but I had smiled at little black girls on the street and imagined their joy as they double Dutched or hopscotched or played hand games that boys never played.

By the end of the song, we learn that the dude ran off and left her, and she was saddled with raising the baby alone because her community thought of her as "fass."

I remember a kid in a grocery store when I was in junior high. It was down on Fifty-Seventh and Prospect. He was probably six or seven, looking to buy a candy bar. He reached up and put the item on the counter then laid a quarter next to it. He was a cute little black boy in a ragged, oversize stocking cap and hand-me-down brown coat. I smiled at him because he looked up and smiled at me. He seemed proud that he had enough money to purchase what he wanted. I touched his head, like a big brother might do. That's when the white store clerk grabbed the quarter and slammed it into the cash register then put a nickel in its place. He looked at the boy as if he were trash. I frowned, but I was too young to protest. Plus, to be honest, I thought the white man was frowning at the boy's ragged clothes. I, too, had frowned at that—until the child's eyes canceled my judgment. I saw hope and innocence in those beautiful brown eyes, and I knew his condition didn't reveal his value. I guess the white man didn't see what I saw. He might not've looked at him at all.

"Thank you," I mumbled to the clerk, took the nickel and the candy bar, and handed them to the child. He smiled again, put the change in his pocket, and walked out of the store eating what he had bought with his own money. I turned back to the white man and saw hatred glisten in his eyes. He resented the little boy's contentment; I resented his desire to ruin it.

These moments happened throughout my childhood, but I didn't think much of them then. I knew I was black, and I knew many white folks didn't like me, but that didn't matter. Dad and Mom spoke very little about race, so I rarely considered it. Even after we saw *Roots*, I didn't get consumed with white people. The world Dad and Mom created for me was black, so I dealt with white folks only when I had to. Most of the kids at Central High were white, but most of my friends were the few black ones among them. I certainly never thought white kids were better than me. That never crossed my mind. What I did think, though, was that black people had to prove our worth. I believed that because I watched Dad do it every day. He never complained about work although he seemed to hate it. Yet he boasted of going every day, whether he felt like it or not, and I heard pride in his voice when he said it. He had *earned his keep*. That's the phrase he used. He had proved his right to be a man, and he was teaching me to do the same. But I didn't want what he wanted, and that's where we parted ways.

I see now, though, that both of us actually wanted the same thing—the acknowledgment of our worth.

Day 34

Something happened a few years later that almost destroyed my self-worth. I was vulnerable and needed someone to lean upon. That's no excuse for what I did, but it does explain the context—if that matters, which I hope it does.

Microsoft's annual business conference was in Los Angeles that year. Hundreds of people came, from all over the world, and, one night, several black executives ended up drinking pretty heavily. Most attendees were old white men, but a few brothers and sisters seasoned the crowd. One man kept looking at me, and I interpreted his expression as desire, so I gave him my room number and he came. We talked a long while, then messed around a bit. It was sensual and beautiful, and I hoped it might evolve into something long-term. It did. His name was Travis, and he lived in New York, so we flew back and forth, over the next several months, between Chicago and the Big Apple, getting to know each other. Sometimes we spent the entire weekend inside, watching movies and talking.

"You want kids?" I asked one rainy Friday evening in a New York hotel.

"I have them," he said cautiously. "Three of them."

I couldn't disguise my surprise.

"I was gonna tell you."

"When?" I blurted.

"When the time was right. We're still getting to know each other."

"I know, but that kind of information should come up front, don't you think?"

"Maybe. But," he huffed, "I didn't want to run you off too soon."

We lay upon the bed in our underwear, surrounded only by dim lamplight. Travis was a tall guy, six-three or -four, with a slender build and slight muscles. He was handsome—clean shaven, tapered haircut, smooth dark chocolate complexion— but what attracted me was his unmistakable brilliance. He had ideas and thoughts and loved sharing them. He was a reader. He was probably the only man I knew who actually read philosophy for the fun of it. At any given moment, he'd ask me something like "Do you think you're a human being?" and I'd be too stunned to answer. He knew Socrates and Aristotle, but his favorite thinker was Howard Thurman. I think the man had read *Jesus and the Disinherited* ten times.

Sometimes he'd create stories and share them in the dark,

and I'd see them in my mind's eye like a whole cinematic production. His deep, heavy, raspy voice tumbled in my head long after weekends were over. I lost my good sense when he touched me—and he always touched me—softly, tenderly, as if exploring something rare and precious and fragile. I take full responsibility for losing my mind. Although it wasn't my fault, it definitely was.

"How old are your kids?"

"Ten, eight, and five. Two boys and a girl."

He was born in the Bronx and grew up the youngest of five brothers. There were things I didn't want to know, so I didn't ask. I knew I'd pay later.

The only thing he hated, he said, was a weak man.

"What's a weak man?" I asked, knowing I wouldn't agree with his answer.

He squirmed a bit, excited to elaborate. "It's a guy who lets other people walk all over him, one who won't stand up for himself."

I shrugged at first. "I don't know anyone like that."

Travis frowned. "You don't?"

"No, I don't. I know plenty of sweet, sensitive men, but they're not weak."

"Then they're not *sweet* either."

It was my turn to frown. "Why can't they be? What's wrong with a man being sweet? It only means he's thoughtful and caring and attentive. You're definitely that."

Travis's excitement tanked. "Don't ever say that again."

I gawked. Was he serious?

I heard his quick, sudden breath. We stared several intense

seconds, then Travis sighed. "I ain't sweet, man. I don't wanna be sweet. Sorry if I bit your head off." He sat on the edge of the bed like a disobedient child awaiting punishment.

"Travis," I said in slow motion, "I wasn't trying to demean you or anything. I was simply saying you're a kind, caring man, and that's what a sweet person is—someone who cares about other people."

"Then just call me kind. Don't call me sweet."

This was going nowhere. I smiled and changed the subject, one of the greatest errors of my life. I knew what he meant, and I knew that, down the road, we'd clash again. I saw the signs, but I chose to ignore them.

We'd been dating about a year when I decided to fly to New York and surprise him for his birthday. Travis had an apartment in Harlem, on the corner of 135th and Adam Clayton Powell. I got balloons and flowers and made a birthday card. As I approached his apartment, I spotted him across the street. A pretty, shapely, light-skinned woman was clutching his arm. They laughed together, touching playfully and smiling into each other's eyes. I knew who she was to him. I always knew. I thought they were at least separated, and that Travis had his own private residence. Of course the kids might come over, but not her.

I watched them until they disappeared into the brownstone. Then I released the balloons into the sky.

Later that evening, I called and told him I was in New York to hug him for his birthday. He sounded genuinely happy and surprised. We met in my hotel room, as usual, and he spent the night as he always did. I never mentioned seeing him with the woman. There was no need. What would've been the point? I couldn't very well reprimand him for a lie I helped perpetuate. I was a pitiful mess. And still I didn't leave him.

We continued seeing each other for a few years. A few *years*. I tried to tell myself I couldn't do it anymore. I broke up with him once, twice, too many times to count. I cursed myself and begged God to forgive me. I tried to throw his information away, but never quite did. I was so ashamed I couldn't look in the mirror. I flew home from that trip, promising never to see or speak to him again, and I held that promise a good while. Then, late one rainy evening, he showed up.

I recognized the knock. Something told me not to answer, but I couldn't help myself. When I opened the door, there he was, sad-eyed and all.

"I know you know."

"I do. And I'm done. I can't do it anymore."

I tried to close the door, but not really. His foot blocked the way.

"I can't live without you," he said matter-of-factly.

It's all I'd wanted to hear. What could I do?

He came in and we picked up where we'd left off. I know this is disgraceful, but I had no power to resist him, no integrity at all.

He told me he would split his time equally between New York and Chicago, and I agreed. Not verbally but silently. I was the weak man he'd soon reject. I couldn't tell Momma about this. Her disappointment would've killed me. I know

I was wrong, in so many ways, but anything was better than loneliness. That kills a man after a while.

He spent the night, but I didn't sleep. Guilt wouldn't let me. By morning, I tried to put him out, but he wouldn't leave. My final strategy was to make him feel bad about not leaving *her*, but he didn't. He couldn't risk losing his kids, he said. I understood that. So, once again, we were back where we started. There is nothing sensible to say, nothing intelligent I can offer. I can only declare that a desperate man is a sad, pathetic thing. Heaven's disappointment, I'm sure.

Travis died from a brain aneurysm the following spring. I won't try to explain how my whole world fell apart or how sorrow took residence in my heart and refused to leave. Suffice it to say, I took a week off work and grieved as if the world had ended. While mourning, I convinced myself that God took him from me because our relationship wasn't honorable. At the funeral, I cried so badly I had to walk out. At the graveside, his wife thanked me for coming, then asked how I knew Travis. I whispered, "I'm an old friend." She smiled and nodded knowingly. "You're the one from Chicago, aren't you?" Too startled to lie, I said, "Yes." She touched my shoulder and added, "Good. He would've wanted this." I didn't ask what she meant. I think I already knew.

Ricky suggested I find somebody free. "You gotta take a risk to love without hiding, Isaac. Nothing else will do."

I knew he was right. I just wasn't as bold as he was. Not yet. He said his parents loved his partner and his kids. I couldn't imagine my parents embracing such a life. He even takes them to Kansas City for holidays and summer vacation. There was no way I could do that. Or could I? Maybe now Mom and Dad would love whoever I loved. I was an adult, and perhaps they'd grown enough to respect my choices. I'd never considered it. If I wasn't the same, maybe they weren't either. I sighed. I was too afraid to know.

Day 35

My mother got sick during the summer of 1993. Dad called and said I should think about coming home for a visit, but he didn't say why. I'd talked to Mom recently and she sounded fine, so I saw no need to rush.

When that Thanksgiving I saw her, half her size, I froze. I knew something was wrong, but I didn't want to know what it was. I chalked it up to age at first although, of course, she wasn't old. Then I considered that perhaps she'd been dieting since she'd always wanted to lose a few pounds, but the sickness lingering in her eyes told me it wasn't that. So I sighed and smiled, and Dad smiled, and Mom and I hugged, like we always did, and I waited for her to tell me the truth.

When she said the word—*cancer*—my legs gave way and everything in me dropped to the floor. I couldn't help it. I could smell death on her—rank and stale—like the scent of chamomile and old folks' homes. She didn't try to lie or deceive me. She rubbed my head sweetly as I sobbed. People say God knows how much we can bear, but God was wrong that day.

I, snuggled like a toddler, slept with Mom that night. I didn't know how much time she had left, so I tried to capture every moment. As she lay dying, I became frighteningly aware that soon Dad would be all I have.

I would've died with her if I could've. There was no answer to my misery. I asked God why this had to be. He had to know what Mom's death would do to me, and He didn't stop it. I hated Him all over again. If He'd taken my breath that very moment, I would've been grateful.

Sorrow and emptiness consumed my life. After Travis's death, I was depressed for weeks; but after Mom's, my whole world shifted. I considered returning to Kansas City and the house and living out my days there. I even wondered what another country might be like. Then I realized that heartache goes wherever you go, so I sat in my apartment and let grief have its way. For days my world went silent. I didn't hear music, human voices, bird songs, sirens in the street, or noise from the TV. I shut everything and everyone out of my life. Nothing penetrated my distress. Lots of people called, but I don't remember any conversations. What I remember was sitting on my floor with Ricky, fingering strands of carpet, unsure of how I'd survive another day. I lost enough weight that my best black suit hung limp all over me. Nothing fit during those days.

The funeral is a blur except for Miss Ora's solo. She squeezed my shoulders and belted, "'Some glad morning, when this life is O'er, I'll fly away! To a home on God's celestial shore, I'll fly away!'" Then she reached upward and sang, "'I'll fly away, oh Glory, I'll fly away… When I die, Hallelujah by and by… I'll fly away!'" The image of Mom taking to the air and leaving this world behind got me through the day.

After the funeral Dad asked if I was okay. I nodded and he nodded back. We said nothing more.

Later that night, Mom came to me. I saw her as clearly as I see myself now. She looked radiant in the yellow dress and white pearls. I asked her to stay, but she refused. Said nothing was more beautiful than where she was. I didn't beg.

She asked if I loved anyone, and I told her no. She told me to get busy trying. I told her I was tired of trying; she told me to try harder. "Love is all you have," she said. She asked if I had repaired things with Dad, and I said no. "You owe him that," she intoned. I shook my head; she nodded. "Give him what he gave you." Then she went away.

I thought of Dad every day after Mom died. He really was all I had. I have lots of extended family, but I was never really close to them. Aunt Pig's son, Jeffrey, and I talked occasionally, but nothing regular. I wouldn't have gone to him if I'd had a need. I probably wouldn't have gone to anyone. I would've let my needs linger—like most black people do.

I missed Dad most on holidays, when I cooked turkey and ham and greens and dressing and had no one to share it with. Ricky came a few times, but not often. He usually went home to Kansas City, because his mother couldn't share him.

I never understood why they never spoke of his sexuality. He said they didn't need to. I guess closeness doesn't necessarily mean vulnerability.

Ricky had always been in the closet to me. People didn't know his sexuality although they might've suspected it.

"There's nothing to tell," he told me as I dropped him at the airport. "I know who I am, and I'm perfectly fine with it. I can love anybody I choose—male or female. Why do I need to announce it?"

"It's not about announcing it, Ricky. It's about being honest with yourself and the world."

"I *have* been honest! I've been with men and women, although I prefer men. Anyone who knows me knows that. We don't ask straight men to announce their sex partners!"

He had a point. "True, but gay men's freedom is more complicated."

"More complicated than what? And why?"

"Our freedom is the pride of our identity."

"Isn't everybody's?"

I gave up. We were talking in circles. I pulled to the curb and Ricky opened the door.

"I feel no need to justify my attractions to anyone. I'm also not gonna hide them. I'm just gonna be."

He took his suitcase from the trunk and walked away without our usual embrace. He knew far more about freedom than I did.

For months after Mom's death, I lived on the edge. It's a frightening, lonely place. Nothing felt right. I hated my job, I stopped socializing, I couldn't imagine loving again. I needed something to give my life meaning.

So I asked Darcy to have a baby with me. We'd talked about having kids—just not with each other. It made sense though. We were best friends, we shared the same values. We'd be great parents. But I was doing it for myself—not the hope for a family. Darcy wanted a family.

We didn't have to be married or anything, she said, but we had to be a unit. I never understood exactly what she meant, but it was something greater than I wanted. Truth is, I wanted her to have a baby *for* me—not *with* me—and she simply wasn't willing. Said she wouldn't have a child and give it up completely. Absolutely no way.

I wasn't done trying. I started dating a new girl at Microsoft who worked in the software design department. I wasn't in love, but I liked her enough, I thought.

I was tired of being different, sick of being alone. Difference is a drag sometimes, and some days it didn't feel worth it. Verlinda Washington was her name. She was as good as any woman I knew. She asked if I was gay, and I asked why she would ask such a thing, and she said because I was rather effeminate for a straight man, and I told her all straight men aren't the same. That was true, but I had also lied to myself. I had actually convinced myself, for the second time in my life, that I could live as a straight man. That perhaps I hadn't been gay in the first place. Over time, she trusted me, and I loved her for it. I really loved her. I made love to her sincerely, passionately. But I ultimately desired different things sexually. I discovered that all human beings are complicated in some sort

of way. That complexity is my freedom now. Lord knows I
paid dearly for it.

We dated six or eight months before I asked her to marry
me. She accepted right away. I'm ashamed now of what I almost did, both to her and myself. But deep in my heart, I truly
loved her. I just wasn't in love with her. I was in love with
the idea of having children, quieting the naysayers, pleasing
my father. The only problem was that I couldn't imagine joy
in the midst of it all.

The day I proposed, I gave her Mom's wedding ring. I did
the whole knee thing, and Verlinda cried and said it was all
she ever wanted. We were happy that day. At least she was. I
hoped I could keep up the charade.

A week later, the same day I meant to call and give Dad
the good news, she asked me a question: "If we never have
children, will you still want me?" I couldn't answer her. I
thought of a life of nothing *but* her, and the thought wasn't
fulfilling. In fact, I realized, in that moment, that I needed
her biological function, and nothing more. My silence was
shameful. I knew marrying her wouldn't have been fair. We
cried and said goodbye. She returned the ring.

Her final words were, "I hope you find someone you can
actually love."

I spiraled into a second bout of depression. I wanted a
traditional life complete with kids, a house, and some sense
of normalcy. I wanted a wedding, a family, an existence
the world celebrated and supported. But from the looks
of things, I wouldn't have it. I couldn't. I had been born

wrong, oriented toward the unthinkable. I wasn't due what everyone else had coming. All my dreams were illegitimate. That's what I told myself.

"Did you actually *see* your mother after she passed?"

I nodded. "Yes. Yes, I did. Just like I'm looking at you now. But I knew she was in the spirit. I knew that."

"How?"

"Because soft, white light surrounded her. When she called my name, it sounded like an echo of her usual voice."

She looked down.

"You don't believe me, do you?"

"Oh I do," she corrected, looking up quickly. "It's just that I envy that kind of power."

"Do you? Do you really?"

"Oh yes. It's spiritual. I believe in spiritual things."

I was relieved.

"Some people can communicate across realms. Apparently you're one of them."

"Guess so."

She smiled.

"When I was a kid, my father took me to Arkansas and showed me where his folks are buried. In the midst of that cemetery, those ancestors began to speak to me, and I had an out-of-body experience. I heard their wails, their cries of pain and dissatisfaction, and I stumbled to the ground. It felt like someone had taken over my consciousness. I was under a spell. My father thought I was putting on, but I wasn't. I'd never met any of them, but they trusted me and told me their story. I never knew why."

"Perhaps because you're supposed to write it."

"Perhaps."

"It'll all come together one day soon."

"It might, but to be honest, I've moved on."

"Have you? You seem pretty stuck to me." She cackled.

I found nothing funny. "All my life I've tried to write, but nothing comes out quite like I want. Maybe I'm simply supposed to read."

"I doubt that. You don't have the gift simply to observe it. There's a larger purpose somewhere. You have to find out what it is."

Day 36

Jackie and Darcy showed up at my house and resurrected me. I hadn't been out in days, and, according to them, I smelled like a garbage dump.

"Bitch, we don't do this!" Darcy declared playfully. They pinched their noses and frowned at my disarray. "Get your ass in the shower, scrub those balls, and put on some clean clothes. We goin out."

"I don't wanna go out," I whined.

"Well, you goin!" they shouted in chorus.

I didn't fight them. Once I got dressed, we exited and walked a few blocks to a nearby park. It was a beautiful, cool spring day. Their laughter, their love, did the trick.

"You know what you should do, Isaac?" Darcy declared, leaning against a tree. "You should go back to school."

I'd thought of graduate school before, but not seriously. I

was making too much money to leave my job. But now, more than the money, I needed a change.

I applied to University of Chicago's English Master's program and got in. I had planned to specialize in African American Lit.

I took a leave of absence from my job for the first semester, to see if I liked school enough to continue. I had saved a good amount, so, for six months or so, I would be fine.

I registered for three classes: Lit Theory, Proseminar in English, and Shakespeare. I attended the new student orientation, where I met colleagues from across the world. We were a veritable UN, a cluster of scholars who would one day study each other's work. Then classes began, and the truth of our personal tensions came forth.

One day, in my Shakespeare class, we were discussing *Othello*. A white girl tried to argue the irrelevance of race, positing that the play is about love and power—not black and white.

I raised my hand. "Yeah, it's about love and power, but love and power are both circumscribed by race. At least in the West."

She smirked. "There was no real racism in Shakespeare's day. Certainly nothing like now."

I couldn't let her get away with that. "Of course there was. That's why the play's called *Othello, the Moor of Venice*. Shakespeare announces his race because it makes all the difference. It's like he's saying, 'There's a Nigga in town, y'all!'" I hollered at my own joke, but no one else did, especially the professor.

"Can we just talk about the play and not bring our own biases into it?" the white girl whined.

"What? Are you serious? Race isn't *my* bias. If I had my way, I'd get rid of it overnight. It's the creation of Western culture, the signature of what it means to be white."

"I'm not racist just because I'm white!"

"Of course you are! It's your inheritance. I'm not saying you're intentionally racist or evil, but I am saying you can't be a white citizen of the West and not be framed in racism. It's as ubiquitous as air!"

Our professor, an old white man, intervened and said, "Isaac, yes, racism is ever present, but you have to evaluate people on an individual basis."

"I'm sorry, Professor, but I don't. No one decides to be racist in America. You inherit it. Whites also inherit white privilege, just like blacks inherit social abuse and discrimination."

Mitzy sneered, "Then you must be white because you have the privilege of being here with us!"

I almost leaped over that table and whipped her ass. Instead, I said, "Do you really think it's *my* privilege to be here with *you*?"

She didn't answer.

"You've positioned yourself as the natural inheritor of this space and me as a grateful outsider. *You* should be happy to be in here with *me*!"

We went on, back and forth, for several minutes until security burst through the door. I looked around in panic.

"Is there a problem, Professor?" one of the white officers asked, looking at me.

There were three of them, intense, searching, convinced that some imminent danger lingered. My mouth fell open. I studied their faces in stark surprise.

"I think we'll be okay," the professor said.

Mitzy began to cry. The one sista in the class, a second-year PhD student, put her finger to her lips and shook her head.

After class she grabbed me in the hall. "Don't let em destroy you, Isaac," she said. "That's all they're trying to do."

Day 37

I was angry, for sure, but, more, I was disheartened. At Lincoln, where everyone was black, I didn't have to fight for significance. But now, in the middle of Chicago, I was a threat.

I didn't go home immediately after class. I walked the streets of Chicago, noticing how the city was a labyrinth of the haves and have nots, how poverty had permanently undermined blacks and settled into their skin like a rash. I walked Hyde Park, all the way down Seventy-Ninth Street.

Now I understood why Dad had compelled me to be a man. Society didn't care about my sensitivities, my fluidity. It saw only my black skin and responded accordingly. I had a college degree, a damn good job, a solid apartment, and *still* I was a Nigga. At least in their eyes.

I eventually went home, fixed a cup of tea, and grabbed my copy of *The Fire Next Time*. I remembered Baldwin's prophesy around race relations in America, and I needed to hear it again. He told his nephew that America was prepared to destroy him. I didn't know he meant me too. He said one thing that stuck out in my mind: "You were born into a society which spelled out with brutal clarity, and in as many ways as possible, that you were a worthless human being. You were not expected to aspire to excellence: you were expected to make peace with mediocrity." I never forgot that. It's one of the reasons I did well at Lincoln. To prove America wrong, to make them acknowledge black excellence. But, in truth, I was born excellent. I just didn't know it then.

Another thing Baldwin said that stayed in my mind: "If the concept of God has any validity or any use, it can only be to make us larger, freer, and more loving. If God cannot do this, then it is time we got rid of Him." I shook my head just as I'd done the first time I read it. How could a black man say such a thing? Baldwin spoke of dismissing God as if he had the authority to do so. I admired him for that. I hadn't seen how God had changed the condition of black people in America, and, as such, I thought it high time we try something new too.

I called Ricky and told him what happened. He was as furious as I was. But he insisted I stay in school. I told him not to worry. I had no intentions of quitting.

Day 38

For the remainder of the semester, the professor overlooked my raised hand and graded my papers harshly. Regardless of what I said, he deemed my comments *antagonistic*, and suggested, right in front of my peers, that I consider "something other than the academic life." One white boy whispered, "Bullshit. You're a fuckin prick." I didn't know what to say. I was more hurt than embarrassed. I knew what kind of student I was, and I didn't intend for this son of a bitch to make me hate learning. So each class session, I swallowed a little more pride until I almost choked on humiliation.

He gave me a C for the course, effectively suggesting I didn't have any business there. I decided to go see him. Something told me not to, but I couldn't let it go. My Lit Theory professor offered to speak to him, but I begged him not to.

I knocked lightly on his office door, and he said, "Come

in!" with a bright, friendly tone. When he saw me, the smile faded, and he stood like one prepared to defend himself.

"How can I help you, Mr. Swinton?"

"Good afternoon, Professor Taylor."

"What can I do for you?" He refused small talk.

"I want to speak with you about my grade. I don't feel it's justified."

He cleared his throat. "It reflects your performance. I had great hopes for you, but not everyone's cut out to be a scholar."

Another gulp of shame. "I'm an A student, Dr. Taylor."

He chuckled. "Most school's A's are not University of Chicago A's."

"I went to one of the best HBCUs in the country!"

"One of the best *what*?"

I chuckled. "Never mind. Thank you for your time." And left.

The therapist said, "I'm sorry that happened to you. I know how much you liked school."

"Still do. I haven't finished yet, but I'm going to."

"You should. You owe it to yourself."

I agreed. "I think the incident matured me."

"How so?"

"I realized I didn't want to get bogged down in a system rigged against me. I don't want to use my energy reacting to white people. Sometimes we gotta do it; I understand that. But usually it's a waste of time. Our rage doesn't change America. Not fundamentally. It makes America change the rules of the game. I didn't want to play anymore."

She nodded. "None of us do."

We talked about other things, then she asked, "Have you been back to the house in Kansas City since your father died?"

I'm not sure why the question unsettled me. "No, I haven't."

"Don't you think you should go?"

"Why?"

"Because it's yours and it holds memories. It might provide you with some closure."

"I have bad memories of that house."

"Yes, but you have good ones too. They go together—the good and the bad. Your job is to sort through them and choose which ones to keep."

"You can't just keep the memories you want!"

"Of course you can. All memories are constructed, Isaac. We create them. They're not pieces of pure history or snapshots of truth. They're our arrangement of how we feel about things. You get to have whatever memories you want."

"I thought about selling the house."

"Maybe you will, but before you do, go sit in it and gather the memories you want to keep. You come from amazing parents, according to your story. Don't throw everything away."

Day 39

A week before my thirty-fifth birthday, I drove to Kansas City. It snowed lightly along the way, calming time and easing my anxieties. Jackie and Darcy offered to ride with me, but I had to do this alone.

I arrived at dusk and sat in the driveway a long time. The house seemed sad. Or lonely. I'd kept the utilities paid so that when this moment came, I wouldn't be in the dark. I don't know what I feared. I saw myself as a little boy again, longing for Daddy's attention and affirmation, while hiding behind Momma's dress tail. We sat at the little oval breakfast table, and Dad asked about my grades, and Mom let me speak for myself, but she never failed to express her joy. The question was really a warning, an announcement that failure was unacceptable. He took no joy in my good grades. They were simply a measure of what I owed the family.

"You're procrastinating, Isaac," I said to myself and flung the door open. Only the little sapling, which was bigger now, welcomed me home. With the wind's assistance, it waved a greeting that made me smile. That was the same tree that had shaded Ricky and me on prom night. It had grown tremendously. So had I.

I forced the key into the rusty keyhole and turned it carefully. The lock surrendered, and the door moaned softly as I pushed gently. I closed it before touching the light switch. There in the dark I saw it all: pain, love, frustration, hurt. They greeted me like royalty, welcoming me back to the throne. *This is your home*, they said. *You're king of the palace! Take your place!* In Dad's voice, something said, *We've been waiting for you.*

And when I turned on the light, I blinked several times then covered my mouth with surprise. Scattered across the coffee table were letters—dozens of letters—addressed to me.

I approached the pile as one might the Ark of the Covenant. They were everywhere, these letters, even on the floor and the sofa.

"What the hell?" I murmured, bending for a closer look. It was definitely Dad's rough, childlike penmanship. I would know it anywhere. He'd never learned cursive, so his letters overlapped like fallen leaves. I didn't understand. Each envelope bore my name, but no address. They were not to be mailed. They were to be found. And I had found them.

I gathered them, one by one, and ordered them chronologically. I even noticed how his penmanship deteriorated over time. I could hardly read my name on the last letter. Yet, for some reason, that's where I started reading:

Dear Isaac,

I can see the Old Ship of Zion now, easing across the water, coming quietly for me. You are in the prime of your life, loving some man freely, I suppose, but yourself mostly, I pray. If not, start doing it. Time waits for no man, Granddaddy used to say. And this is true.

When you read this, I'll be in the next world. Don't cry for me, son. I've cried enough for myself. And have no regrets about us. There is nothing for which you are to blame, unless you've now made your own mistakes and hurt others, which you may have. Every man has. But most of those hurts—at least many of them—are blooms of seeds I planted in you. You must learn to up-root unwanted seeds without destroying the entire harvest. This is the son's lesson. Nurture good sprouts, Isaac. Toss weeds aside and never think of them again. Just re-member that sprouts and weeds are planted together, and weeds have a valuable function. They teach you what to avoid, what not to embrace. There is no good plant-ing without them.

All I think of now is you. This means I love you. I feel it in my heart—that sense that nothing and no one else matters. I've always wanted to know that feeling, and now I do. The sad thing is that you won't hear me say I'm sorry. But I did say it. Perhaps in this letter you'll feel it, hear it in my tone, and let my words love you bet-ter than I ever did.

Just one last request: tell people I tried. If there is a funeral, and if you attend it, please tell them I tried. You are free to say I failed, too, for, in so many ways, that is the gospel truth, but at least say I tried. Recall, if you will, the few joys we shared—you, your mother, and I—and tell them I left you the house although you didn't want it. Tell them about our trip to the land, how you loved it and later painted it more beautifully than I had remembered. Tell them you graduated from college debt free because I paid the tuition. Tell them I wasn't always a good father, but I was always a man.

And, if at all possible, take me home. Whether in a casket or a vase, please take me home. Don't leave me in Kansas City. Honeysuckles don't bloom here in springtime. Neighbors don't drop by if they haven't seen you in a while. This is not my home. I can't stay here. Lay me next to my brother, beneath the little tree in the cemetery. I'll have peace then. If what black people say is true, I'll meet Esau again and never long for this world. I'll meet my mother, too, and hopefully, she'll love me the way your mother loved you. I'll confront Granddaddy about what he did and maybe he'll apologize, and we'll all be happy in eternity. I'll tell Grandma that her dream came true: her great-grandson got a college education. But she probably already knows.

This is all I have to say. If this isn't enough, I have nothing else to give. I would give you my life, but it's already spent. The most precious thing I leave you is the land. It's yours. Never sell it. It will support you when the world casts you aside. If you end up like me, with nothing and no one, you can always return to it, and it will love you and sustain you without judgment. If you don't think you want it, keep it anyway. It may be all you have one day.

Finally, I leave you this charge: Live your life freely, Isaac. Rise above our history and be your unapologetic self. Just remember that I meant well. Even in my failure, I truly meant well.

Your Father,
Jacob

At the last word, I returned the letter to the envelope and cried. Eventually, I took Mom's old reading chair and panted til my heart calmed. I must've sat there, sniffling regret and sadness, for hours. Soon, I went to the bathroom, blew my nose, washed my face, and returned to the judgment seat.

There was only silence in the house. What had my father done? Why had he written these letters? Could I handle what I was about to learn?

I saw Mom's face, smiling and nodding. The time had come. She knew there'd be a reckoning one day between Dad and me, and it had finally come.

The first letter basically said I'm sorry. For hurting me, misunderstanding me, calling me names, not wanting me. I never thought he'd apologize, but he did. And it wasn't the words that moved me so much as the sincerity of his heart. I'd never seen it, his heart, and now, staring at it, it looked and felt familiar, like it was my own. His words were heavy and murky, like thick, muddy water, but they flowed easily.

He asked me not to cry, but I couldn't help it. He wrote about his childhood, and I saw him as a little boy—he and his brother, Esau—and I felt compassion for them. He spoke of himself as a fragile human being—something I'd never imagined—and exposed the bruises of rural country life. I understood him better after just one letter. I had a mountain to go.

I determined to read them all before I left that house. I'd planned to stay the weekend, but I would stay longer if necessary. I was still on leave from work, so I had some flexibility.

I made a cup of tea and perched, once again, in Mom's reading chair. Letter by letter, I discovered the nuances of my father's soul. He was simply what the world said he should be: hardworking, emotionally unavailable, patriarchal. As a child, he'd tried to resist, but with no personal or cultural allies, he failed miserably. Early on, his entire world consisted of feeding livestock, raising spring crops, and hunting or fishing for the evening meal. No one asked what he thought. How he felt. What he dreamed of. Finally, I comprehended the foundation of his misery.

Part of Dad's anger was his abandonment. He'd always wanted his mother's love, but he never got it. She died in his infancy. Then when he married my mother and witnessed our impenetrable bond, his maternal longing resurfaced. All our cackling and private conversations merely reminded him of his loss.

His troubles with Mom were more intense than I knew. Really, they had very little in common. I'm not sure why they ever married except that both needed someone. I think Mom's intelligence intimidated Dad, but he would never have admitted it. Instead, he questioned everything she said and did and watched her like a guard dog. I'm surprised the relationship lasted as long as it did.

Everything he said about the way he treated me was true. And horrible. No father should treat his son that way. Dad called me sissy and punk and girly, and rarely said he was proud of me. Those wounds never heal.

Yet he did teach me how to work. Discipline got me through school without debt. Work study plus scholarships covered me, and very few college students, black or white, can say that. I have several talents only because Dad wouldn't let me quit anything I started. I laugh about it now, but as a kid, I hated his rigidity. In truth, it's the only thing that saved me.

Dad's letters were more writing than I'd ever done. How funny was that? The man I thought couldn't read actually became a writer.

I wish now I would've called him more often.

Day 40

Hour after creeping hour, I pieced together Dad's complicated life.

His early years fascinated me. The one thing he wanted as a boy was to play baseball. I knew he liked sports, but I never knew he considered a career in the Negro Leagues. I thought he'd tortured me with Saturday-morning practices to make a man out of me, but perhaps, in his heart, he meant to invite me into his dream.

Still, he was a hard man. I lived on edge whenever Dad was around. In his letters, I heard his apologies, but they weren't healing my wounded heart. Should they?

Most surprising was how much he enjoyed taking me to Arkansas. I appreciated the trip, but, in his letters, Dad speaks of it as a father-son journey to paradise. The land was beautiful and pastoral in an idyllic sort of way, but I wouldn't have moved there. I had no sense that life would've been sweeter in the country than in Kansas City. If Dad was any indication of the people, I knew for sure they wouldn't have liked me. No, the country wasn't my home. But Dad transmuted into something beautiful down there. He seemed to be part of the landscape itself, as if the very soil had nurtured and grown him. The trees, the golden river, the wind all knew him. Throughout the day, he murmured things I couldn't discern. It was a language only he and nature shared.

The letters reminded me how much I yearned for his approval. Every girl I dated was with the hope that he'd be proud of me. But I couldn't keep up the act. I hear his regret in his tone, and I'm relieved to know he knows how hard I tried.

He started reading one day because Mom gave him a book. She was the real reader in the family. Too destitute to do anything else, and too sick to move, Dad inched his way through one book then another until he learned to construct meaning. I was fascinated by his perseverance. Most people would've quit, but of course Dad wasn't a quitter. He worked at the post office thirty years without missing one day. If that's not excellence, I don't know what is.

Leaning back in the chair, I closed my eyes and sighed, knowing that Dad was never a failure. We lived totally separate lives as grown men, each searching for meaning in this world. When Mom died, instead of coming together, we retreated into our own private sorrow. He really loved her. I was happy to read that. He just didn't know how to make space for her in his heart. He'd been taught to rule and control women, and Mom wasn't having it. But he took care of her. Even when they split up. She never wanted for anything—except a man she could grow with. His growth came much too late.

Now I know Dad met Adam. He was in a bad state that day. His fragility scared Dad beyond belief. He was always small, but by the time he came to the house, he was frail, and dying. I think Dad saw my face in Adam's and couldn't handle what it might mean. If he'd seen me that way, covered in dark purple splotches, he would've been ashamed. He would also have known the cost of my kind of love. What Dad didn't know was the strength and boldness of so many of us back then. Some fought the government for gay rights, others argued against the church for their very souls, and a few wrote books and created art that forced the world to see our humanity. He never considered what black people made gay boys pay for authenticity, how it separated us from families, communities, the world, God. It probably never crossed his mind that he'd birthed a son who had to justify his existence, a boy who would spend a lifetime begging for permission to be, to love, to live. But when he saw Adam, desperate and alone, I think he saw the manifestation of his own narrow-mindedness. According to the letter, he realized that what he hated he created.

With me far away and Mom in eternity, Dad had no choice but to examine himself. Inevitably, he concluded that his errors were too big, too serious, to fix. There was no way to reverse time and love his family the way he should've, no way to refashion my self-worth with his affirmation at the center. That was wishful thinking. Yet there was something he could do that would mean the world to me one day, and he did it.

But, like me, he had to go home first. Somehow, in his spirit, he discovered that the only real legacy a father leaves a son is a connection to his past. So, with his last dime, he built for me a labyrinth of history. Sitting atop every Swinton grave is a tombstone of names and dates which, if I can align them, will tell me the story of my people. There, of course, will be gaps in details and information, but that's my job to find out or fill in. It's the perfect gift to a writer—if I ever become one.

Dad asked only one thing of me: "take me home." He begged me not to leave him in Kansas City. It was an earnest plea, like a man begging for one more precious breath. I vowed to honor his request, and I did. Whether I can forgive him or not is another matter.

"You're not gonna believe this!" I shouted when the therapist entered.

I was already pacing in the waiting area. Her countenance brightened with excitement.

"What happened?" she sang.

"I went home! That's what happened. And found letters written by my father while he was dying."

She led the way into her office, where she took a seat behind the desk. I continued pacing as I told her about the discovery.

"Dad apologized. For everything. The way he treated me, the way he treated Mom, what he didn't know, what he didn't understand. Who he was, who he wasn't. Everything."

She stared at me, trying, presumably, to see if I had changed. "How did they make you feel?"

My foot tapped the hardwood floor. "Exonerated, I think. Relieved. I don't know. Angry, maybe."

"Why angry?"

"Because we won't get to work this out together."

"Maybe you will," she said. "Through these letters. He gave you the material with which to heal both of you." Excitement and expectation glimmered in her eyes. "He's talking to you right now, across time. It's up to you to talk back."

Day 41

I submitted my resignation at work on Dad's birthday. It was May 24th, a beautiful Friday afternoon. I remember getting up that morning and saying, "That's it. I've had enough." That's all I said. I had spent a year—no, a lifetime—ducking in and out of depression, and I was sick of it. I had worked too hard not to be happy. I loved people too much to spend a lifetime alone.

Dad had planted seeds of self-rejection in me, but I had watered and fertilized them over the years. Even after I knew better, I still surrendered to self-doubt and self-criticism. Perhaps this is simply the human dilemma. Nevertheless, I decided that if I grew those seeds, I could uproot them too.

I went home and got a yellow legal pad. Somewhere in my imagination, words for my first novel poured like an ever-flowing fountain onto the empty page. Simple as that. But that's not what happened. I stared at the blank paper, waiting impatiently, but nothing came. I got up and walked around a bit and still nothing. I realized I needed a story. I had experienced many things, but my life wasn't compelling. Each time I tried to write about it, the narrative felt contrived and stereotypical, so I stopped. I needed something larger than myself, something that included me perhaps, but wasn't limited to me. Something that might change a reader. A writer too.

I conceived a tale of two brothers, separated during slavery. One was three, the other five. Initially, their names were Aaron and Anthony, but I realized that couldn't be right. Those names were too…contemporary. They didn't fit little black boys on a Southern plantation. So, for a while, I called them John and James, but that wasn't right either. I saw the boys in my head, cloaked in ragged gray-and-brown garments, but bright-eyed and innocent. The five-year-old stood slightly taller than his brother and maintained a sense of protection over him that lasted a lifetime. The younger was darker with a round, handsome face. Both had the flat, wide African nose of their father, but the reddish-brown complexion of their mother. All of this, and I hadn't written one word.

It just wouldn't come. I had the idea, but I couldn't figure out how to start. I bet I threw away twenty pages. Was this the writerly life?

The next day was no better. I couldn't write a thing, but the story evolved. Those little boys' names finally came: Matthew, the oldest, and Jesse Lee, the baby. They were sold to separate plantations, one in Mississippi, the other in Louisiana. Their parents were inconsolable, screaming at and fighting slave traders as they dragged their babies away. It was a pain-

ful story, but one I wanted to write. I started jotting notes so
I wouldn't forget things. My dream of writing a novel had
begun, but it was unimpressive. I mean, anyone could think
of a good story, right? I wanted a manuscript! But it was a
long way away.

Days later, I was still taking notes. Matthew endured hard
labor in Mississippi. Their mother, Beulah, was too devastated
to eat. That's all I knew about her. Their father, Henry Joe,
went to the field as usual but stopped talking. His heart ached.
Every few minutes he looked down the dirt lane, hoping to
see his boys returned, but all he saw was circles and circles
of reddish-brown dust. Sometimes he cried. Sometimes he
prayed and asked God to take care of his boys until he got
free and could find them. At night, he and Beulah lay in bed,
side by side, in complete silence. They didn't touch or look
at each other. I saw them, stretched out on an old wire bed
in a room so small either could've touched the wall without
rising. It was a two-room shack, with almost no furniture
and no hanging pictures. A kettle rested atop a woodstove,
and four fragile wooden chairs sat beneath a small rectan-
gular table. I saw it all in my mind. It was like a personal
memory—vivid, specific, spectacular. I closed my eyes to see
more clearly, and that's when I realized there were no lights.
No lamps, no candles, no nothing. They lived in darkness.
I knew, of course, the evils of slavery, but I'd never considered the depth of darkness enslaved people endured. I'd never
thought of light as a luxury. Human bondage really is un-
imaginable. Yet there I was, imagining it! I saw a small pallet on the floor on the other side of the room and guessed

that that had been the boys' sleeping place. It was neat and clean—and empty.

I tried to write this, but the language didn't pop. It sounded drab and ordinary, nothing like the melodious phrasing of a real writer. I paused. I was embarrassed. I'd gone to school and read more books than most, I believed, and *still* I couldn't write a beautiful sentence? I almost abandoned the project, but the story kept coming.

I realized, after days of trying, that, if something didn't happen soon, I'd be a broke, homeless writer. No, just broke and homeless. I hadn't written anything. I'd saved enough, thank God, to take care of myself for a few more months, but no longer. At the rate I was going, I was about to be in trouble. But I couldn't write just anything. That's not a writer. A writer creates language that moves the heart or touches the emotions or at least delights the mind. Everything I wrote sounded plain. When I tried to beautify my expressions, the language seemed forced and unnatural—nothing like the smooth, easy sea of words I'd encountered a lifetime.

Every day I wrote something, played with phrases and word arrangements, but only made a mess of things. I recall one sentence that made me laugh out loud: "The boys, the angels of Eden, were divided like a whole number into fractions." Isn't that the worst? What does that even mean?

Anyway, the story kept coming. Matthew was taken in by an old woman who treated him like her own. Her name was Sally. I heard it clearly. She was a small, stout, dark-skinned woman with a short black and gray afro. She was as strong as any man around, and folks respected her for it. She'd lost a son many years ago, so when the boy arrived and ended up in her cabin, she gladly took him in. He stared at her and wondered if she knew his mother. He didn't speak at first. Then, practically starving, he asked for food and Sally smiled and buttered a cornbread square and gave it to him. Their bond would never be broken.

Jesse Lee's fate wasn't so encouraging. He was a sickly child, coughing and wheezing the while, and most didn't want the responsibility of his healing. Yet one man took it. He saw hope in the boy's eyes and remembered what it was like to lose a father. His name was Elijah. He had a four-year-old daughter who took to Jesse the minute she saw him. She'd always wanted a sibling, and now she had one. Soon, they were inseparable. Jesse Lee didn't know the man was a healer until, one starry night, they stood beneath a full moon and the man gave Jesse a potion to drink. Jesse Lee winced and swallowed the foulest drink he'd ever tasted. But he never coughed again.

Their captor told Elijah, "You's bout the hardest-working nigger I got. Raise that boy to be the same." He put the child in the man's cabin and returned to his mansion. Elijah loved the boy the way he'd dreamed his father loved him. He spread an old, prickly blanket on the floor and told the boy, "This just til yo daddy comes," and kissed the crown of Jesse Lee's soft, curly hair. The little girl admired him. He was beautiful and sweet and obedient, and she believed he'd protect her a lifetime. She asked if he could share her narrow, wooden bed, but her parents wouldn't allow it. So she spent the night leaning over her bedside, staring at the new child in the family, wondering where he'd come from.

I had a notebook full of notes but no novel. Something about creative writing intimidated me. Yet I felt obligated to continue. I owed those boys something. They had entrusted their story to me, and the least I could do was write it, I thought, even though I was struggling. The story kept materializing in my mind, but few words made it to the paper. Still, I had to try.

I paced the house for weeks, conceiving almost the totality of a tale.

Matthew grew quickly and found favor with most others on the plantation. Sally caught pneumonia one winter and died, but not before telling him how to escape north.

"Which way?" he asked.

"Shhhhh," she whispered, closing her eyes. "Ears all round, waitin to hear anything they can report back. Be careful who you talk to."

He nodded.

"Nature'll lead you if you'll follow it. In the dark, all you gotta do is hug a tree and when you feel the moss, walk in that direction. It's always pointin north. You can look up, too, on a clear night, and see that star yonder—the one shinin bright all by itself—and walk straight toward it. Either one'll get you where you wanna go."

"I'm goin first to get my brother."

"How you gon do dat? You don't know where he is."

"They sold him to Lou'sana, I heard."

"You don't know which direction dat is. You might be worse off tryin."

"Might be, but he's my brother. We was li'l boys when they separated us. My heart ain't been right since."

She touched his hand in the dark. "I understand. I had a boy once. They took him when he was five—just old enough to remember me and this here place. I'm stickin round in case he come back."

"What if he don't?"

"He will. I believe it like you believe yo brother waitin on you."

They sighed together.

"Shame to be a slave," she added, "*and* have nothin to believe in, ain't it?"

"Guess it is."

I thought about that. How black people survived bondage *and* emotional trauma by believing in the Invisible. When you consider it, they should've given up and died. Every single one of them. But for some reason, they didn't.

Matthew, at seventeen, ran away but didn't find Jesse Lee. He scoured the Deep South, hiding in barns and wooded areas, stealing half-rotten fruit, stale bread, and well water every chance he got. Nothing came of it. Eventually, at nineteen, he escaped north and ended up in a place called Philadelphia—where Negroes roamed free and unchained. *I could live here*, he thought, *but not without my brother.*

Day 42

Meanwhile, Jesse Lee's captor beat him for the least infraction and, sometimes, for no reason at all. By his eighteenth year, very little flesh remained on his back, and, a few times, the mean bastard beat his naked front. Jesse Lee wailed until the forest cried with him, then cried for him. Elijah, his adopted father, nurtured his wounds and reminded him that he was more than what white folks said. Jesse Lee wasn't so sure. He regretted the gift of beauty God had given him—or, perhaps, he hated that it solicited Massa Robert's desire. The white man, smelling of spoiled fish and lust, spent his days watching the young man, waiting for any reason to strip him down and whip him. It was his nakedness the man enjoyed, and once Jesse Lee discovered this, he tried to hide his six-foot muscular form with oversize clothes and self-degrading comments, which, he hoped, might dissuade Massa Robert's affections, but they didn't. Actually, they made him touch Jesse Lee more sensually, believing the boy to possess some private pleasure Massa Robert had not experienced.

Once, while beating Jesse Lee simply for an unblemished complexion, Massa Robert threw down the whip and ran forward, penis erect and throbbing. He forced himself into Jesse Lee's mouth and stayed there until the ecstasy subsided. Jesse Lee shrieked like a soul in Hell. Everyone knew something terrible, something revolting and reprehensible, had happened. No one had ever wailed like that, they said.

Jesse Lee vomited bile, spewed blood, then gave up the ghost. Everyone thought he was dead. He wanted to be dead, but God wouldn't take him. Not yet. Not before Matthew found him. Elijah, cursing God the while, carried the young man's limp form into the cabin and anointed it with oil, begging God to destroy the white man's insatiable appetite for black flesh. He also prayed the boy would live to see his vengeance. Others begged Jesse Lee not to give up. He didn't hear any of them.

I don't know why I had conceived such a story. It felt so real. And personal. As if I knew these boys, as if we shared blood, and that blood insisted I tell the tale. It was very strange. I couldn't deny it. And I couldn't think about anything else.

I walked the streets of my neighborhood, trying to visualize the opening sentence. "This is the story of two boys and a tragedy." *Yuck!* "Long ago, something happened that most will find unbelievable." *Elementary.* "The boys' last memory was the horror in their mother's eyes." Not bad, but still not what I wanted. I was missing something. This wasn't supposed to be this hard, was it?

Maybe it was. Perhaps I'd been arrogant to think that, just because I could read, I could write. Writing was certainly an art, a skill most didn't possess, but, again, since I'd always read, I believed writing should come easily for me. Man, was I wrong.

Ricky called me a fool for leaving my job. "Shit, why can't you write on the side? You gon fuck around and be broke as hell!" He laughed, although he wasn't joking.

There was no way to write *on the side*. It was too hard. It took too much time. Hell, I couldn't write at all. Now I appreciated the work of producing a whole book, especially a novel. Each sentence is a labor. I'd taken for granted how easily I could consume a book and had sometimes wished writers would hurry and publish another. Damn, that's rude.

But back to the story.

I kept taking notes. Matthew was free, but his soul wasn't satisfied. He met a young lady and fell in love, but he couldn't marry her. Guilt teased him each day about having left Jesse Lee in bondage. I saw him, pacing the streets of Philadelphia in a cloud of remorse, attending abolitionist meetings in hopes of hearing something about slaves in Louisiana. He had no idea how big Louisiana was. Unable to read, he couldn't consult printed material for help. Yet, one day, he heard a white man say he'd come from a place called New Orleans, Louisiana. He asked the man if they had slaves there, and the man said unfortunately yes. He didn't have any himself, but many of his neighbors did. The man appeared wealthy, cloaked in a long blue suit jacket with a pristine white ruffled shirt. Matthew took a chance and asked how far New Orleans was. "A mighty long way," the white man said, nodding slowly. Matthew wasn't discouraged. He told the man his story and the white man said, "Louisiana is a big place. Your brother could be anywhere." Matthew said, "As long as he's somewhere, I can find him."

"You can't travel alone. Slave catchers always looking for free Nigras to kidnap back into slavery."

"Is you goin back anytime soon?"

"In fact, I am. Next week."

"Well, maybe I could go with you."

He shook his head. "Traveling as a free Nigra is dangerous in the South. They'd capture you for sure."

"Then what if I went as yo slave? You know, a boy who takes care o his massa?"

The white man didn't like the idea, but he understood Matthew's desperation. "I suppose that could work. I'd have to treat you like a real slave though. To make it believable. That's nothing nice."

"Oh I know. Believe me, I know. But it's the only way I can get to Lou'sana."

"God only knows where your brother is. The state is hundreds of miles wide."

"I'll walk it if I have to."

They agreed to meet at the train depot the following Saturday morning at seven. Matthew was there at six biting his nails, hoping Jesse Lee hadn't given up on him. The white man—whose name I couldn't figure out—handed Matthew a navy blue pinstriped suit with a white ruffled shirt and said, "Put this on. If you're a white man's traveling boy, you gotta look the part." Then he gave him shiny, black buckled shoes. The suit fit a bit snug—so did the shoes—but Matthew made them work. He'd never worn a suit before. It felt strange and heavy and tight, but he didn't complain.

"Now. You gotta call me Massa. Much as I hate this, we have to make it real or both of us will pay."

Matthew understood. "Yessuh. No problem, suh." The white man sighed. "I'll call you Jim. That's a common slave name."

"Matthew's my name. You could just call me that."

He disagreed. "Naw, better call you Jim. Matthew's got too much dignity. Wouldn't want folks to find us out."

They shook hands firmly. And with that, they were off.

Something about the man troubled Matthew. The moment they stepped onto the train, the insults began. It seemed genuine and heartfelt—not the least bit contrived as they had planned. In fact, the man appeared to enjoy it, as if, deep inside, he'd waited a lifetime for this opportunity.

"Sit down, Nigra boy!" he shouted repeatedly along the way, snatching Matthew's sleeve so hard he nearly fell over. Sometimes, the man slapped his cheeks, too, leaving them sore and tender. But Matthew endured. If this were the cost of finding Jesse Lee, he'd gladly pay.

"I read your last entry, and I love the story. So intriguing. I want the boys to find each other."

"Me too!"

"Well, can't you make them? You're the writer!" She cackled as if I didn't know.

"It's not that simple. Stories assume a life of their own, and sometimes characters do things authors don't like. Or prefer."

She frowned. "You don't create the characters?"

"Yes, I do, but I don't own them. They act on their own. I know that sounds a little crazy, but it's true. It has to be true, or characters would simply be manifestations of the author."

"I see," she said, rather disappointed. "I still hope they find each other. We need stories where black people win."

"I agree. I'll see what I can do, but I can't make any promises. Just know that I agree."

Her facial expression softened, and she asked, "Does your family have family reunions?"

I nodded. "Yes. On my mother's side. Every Fourth of July weekend."

"Did you go to the last one?"

"I did."

"Where was it?"

"Kansas City."

"Did you learn anything you didn't know?"

"Actually, I did. More folks came than usual. There was enough liquor to fill a small pond and enough cigarette and marijuana smoke to cloud the entire Midwestern sky. I think every adult, except me, was either drunk or high by the time we gathered to eat. It was good to see Aunt Pig and Uncle Joe and all my cousins. Folks spoke of Momma like she was sitting there. I heard stories I'd never heard before. One of them disturbed me a little, although I guess it shouldn't have.

'Y'all remember that boy Rachel was so crazy about in high school?' Uncle Joe began.

'You mean my dad?' I asked.

"Everyone roared, 'Hell, naw!' and laughed hysterically. 'He wunnit the one she *really* loved. She married yo daddy cause she thought she was pregnant.'

"I gasped.

'Y'all shouldn't do that,' Aunt Clarece admonished. 'This boy ain't got no business knowin all o that.'

'He a grown man. Shit! He oughta know. Ain't nothin wrong wit knowin.'

"She walked away with a cup of something so strong I smelled it when she passed. Everyone else waited for the story although, apparently, they already knew it.

'She wunnit pregnant though. Jes thought she was.'

"I got a beer from the nearest cooler and joined in. I had a feeling I might need a little help swallowing this one.

'What was dat boy's name?'

'David or Darrell or Donnie something,' someone volunteered.

'Yeah! That's it. Donnie.'

"People mumbled his name in agreement.

'He was sharp as a tack! Wunnit he, Charles Earl?'

'You betta believe it. Walked around like Rockefella!'

"Folks screeched.

'Only young man I ever knowed what could wear white all year long,' Uncle Joe touted. 'Hot or cold, didn't matter. Never wore the same suit twice. Just classy. That's what he was. Just classy.'

"Elders murmured pride and admiration.

'He wunnit hard to look at either!' Uncle Joe added. 'I can tell you that!'

'Easy on the eye!' Aunt Pig affirmed. 'Tall boy, soft pretty hair, brown skin smooth as peanut butter! Yessuh! He was a looker fo sho!'

'And crazy bout Rachel! Lord have mercy! Come by the house nearbout every day askin after that girl.'

'She wunnit stuttin him at first. Least she acted like she wunnit,' Aunt Pig said.

'She liked him from de start,' Uncle Joe stated confidently. 'I could tell. Anybody could.'

'Now she wunnit no slouch either!' Aunt Pig's sister, Aunt Macy, intoned. 'Rachel had a figure like a Coca-Cola bottle!' Heads nodded at different speeds. She went on, 'Thick, wavy hair, shapely legs, and a smile that'd make a man look twice any day.' She turned to me. 'Yo momma was a beautiful lady, son. Don't you never forget it!' She slapped my leg.

"Uncle Joe resumed. 'We thought fo sho dey was gon hook up and get married and all.'

'Why didn't they?' I asked.

"Everyone quieted sadly. Aunt Macy stared across the horizon, shaking her head. Uncle Joe's energy calmed. 'Somebody killed him at a club down on Thirty-Sixth and Prospect. Said he thought he was better than other folks. Maybe he did. Maybe he was.'

'Ain't no reason to kill nobody,' Aunt Macy said.

'Folks don't need no reason.'

'When yo momma heard, she took off runnin down the street, screamin and hollin like God had died. Everybody heard her and ran outside to see what was the matter. I ran after her and caught her. I was skinny back then.'

'Shiiiid!' folks yelled excitedly. 'Now we know you lyin!'

'No, I ain't! I coulda outrun any o y'all in my heyday!'

'You wunnit *neva* skinny,' Aunt Macy emphasized. 'You was a *li'l smaller*, but you wunnit *neva* skinny.'

"Uncle Joe had always been large. I couldn't imagine him skinny.

'Anyway!' he sneered, laughing along. 'Yo momma wunnit no good after that. She was bout se'umteen, I guess. In her last year o school.'

'That's right, that's right,' Aunt Macy confirmed.

'Couldn't eat, couldn't sleep, couldn't do nothin. Just down. Neva seen nobody like that. Scared us half to death.'

"I'd never heard this story. Mom never mentioned Donnie to me.

"Uncle Joe said, 'Then one day, she got up and said he come to her in a dream and told her to live, so she owned him that much. She wunnit herself, though, but she was better than she'd been. Her momma told her she needed to get away and get her mind off that boy, so she sent her to Arkansas to her aunty. Guess it helped. Yo daddy kinda reminded her of Donnie, I think, but he wunnit nearly as classy.'

"I should've been offended, but I wasn't. I hadn't even gone to see Dad and I was no more than five miles from him. People asked how he was doing, and I said fine. They didn't inquire further. Now I know why. I must admit the story hurt my feelings a little. I'd never heard of any other man my mother loved. But I guess she was as human as the rest of us.

"The story proved that you never know another person completely. I'm sure Mom loved Dad. I'm just not sure he's the only man she ever loved. This fascinates me because it makes me consider that I didn't know her at all. Isn't that something? That you can know a person your whole life and share everything you ever thought, only to discover they never shared their whole selves with you? I knew Mom and Dad had tough times, but I also thought they had never loved anyone else. Now I know both of them did. Of course this isn't wrong; it's just, well, surprising. Each told me what they thought I could handle. I suppose I did the same.

"I went by the house later that night. I parked on the street and sat in my car a long while, trying to find something to say to Dad. The mere thought of talking to him made me emotional, and the last thing I wanted was to cry in front of him, so I left. Too many difficult memories. My heart was beating so fast I could hardly breathe. I felt awful for not seeing him, but I didn't turn around." I paused for a minute, gazing at my therapist. "I hope my father is happy in eternity."

"I'm sure he is, Isaac. Do you believe in that? That people keep their consciousness, even after they die?"

"Absolutely. We studied African ancestral reverence in college, and my professor spoke of ancestors as real people—with emotions and opinions and preferences like other living beings. Just without a body. I think I've always believed that. Even as a kid, I knew dead people weren't dead. When we went to Arkansas, I felt my grandmother and Uncle Esau as sure as I feel my own being. It's hard to explain, but it's true. A feeling comes over me, and I sense everything they feel as if they occupy my body. I don't fight it anymore. I just let it be. It's sorta weird, I know. Some call it a spiritual gift. Sadness, joy, frustration, uncertainty, whatever. I can feel it, and I can usually distinguish one emotion from another."

"That's pretty amazing. And pretty rare, I'm sure."

"Probably. I'd give it away if I could."

"I'm glad you haven't. You need it now."

I chuckled. "You're right. I felt my father's spirit as I was reading his letters. He was sitting on the sofa, staring at me, hoping I understood everything he'd written, praying I would learn enough to forgive him completely. He cried a few times, and that's something I never thought I'd see. Well, I didn't *see* it, but I sensed it, and it mingled with my own emotions, and, this time, I struggled to keep his feelings separate from mine. It didn't really matter though. It's the most authentic we'd ever been with each other. It means we finally saw each other's heart."

The therapist smiled and said, "There's another level, Isaac. You're almost at the mountaintop."

I sighed and said, "Maybe the mountain's too high. I'm tired of climbing!"

She dismissed my complaint. "You'll see everything soon enough." She threw her head back playfully and sang, off-key, "'Ain't no mountain high enough!'"

I laughed along uneasily.

Day 43

Christmas of 2004 came as the novel continued to evolve. I've always loved Christmas—the lights, decorations, shopping, food. I love holiday movies and music, and snow in the midst of it all. It snowed that Christmas in Chicago—and damn near every Christmas thereafter!—so I got a big, live tree and spent hours hanging tinsel and silver-and-gold ornaments all over it. I draped it with white lights and topped it with a black angel I'd bought at an African shop downtown. I sipped warm apple cider and listened to R&B Christmas songs like "All I Want for Christmas Is You" and "Santa Baby" and of course the Temptations' "Silent Night." I turned off all the lights in the house and plugged in the Christmas tree and chilled out with spiked eggnog.

Dad told me and Mom once that he got nigga toes for Christmas.

Mom gasped with laughter. "What did you say?"

Dad held a stern expression. "That's right! You ain't never heard o nigga toes?"

"Stop it, Jacob. Just cut it out. There's nothing called that. Nothing."

Dad stepped forward. "What? Is you crazy, woman? Sho it's such a thang as nigga toes. We ate em all de time!"

She surrendered. "What in God's name are nigga toes, Jacob Swinton?"

Dad hollered, "They're Brazil nuts," and collapsed with laughter. Mom stared at him incredulously. She wanted to laugh—I saw the corners of her mouth twitch—but she refused to participate in his foolish, as she called it. The whole thing cracked me up.

"They gave you that *for Christmas*?"

"Shit yeah!"

She waved Dad's truth away. "Cut it out, man! You need to stop tellin lies!"

"I ain't lyin! That's what we got. And we wuz glad to get it." He paused. "Pecans, nigga toes, walnuts, peanuts, oranges, apples, and a candy cane. That's what we got."

Mom rolled her eyes and continued whatever she was doing. I think back now with the deepest gratitude. Dad couldn't have made more than what? Two dollars an hour? Of course things were cheaper then, but still he wasn't making much money. He was also paying for a house, car, and everything else we needed. Mom never worked outside the home. Only his income covered us. How in the world did he do that AND pay part of my college tuition? Lord. He sacrificed more than I ever knew.

★ ★ ★

By New Year's night, Matthew and White Man had crossed the Mason-Dixon Line. He called him "Nigger" and ordered him around like a work mule. White passengers nodded their approval, confirming that White Man was performing his citizen's duty. Matthew stomached the torture, believing Jesse Lee's face would be worth the effort.

At one point, as the train zoomed past a setting sun, White Man said loudly, "Nigger, fetch me a cool drink of water."

Matthew swallowed rage. Where was he supposed to get water from?

"Yessuh, Massa, but I cain't go to de kitchen alone. You knows dat."

"Well, figure it out, Nigger boy!"

White Man kicked him in the rear. Passengers burst into triumphant laughter. Matthew's fists balled and trembled, but he held his peace. Slowly, timidly, he walked the narrow aisle, unsure of where he was going and what train officials would say, but he had to try.

He passed from one car into another as whites stared and pointed. One man asked, "Who is you, boy?"

I'm not a boy! I'm a man! Matthew wanted to say, but, re-membering the goal, humbled himself and answered, "I's my massa's traveling companion."

"Well, what you doin walkin the train by yourself?"

"I's fetchin him a cool drink o water, suh. He sunt me after it."

"Well, you just hurry up and find it. Boy like you could get in a lotta trouble witout his master beside him."

"Yessuh."

Matthew moved on. When he reached the kitchen car, he cleared his throat and bowed. A waiter inquired of his business and Matthew said, "Cool drink o water for my massa, suh."

The waiter shoved it at him, and Matthew took it, careful not to spill any more. When he returned, White Man shouted, "What took you so long, boy?" after snatching the glass from Matthew's hand. "I sent you a long time ago!"

"Nawsuh, you sunt me just a few minutes ago, suh."

"You contradictin me, boy?"

"Nawsuh."

Matthew licked dry lips and braced himself. He saw real anger in White Man's eyes. He didn't understand. Wasn't the man acting? Wasn't this all a facade?

The backhand came so hard and fast it left Matthew dazed. For a moment, everything went silent. He lost balance and fell to the floor. The train seemed to move in opposite directions at once. Matthew tried to stand but couldn't.

"Get up, you black son of a bitch!"

Somehow he managed, only to be knocked down again. Passengers looked on with carefree amusement.

"But Massa, I went fast as I could," Matthew mumbled. "They don't low no runnin in de train, suh, but a man stopped me and asked—"

Wham! White Man's foot vibrated in his gut. Matthew frowned and groaned. Were they still acting? Why did this feel so real?

White Man knelt quickly and whispered, "Just keep playing along. It'll be over afterwhile."

Matthew tried to say this didn't feel right. That there was

no excuse for such excessive behavior, but he never got the chance.

"That's right! Make him obey you!" another white man charged. "They'll get outta hand if you don't."

White Man laid more blows on Matthew's body and left him on the floor. Hours passed before he gained enough strength to stand. When he did, White Man instructed him to sit beside him and keep his mouth shut. Matthew obeyed and eventually fell asleep. But something was wrong. It wasn't supposed to be this way. Yes, they were disguised as master and slave, but the abuse far exceeded the plan. Still, he went along, hoping the end would justify the means.

Jesse Lee needed him now more than ever. His master's hands couldn't resist his flesh, squeezing and massaging every private place. Jesse Lee was marrying age but couldn't face a woman. Most nights, he lay chained to a post in the barn, ever ready for Master's unthinkable, insatiable appetite.

Occasionally, he heard his mother call his name: *Jesse Lee.* Then she told him to be strong: *Someone's coming for you.* He heard it clearly, as if she stood before him. And he believed it. He needed to believe it, for he'd become obsessed with one desire: Massa Robert's destruction. Nothing else mattered. The white man would never stop, he would never repent, he would never apologize for the ungodly things he'd done. As long as Jesse Lee lived, the abuse would continue. He was convinced of that. So he had to end it. And soon. His pride, his breath, was slipping away. He didn't know how to talk about it. He wanted to answer his adopted father's questions—*Is you okay? Do you know you stronger than he is?*—

but words wouldn't come. His mouth moved, tears streamed, but no sound emitted. Were there words to describe this horror? In Jesse Lee's mind, even God had failed him.

Day 44

At night, I cried for Jesse Lee. Then, each day, I sank deeper into the narrative, hoping for the boys an ending that would honor their fight. I paced the floor, talking aloud as if they were real people. I stepped back in time and saw everything distinctly. They wanted me to write this story. But, for some reason, I couldn't.

I called Ricky and told him my dilemma. He said he always knew I'd be a writer. Or a teacher. I told him I never wanted to teach. I wasn't sure I'd write either.

"You gotta. It's just in you. Always has been. Most people ain't that smart, but you are. I've known that since the day I met you."

"Then why can't I write? Every time I try, I go blank. I can see the story in my mind, but I can't put it on paper."

"I don't know. I ain't no writer. Maybe it's your process. They say different writers have different ways of writing. It'll come. Just keep trying."

His encouragement irritated me. I was already trying—and failing. I had a story—a damn good one, I think—but I had underestimated the craft of writing it. I wasn't a writer yet. I was only a reader. There is a difference.

After weeks of struggling, I almost quit. The story kept coming, and I liked it a lot, but the inability to write it made me doubt myself. I'd never been insecure about anything academic. School was my thing. But now my intellectual confidence eroded, which scared the heck out of me. I couldn't find my narrative voice, and looking for it was too stressful, too slow, too incremental. It didn't seem worth the turmoil and trouble. Of course, I had quit my day job, so I wasn't sure what I'd do, but I still had some savings so I packed a light bag and started driving.

I think I drove every street in Chicago twice. I listened to Stevie Wonder, Aretha, Whitney, Common, Nas and every other artist I liked. I drove along Lake Michigan; I drove by the DuSable Museum, passed the University of Chicago and the Cabrini-Green towers. Those projects fascinated me because they were always gray, regardless of the weather. I saw two little boys who reminded me of the brothers in my story. I guessed they were brothers because they looked alike. They wore torn, battered coats and ragged knit beanies, far too big for their heads. Yet, consumed in a game of tag presumably, their joy was unmistakable. Each possessed bright, round eyes and jubilant voices that carried with the wind. The only sad thing was that, if history had its way, they would probably submit to the notion of their own inferiority one day.

Mom always said I was as good as any kid out there, and I believed her. Dad didn't say this, but his standard for me implied it. Report card day rewarded it. I'd lay the index-size cards on the kitchen table and go to my room, waiting to be called forth. It never failed.

It started with Mom's "oohs" and "aahs." I'd smile from the bedroom, glad that something about me brought pleasure to the house.

"Lord have mercy," she'd declare. "Do you see this boy's grades?"

Dad tried not to rejoice, but, as he used to say, *excellence can't be overlooked*. He'd take the cards and read aloud: "English, 98. Geometry, 96. American History, 99. Civics, 95. Geography, 100." I'd peek around the corner and see Mom looking at him, daring him not to celebrate. He'd chuckle and say, "Damn." Mom would clap and dance a bit. "Damn right!" She rarely cursed, but she wouldn't take it back. She'd holler for me—"Isaac, honey!"—and I'd pause before rounding the corner, wanting the moment to last forever.

"You done good, boy!" Dad would say. "Got some good marks."

"Not good—excellent!" Mom corrected and applauded. "You gon be a college professor or a philosopher one day. Mark my word."

"Do they make any money?" Dad would ask.

Mom would add, "If they don't, they make a lotta influence."

I liked that. That there are people in the world whose influence exceeds anyone's money. The people I admired most, the ones whose names lingered in my mind, weren't rich. Yet they had changed the world.

When I left the projects, Matthew started speaking again. Something about those boys, wrapped in poverty and joy, seemed to inspire him onward. He said that, when the train got to New Orleans, White Man tried to sell him back into slavery. The whole thing was a fraud, a trick. He'd trusted White Man out of desperation, but the cracker had deceived him. Nonetheless, he would never be a slave again. He'd promised himself that. So after having been bought, sometime during the night, he escaped and found himself in the middle of a swamp. Nighttime noises startled him—the screeching, howling, hooting, hissing. He couldn't discern the sources, but, even so, nothing frightened him like the depth of White Man's lies. So he kept running. Murky water swirled about, thick and smelly like dead fish. The greatest nuisance, however, was the mosquitoes. They attacked Matthew like a formidable army. They bit his exposed flesh and hummed in his ears.

After stomping around trees and stumps and thorny bushes for hours, he heard footsteps and froze. Someone was coming toward him.

A black man, cloaked in a black coat, whispered simply, "Follow me," and, knowing nothing of the woods except his desperate desire to escape them, Matthew obeyed. Soon, the phantom led him to a small hovel of branches in a clearing.

The man bent to enter first and, having trusted him thus far, Matthew followed. The man lit a small coal oil lamp and exposed his middle-aged face. His wild beard was thick and coarse and black with gray strands pointing in every direction. Bulbous eyes flashed clear and white like stars on an uncloudy night. There was almost no flesh on him.

"Mosquitoes eat you alive befo you get to freedom."

The man reached into a corner and handed Matthew a bottle.

"Rub this on. Don't smell good, but it'll keep em away. Keep you from scratchin yoself to death."

"Thank you, suh," Matthew mumbled. He had a thousand questions but decided to let the man tell him whatever he wanted him to know.

"You pretty lucky, fella. Nough in these here swamps to kill you in no time. Snakes, gators, poisonous frogs. Slave catchers don't come out here. They figure the swamp'll kill ya sooner'n they can."

Matthew rubbed the foul ointment over his face and arms.

"Smell'll wear off in a day or two. You stay out here, you'll be glad about it."

They sat for a while, sipping strong, bland tea. Matthew gathered enough courage to ask, "You live out here?"

The man nodded. "Only home I got. Ran away a few years ago, driftin here and yonda, til I settled in this spot. Met some folks what taught me what I know. It ain't a bad livin. Just lonely sometimes."

"You got family somewhere?"

"Everybody got family somewhere. Just don't know where mine at." He paused. "You?"

"Yeah. A baby brother somewhere in Lou'sana, I think. I'm trying to find him now. We wuz sold from our momma and daddy years ago."

"You gotta lotta lookin to do. This here a big place."

"I thank you for helpin me out. Mosquitoes almost carried me off."

"Awww, ain't no problem. Somebody helped me once. Least I can do."

Matthew slept on a pallet on the dirt floor while the man rested in a makeshift wooden cot. Next morning, they shared bread and some kind of jam as the man explained how to travel north. "You's at the bottom of the land," he said. "You got to go upward to see the rest." He gave Matthew a cloth sack of berries, roots, and dried meat and sent him on his way.

As evening turned to dusk, I stared into a purple-orange Midwestern sky. Within minutes, I merged onto I-90 North. Soon, Matthew shot past me like a lightning bolt. The cloth sack dangled from his right hand while his left swung empty, keeping time and balance. He ran parallel to my car. I literally saw him, bare feet and all, rail thin, but muscular with almond-shaped eyes so intense they glowed in the dark. His navy-black skin melded perfectly with the night, such that his ragged garments seemed to float midair. Matthew was running for his life. So was I.

After a while, I needed gas, so I stopped and filled up at a Conoco station near Evanston. An old white woman lowered her car window and said, "Be careful, young man. Everybody ain't friendly out here," then drove away. It was a strange comment, a kind of warning, it seemed. I knew I wasn't on the South Side of Chicago anymore, but did something sinister await me? Was the Klan hiding out nearby? What did the woman know that I didn't? Her statement frightened me, so I got back in the car, with only half a tank, and sped away. Once my nerves settled, I saw Matthew again, racing beside me, chasing a hope more precious than gold. The faster I drove, the faster he ran, until his feet blurred beneath him. I smiled at his determination. I loved him for loving his brother like that, for doing everything in his power to keep his promise. I wanted their family together again. I know most stories don't have happy endings, but why couldn't mine?

The more Matthew ran, the more I drove, until, somehow, I found myself on I-57 South headed to Arkansas.

I hadn't planned to go. Hadn't even considered it. But Matthew seemed to be leading me, deeper and deeper into the South, into our history, where, only weeks earlier, I had laid my father to rest. I had nothing with me: no clothes, no food, no extra money. Nothing at all—except a hell of a story.

Jesse Lee knew Matthew was coming. He felt it in his spirit. Yet he feared that time was running out. He wouldn't let Massa Robert touch him again. He promised himself that. And he kept that promise.

It didn't take long for Massa Robert to try. One hot Sunday afternoon, he cornered Jesse Lee behind the barn where the violation often began. But this time, Jesse Lee was ready. Massa Robert sensed something different in the boy's countenance, so he warned, "Just take it easy, boy. It'll be over soon." Yet the moment Massa's right hand reached forth, Jesse Lee severed it with one swift blow of the scythe. Massa Robert collapsed to the ground, squeezing his throbbing, handless, bloody right wrist with his trembling left hand. Blood spewed from the wound like a mighty rushing river. Massa Robert's bellow rang across trees and crops, shacks and mansions, as swift as a thought. Field hands gathered quickly as did the overseer who, upon seeing the limp, lifeless white hand on the ground, searched black faces for expressions of fear and guilt. Jesse Lee saved him the trouble. "I did it," he declared, "and I'd do it again." His resolve trumped the overseer's rage. For an instant, the man feared him, having never seen a slave resist with impunity a white man's aggression. The bloody scythe, shivering in Jesse Lee's hand, convinced the overseer not to press the young man further. He'd proved what he would do. Surely he'd do it again.

"Fuckin Nigger!" the overseer yelled, kneeling to assist Massa Robert. He lifted the ailing man from the earth.

"You'll never get away with this," Massa Robert promised, barely able to speak. "You'll be dead by sunset! Mark my word!"

The overseer accompanied Massa Robert into the big house. The enslaved began to whisper and wonder what would happen next.

Elijah approached cautiously, watching terror and pride dance in the boy's eyes. "You gotta leave here!" he said suddenly. "Now." He took the scythe from Jesse Lee's hand.

Tears came, for both of them, and they embraced tighter than they'd ever hugged before.

"You's the onliest son I ever knowed," he whispered, staring at Jesse Lee's long, flat feet. "If I don't see you no mo, I'll meet you again on the other side." Jesse Lee knew what he meant. But he had another plan.

"I ain't leavin," he said. "My brother's coming for me."

"You got to!" Elijah demanded. "They'll kill you shonuff!"

"Ain't leavin til my brother gets here!" he repeated louder, shaking his head.

Others whispered and frowned with curiosity and confusion. Jesse Lee stared across the land and into an uncertain future.

"What you gon do?" Elijah pleaded. "We cain't protect you. Not from something like this."

They didn't know that, from the day Massa Robert first touched him, Jesse Lee had spent many nights building a shelter where no one would think to look. He'd kept the project from everyone, including Elijah and Ella Mae, his sister, both of whom he needed now if he were to survive.

He quickly ushered them to the slave cemetery. Beneath overgrown grass, weeds, and wild shrubs, he revealed a trapdoor. They looked at each other, stunned.

"Just need a little food and water. Til my brother comes."

They promised to help.

"I'll wipe yo scent away," Elijah said, "and bring you a slop jar for yo business."

Ella Mae touched his arm and said, "I knowed you was special the day you got here. You gon live, Jesse Lee. Just wait and see."

He lifted the small debris-covered door.

"And one more thing," Ella Mae said, pausing his descension into the earth. "Yo brotha *is* comin. Don't ever stop believin."

Jesse Lee nodded and sank slowly into the living grave.

Day 45

I stopped around midnight for gas and a cup of coffee, which I don't normally drink. I wasn't sleepy, but I feared I might be soon.

All the while Matthew kept running. He didn't know what I knew—that his little brother lay trembling in a hole in the ground, waiting for him—but he believed Jesse Lee knew he was coming. And with everything in him, he *was* coming.

I exited at Blackwell at 2:16 a.m. When I got to the land, I couldn't see anything but the outline of the old shack and a wall of trees in the distance. I killed the engine, lowered my window, and sat still a long while. I'd never heard the song of silence. It's not completely soundless, but rather a faint whirring, a kind of barely audible humming that can hypnotize the hearer. Perhaps this was peace of mind, I thought.

Dad had told me about silence. He'd boasted of a life in the country without worry or stress, and I'd wondered—

"Oh shit," I murmured, reaching for the interior cargo light. "That's it!"

I could almost see the revelation before me.

I grabbed my notepad from the passenger seat and scribbled, "Matthew is Uncle Esau!"

"Of course you are," I cackled. "You're big brother. That's why you brought me here. To tell me the rest of the story."

And that's when he stopped running. I saw it in my mind's eye. Sweat drenched his brows, and he leaned forward, resting upon his knees. His face was as dark, as magical, as the night. "You'll find your brother," I said. "I promise. I'm writing the story." He nodded and cried.

I couldn't believe I'd missed it. It had never crossed my mind. Yes, there were two brothers in the tale, but that was where the parallels ended for me. Dad and I had had so much tension that no one could've convinced me I'd one day write his story. I'd wanted nothing to do with him. He'd wanted nothing to do with me. But there I was, standing in the middle of the land, the last keeper of our legacy, very possibly the last Swinton, talking to his big brother. I knew it was him. He looked exactly as Dad had described. Because of that, I knew Dad was Jesse Lee. It all came together. Then I remembered where Jesse Lee was and the fragile hope keeping him alive, and I covered my mouth. I didn't know how the story would end, but somehow, someway their hope had to be rewarded.

The context of the story was slavery because that's where it all began—the forced separation of black men from each other: fathers and sons, uncles and nephews, brothers and brothers. I

had studied enough of this in college to know the weight of
what we bore, what we endured, what we carried and passed
along for generations. I'd read Frederick Douglass's narrative
and Linda Brent's account of the physical violation of men. I'd
studied slave rebellions, African retentions in the diaspora, and
black familial trauma. I knew something about black struggle
and the hope for freedom. So establishing the framework for
the novel wasn't difficult. The hard part was exposing black
men's hearts. That made me uneasy and insecure. I knew what
I felt, what we felt, but I never wanted to surrender our vulnerability for public pleasure. Yet by exploring the lives of
these precious brothers, I discovered that all men want the
same things: validation, worth, purpose. They just never say it.
That's why some men dislike me—I'm willing to say it. That's
also why I have to tell this story. Because it's a love song, a
black male ballad, a lullaby most brothers can't sing. But I can.

Sitting in the car in the dark, I finally conceived the opening lines:

The day they were sold away, the sun stood still. Their
small hands trembled, meshed together in an attempt to
stay together as slavery pulled them apart. One would
go to Louisiana, the other to Mississippi. They were babies then—three and five years old—listening to their
mother scream and their father wail the promise of their
reunion. They would remember that day, the rank smell
of horse manure, the dry taste of dust particles, the hot
summer breeze that made trees wave goodbye. It was
a quick separation, each snatched in an instant, but, in
their hearts, their parents' cries lingered.

The boys believed one thing: they would be together again. Their precious, naive hearts supported their hope that tomorrow or tomorrow's tomorrow would grant them another day to play beneath the old, raised shack in which they were born. They didn't know, however, that it would take a lifetime. Yet they never stopped believing. This is the story of that belief—and what it took to keep it.

Yes. I liked it. I reclined in the seat and read the sentences many times as the roar of silence deafened me. The words weren't perfect, but they were pretty good. It was coming together now. Everything Dad told me about Uncle Esau in his letters was precisely what Matthew felt for Jesse Lee. It was also every black boy's dream of a brother. I'd never read a novel about regular, everyday black men loving each other. So I had to write it.

Dad's body was gone, but he was there with me, in the pitch black of our history. I suppose he needed to tell me something in those letters, to make sure I understood whatever he had come to know or admit to himself. He had to write what he couldn't say, what black men dare not speak. He wanted me to translate it creatively because, knowing me, I wasn't afraid to cry, which is what we're going to do if we ever tell the truth. My resistance to him all those years finally paid off. It prepared me to heal him. And me.

I'm still not totally free. I can admit who I love, but I'm afraid to love them. That's why starting this story was hard for me—because I've wanted a private freedom. Yet freedom is never private. It will not hide for you. It will not disguise itself. It takes no refuge in safety. It's a declaration to the world of one's refusal to be bound. And that's the role of the writer—to force the reader's freedom—even when bondage is the preference.

I'd wanted to write a benign story, one I could control. I didn't want to write ours. Ours is messy, complicated, burdened, painful. Difficult to translate into pretty sentences. But it's the only real story I know, the one I've been sent to tell. Generations of wounded, black hearts are waiting for my boldness. This is why I was born. This is why I was sitting there in the dark. Because our American story began in the dark, in the bottom of slave ships. In endless fields of cotton. In miles and miles of treacherous marching. My job was to write, not our facts but our feelings. And that's what I intended to do.

Quiet and alone, I turned off the interior light, exited the car, and leaned upon it. There was no fear. I was home. Soon my eyes adjusted, and levels of darkness vanished. I could see pretty much everything. It was exactly as it had always been, a frozen time and place as fixed as a Polaroid picture. But the more I studied it, the more I realized I was wrong. It wasn't the same. Something had changed.

In the distance down the road, a large tree had fallen. It lay perfectly horizontal, like a corpse, with roots on one end pointing in every direction and branches waving sadly on the other. Also, the old house bent more severely now, as if, any minute, it would give up the fight and simply fall over. It was strange to me that that little house once stood as Granddaddy's pride. Dad said folks came from all over the county when he finished building, marveling at the craftsmanship. Now, all that excellence was gone. Or was it?

I jumped back in the car, turned on the light, and started writing again. I asked Dad and Uncle Esau to tell me everything. Matthew started running again. I was confused. Of course he wanted to find Jesse Lee, but was he inexhaustible? I saw him sprint across the open field before me and dash into the thick forest of trees and thorny shrubs. I saw him wade through rushing rivers and wince beneath torrential rain. I saw him climb trees to see across horizons then climb down to continue running. Every now and then he'd wipe his brow with his sleeve, but he wouldn't stop. Occasionally, he'd look around and open his mouth, but nothing came forth. He just kept running. He was searching for something beyond his brother, something greater than what he thought he'd lost.

I saw Jesse Lee, too, sitting in that hole, cold and horrified. He would've died except he meant to see his brother again. He heard slave catchers and hounds running back and forth across the land, and he gave thanks for a healing father who knew how to wipe a man's scent from the earth. Massa Robert's only desire was Jesse Lee's complete annihilation. He knew that. And every day Jesse Lee lived, he smiled and gave thanks that everything in the grave ain't dead.

It's funny that, in my imagination, Dad experienced the horror of same-sex violence. Maybe that's what he feared for me—that some man would misuse me or strip my innocence and I'd never know joy again. That was a measure of love. And maybe that's why I loved when Jesse Lee dismembered Massa's hand. Because by severing his hand, he dismantled his power. I don't know. But I wanted to reach through the story and free him. I would've whipped that white man's ass if I could've.

Yet it wasn't that simple. I was the writer, but not the characters' consciousness. I couldn't make them do what I liked or force situations to go as I preferred. I was the conduit, not the creator. My job was to tell the story—not to fix it.

Suddenly, I heard Dad weeping. I stopped writing and laid the pad and pen on the dashboard. His letters had told me that, for the most part, he'd been a slave. Everything about his rural rearing was a limitation, a restraint that he had no way of escaping. He told me he felt like a slave, and I laughed, but he was serious. I didn't understand what he meant. *Everybody's free*, I thought. But everybody's not free. The terms of black bondage shifted, he was trying to say, but they didn't vanish. If he'd been a scholar, he might've said they *transmuted form*, but they did not disappear. I understand this now. He provided for Mom and me so well that, as a child, I didn't see it—black limitation—and that's the achievement of his life: that a slave raised a free man. Only in that dark moment, with ancestors beside me, did I see it, and I've never cried like I did right then.

Dad's weeping turned to wailing. At first, I couldn't see him, but I heard him. His unrestrained heart made me anxious. Then he said, "Look at me, son. Let's not be ashamed this time," and I obeyed, and suddenly there he was, in the passenger seat beside me. I saw myself in his watery gaze. We looked alike now, different versions of the same self, the same life, the same past. He stared at me without blinking. He saw me without shame or disappointment. He shook his head slowly, presumably at all he'd misunderstood, and his tears anointed the floor and console of my car. I reached toward him, but he pulled away. Touching was not allowed. I knew that. Still, I think I would've traded a lifetime for the ability to hold his hand.

The best I could do was stare at him. No son can watch his father cry without crying himself. Those chains fell off, and he quivered with light and revelation. I saw him as clearly as I see myself. He lifted his large hands, palms toward me, and I did the same, and suddenly energy vibrated between us. It felt like fire. And unbridled love. His weepy eyes never left mine. I tried to blink, to look away for comfort, but his gaze held me captive. He'd avoided my heart a lifetime; he wouldn't do it in the spirit.

"Finish the story, son," he said.

I promised I would.

"It shall be worth it all."

I believed him.

"Every generation owes a debt."

I understood that.

"It's always because of—not in spite of."

I agreed.

"Love your people, but love yourself first."

I respected that.

Finally, he said, "Write until your hero wins."

I didn't understand that. But I soon would.

He vanished, and I reassumed the pen and pad and wrote through the night. Matthew got as far as Baton Rouge before pausing. His breath simply gave out. Much as he wanted to press on, he had no strength. He lay in the woods two whole days before moving again. Each hour of rest increased his guilt, but his body wouldn't move. "Hold on, little brother," he murmured as he recovered. "I'm on the way."

Jesse Lee spent dark days in that grave. Elijah and Ella Mae sneaked food and other supplies when they could, but sometimes they couldn't. He emptied his slop jar only when he had to, then returned to the hole to wait for Matthew. Some days, field hands sang loudly, "'I gotta home in glory land that outshines the sun!'" and "'One of these days, my savior is coming!'" Jesse Lee nodded. He believed that.

Some nights, when he resurrected long enough to breathe God's fresh air, he wondered where he and Matthew would go. Could they live somewhere unhunted, unsurveilled, unaccused? Jesse Lee feared he'd spend a lifetime glancing over his shoulder, waiting for Massa Robert to grow another hand and reprimand him for what he'd done. But perhaps, this time, this one rare time, the slave might win.

White folks never stopped searching for Jesse Lee. Day and night, they scoured the forest with howling hounds, which, some days, barked only a few feet above him. Yet Jesse Lee lay quiet in the womb of Mother Earth, savoring the sweetness of revenge. However, if Massa Robert ever had his way, Jesse Lee would be dismembered, one limb at a time. So, for now, like a seed, he germinated in the soil, prepared to burst forth and bloom the day his big brother arrived.

One afternoon during water break, an old woman found her way to the cemetery and began to stomp about, speaking modified Scripture:

"For de Lord shall descend from heaven wit a shout, wit

de voice of de archangel, and He shall gather up his chil'ren unto himself: and de dead in Christ shall rise first, and they shall be delivered into de hands of de Father." She clapped and stomped, speaking life into the dead and the waiting. "Therefo, my beloved bredren, be ye steadfas, unmoveable, always aboundin in the work of de Lawd, for one day, your labor shall not be in vain." She laughed and clapped louder and walked circles around arbitrary stones, which marked lives of people most found worthless. Yet she knew there was value in the dead. And in those who dwelled among them.

I wrote until the sun peaked the eastern horizon. I had almost twenty pages when I looked up and saw light illumine everything my father loved.

I exited the car and welcomed a new day. So many thoughts swirled in my mind. I wasn't sure how to make Matthew find Jesse Lee. I wanted the fateful reunion, but it had to make sense. I also wasn't sure what to say to Ricky and Darcy, who had phoned me throughout the night. They wouldn't believe I was in Arkansas, writing, finally, the story I'd told both of them about. They loved me, but they didn't understand why, as smart as I was, I couldn't write just anywhere. I didn't understand either. But now I knew. I needed the sanction of my ancestors, my father's blessing, to tell this story. I needed the truth and freedom of our past, our legacy, to get voices and details right. It's the only way we could heal completely.

Before that trip, I had written only a paragraph or two. Never a whole page. Every now and then, only a few sentences. Now, in the darkness of night, in the middle of my people's land, I had written the first chapter of a powerful story. I'd thought writing was a romantic art, filled with glorious epiphanies and melodious expressions that poured from a writer's pen. I never knew you could write for hours and come away with nothing. At least nothing useful. It made me wonder how much time Baldwin, Morrison, and other greats had spent writing books filled with lyrical sentences and polyrhythmic phrases.

I think I was trying to give my life meaning—like Dad when he wrote those letters. Words let you outlive yourself. They take your energy, your life force, and speak for you long after you're gone. Funny that I'm writing about Dad, although I'm talking to myself. He's here, however, listening to every word I mumble. Still, I have to write it. Something about language makes a thing real. It makes thoughts tangible. You can lie to your thoughts, and they'll lie back to you— until you write them down. Then, before scrutinizing eyes, they won't lie any longer. I didn't know, at the time, that I was searching for something absolutely true, something that wasn't a lie, something no man's hands had tainted. I wanted something to prove I was more than what my father thought I was. I hoped that, if I could write a great book, Dad might see me, even from afar, and apologize for having underestimated me.

Yet I was a long way from a great book. I realized as I was driving that I couldn't simultaneously conceive and write a story. It just didn't work for me. I had to birth the whole thing in my mind first. In fact, I had to outline it. I had to get out of my head, out of my own way, and let the story evolve uninterrupted. When, overnight, I did that, my anxiety calmed, and the tale unfolded before me. Just like that. Each character had a mind of his or her own, and I couldn't make them do as I preferred. But I could create situations and circumstances that, in some instances, forced certain behavior and decisions, and that's precisely what I intended to do. It's what all writers do. It's what people call creativity.

I see it now. I tried to make Matthew return to Philadelphia, to regroup and get some help, but he wouldn't go. He was determined to find Jesse Lee or die trying. I didn't want him to die trying. I wanted him to live and prosper, and I wanted Jesse Lee to survive belowground until Matthew got there. I just wasn't sure how to make all the ends meet. But somehow, they were going to meet—if I had my way.

I think I was Jesse Lee, too, waiting for Dad. I'd spent a lifetime trying to please him, hoping he'd one day love and celebrate me just as I am. But he's not coming. From his letters I saw that he went as far as he could go. Yet Lord knows he came a mighty long way. He changed so much I didn't recognize him. Yet I heard love in his words, and that's more than I ever felt from his heart.

We're still not healed. He apologized for so many things, but I've not totally forgiven him. I understand the weight he carried, and I'm not mad anymore, but that's not the same as forgiveness. Forgiveness means I let it go. I'm not sure I'm ready for that. Still, there's nothing more for him to do. Everything else is my work.

Suddenly, once again, I heard Mom call my name: "Isaac."

I looked around the land, afraid that perhaps I was merely hearing things, but then I sighed and relaxed. I know my mother's voice. "Yes ma'am," I returned and closed my eyes.

She sang softly, musically, "Sweet, sweet Isaac. Heal us all."
And I knew what to do.

I got back in the car and drove to the main road, where
I stopped at a convenience store and bought several bottles
of water.

Within minutes, I stood in the center of Rose of Sharon
Cemetery, at the foot of my father's grave. I had a feeling this
wasn't going to be easy.

"Forgive him," she said. "And all of us." I waited, but nothing else was said.

"How?" I muttered. "Just let it all go?"

Silence.

I bowed to my knees and opened one of the water bottles.

Yes, she whispered.

I stayed in that position a long time before uttering a word.
She didn't rush me. She knew what was at stake.

Eventually, I took a deep breath and called Dad's name:
"Jacob Swinton." It sounded awkward and uneasy. I'd never
heard the melody of Dad's name in my mouth. I had always
called him by his function—"Dad"—but in that moment, I
wanted to honor his being, his existence, so I called it again:
"Jacob Swinton, son of Sarah Swinton, grandson of Abraham Swinton. You are more than my father. You are a man.
A very good man. *Asé*."

I poured a little water atop his grave.

I can't explain why I said that, but immediately I felt his excitement like a dull vibration crawling across my skin. I shuddered but didn't leave. I didn't look up either. I still wanted
my anger, but I had to admit he'd given his all.

"Thank you for your sacrifice, Dad. And for your discipline. It saved me. *Asé*."

I poured more water.

"Yes," Mom whispered.

"And for trying so hard."

Tears came, but I didn't wipe them away.

"Be free now, my father. You raised a man. *Asé*."

More water.

I heard his weeping. It was loud and deep, like the howling of wolves. Something about his moaning connected with my heart, and I wanted only to hold him and kiss the crown of his shiny black head. Mom's quiet, comforting voice lingered in my ears: *Yes, baby. Yes.*

"I didn't fail, Daddy. You and Mom taught me everything I needed to know. *Asé*."

After each statement, I poured a little more water across the mound and waited for Mom's murmured affirmation.

"You hurt me, too, Dad. I need to say that."

"YES!" Mom declared.

"You said some things no father should ever say to his son."

"That's right."

His lamenting intensified, and so did the cracking of my voice. Myriad ancestors joined in, creating a chorus of mourning that made me cover my ears and squeeze my head tightly. Echoing through my mind were centuries of elders' apologies and confessions never spoken: *We're sorry… Forgive us… It's not what we meant… Be better than we were!*

Their sincerity resonated. So many wounded hearts finally accounted for, so many broken hopes, borne a lifetime, mended in an instant.

"*Yes*, baby! Do what only you can do!"

"Everything I am is what I'm supposed to be. God sent

me just like He sent you. We're not the same, but we're both made in God's divine image. *Asé*."

I poured a little more water. Ancestral heads nodded, confirming my statement.

"I'm grateful you were my father, but I hate that you didn't see me. Now I know why. I didn't see you either. I'm sorry for that, too. *Asé*."

"*Yes.*"

More water.

"You were not a failure. You were not dumb. Your work ethic fed our family. You were strong and steady like a rock. You were…beautiful. *Asé*."

Water.

Spirits danced right there in the cemetery. I looked up, finally, and saw, just above my head, a red bird perched on a limb, watching my every move.

Once again, Dad's image materialized before me. He was an old man now, with a shadowy gray beard and a receding hairline, yet his eyes were as strong as ever. To my surprise, he still wore his one good suit. I thought Heaven might've given him a long white robe, but perhaps he'd denied it. It would've been like him to reject a dress-like garment—even in Heaven.

"Your letters taught me an amazing thing: all a man can do is try. It's the only thing that counts. We all fail. No life succeeds forever. Trying is the key; it's the only real achievement. I see that clearly now, how hard you tried, and for that, I love you. *Asé*."

I drizzled rivers of living water all over that raised mound. Mom began to sing my childhood lullaby as I continued sobbing. Dad's celestial mouth trembled, but he didn't speak. I think his heart was overwhelmed.

Minutes later, Mom went silent. I did too. The red bird lifted into the sky.

The last drops of water I poured for fathers who'd spent a lifetime trying—and sons who'd missed it. Then, I stood, brushed my knees, and returned to the car, where, assuming the pen and notepad, Matthew told me the rest of the story.

★ ★ ★ ★ ★